THE MOST ELIGIBLE BACHELOR

OrangeBooks Publication

1st Floor, Rajhans Arcade, Mall Road, Kohka, Bhilai, Chhattisgarh 490020

Website: **www.orangebooks.in**

© Copyright, 2024, Author

All rights reserved. No part of this book may be reproduced, stored in a retrieval system, or transmitted, in any form by any means, electronic, mechanical, magnetic, optical, chemical, manual, photocopying, recording or otherwise, without the prior written consent of its writer.

First Edition, 2024

THE MOST ELIGIBLE *Bachelor*

K PRANEETH, K PREETHAM

OrangeBooks Publication
www.orangebooks.in

SYNOPSIS

The story is about a strange deal that took place more than two decades ago. The deal was between a villager Ravikant Varma (or as the people of his village called him 'Vantala Varma') who is looking for whatever he could get to start his own restaurant and Sharada Devi (whom the villagers called capricious, chaotic and a highly educated mad woman).

The conditions of the deal go thus. The borrower i.e., Varma would be given the amount he requested for (a few thousand rupees) without any security or guarantee from his end. However, in case he doesn't repay Sharada before the due date, he would either have to get his son Raj Varma (a mere toddler when the deal was entered into) hitched to Sharada Devi's daughter or give her as much money as she would ask of him then. If none of the above are possible, then Ravikant Varma would be imprisoned for a duration of Sharada's choosing.

Twenty-five years later. Mr. Varma is now the chairman and founding director of the 'RV restaurant chain', one of the most successful food chains globally, headquartered in New York. His son Raj Varma is in the running to enter the coveted list of Vogue's top 10 most eligible bachelors of the world. Just as Mr. Varma plans to take his company public, he is reminded of the long forgotten deal and the long lost contract he entered into all those years ago by his lender Sharada.

She just waited and waited all these years as she saw her borrower earn millions, hoping against hope he forgets to pay her. And now that he did, she would stop at nothing short of ownership of Varma's empire or his son.

Now it is upto Raj the heir to Varma's empire, to decide what to do. Should he marry a woman he had never seen before in his entire life or forgo his inheritance worth millions or allow the imprisonment of his father?

Race through the pages to be a part of this game filled with equal doses of fun, thrill, twists and turns in every chapter.

CONTENTS

Chapter - 1 1
Ravikant Varma's D-Day

Chapter - 2 9
Sharada Devi's D-Day

Chapter - 3 14
D+1-Day

Chapter - 4 20
The Deal

Chapter - 5 32
The Actual Debt

Chapter - 6 39
The Bargain

Chapter -7 47
The Escape

Chapter - 8 55
The Journey

Chapter - 9 65
Gotcha

Chapter - 10 74
The Arrival

Chapter - 11 .... **92**
    Plan Of Action

Chapter - 12 .... **105**
    The Unexpected

Chapter - 13 .... **115**
    And So It Begins

Chapter - 14 .... **126**
    The Elephant In The Room

Chapter - 15 .... **135**
    Marriage Fixed

Chapter - 16 .... **148**
    The Queen Steps In

Chapter - 17 .... **161**
    Take A Call

Chapter - 18 .... **170**
    The Challenge

Chapter -19 .... **180**
    The Threats

Chapter - 20 .... **188**
    The Unlikely Pair

Chapter - 21 .... **198**
    The Fight Ahead

Chapter - 22 .... **211**
    The Duel

Chapter - 23 232
    Manoj's Fate

Chapter - 24 246
    Sharada Calls The Bluff

Chapter - 25 260
    Cards On The Table

Chapter - 26 270
    The Secret Sivasamudram

Chapter - 27 281
    The Phone Call

Chapter - 28 292
    Damage And Control

Chapter - 29 306
    Job Done Billion Dollars Transferred

Chapter - 30 324
    All Hands On The Deck

Chapter - 31 335
    Showdown

Chapter - 32 349
    Payback

Chapter - 33 370
    Waves And Tides

Chapter - 1

RAVIKANT VARMA'S D-DAY

It was close to midnight on the 16th of December and it was celebrations time at the Broadway Plaza Hotel in New York. The CEO of the world-renowned RV restaurant chain was sitting in the presidential suite puffing his cigar. He was looking at the speech worded for him by his secretary. It was an early Christmas for the company as it completed 25 successful years and was all set to announce its IPO at the Wall Street.

The CEO, Ravikant Varma took a huge drag from his cigar. How odd it was, he thought to himself. Here I am, a high school dropout from a village in Andhra Pradesh, reading a speech specially curated for me by an MBA pass-out from an IIM. A slightly narcissistic grin spread across his face as he looked at himself in the mirror. He considered his image for a while. He was quite a stout man, with more breadth than height to speak of. He didn't have a big tummy but a look at his shirt buttons could tell someone that he was well fed. He was nearing his 60s but his face was built to cover this up. There were no wrinkles or dark circles to date this man, the only give away would be the patches of silvery hair here and there (which too were left un-coloured purposefully to give an impression of experience).

His face was clean shaven but for a staunch mustache which was jet black in color.

A look at the mirrored image of the paper in his hand brought him back. He must memorize this speech soon, especially the financial jargon or his lack of education would be exposed in front of 30 odd TV channels waiting for him.

He started reading the speech to himself, mouthing a word or two out to get used to the pronunciation.

"It is an extremely prestigious moment for us at the RV family (as we love to call ourselves in our firm) as we complete 25 successful years this midnight. The years have been as delicious and fulfilling as the dishes we make. The company has expanded beyond boundaries and so has our cuisine. This year alone, we have

ventured into the Thai, Spanish and Mexican recipes with a great response from the customers.

At the expense of sounding boastful, I would like to add that we not only make good dishes but also make good profits. The bottom line has grown 1.5x to reach a sum of USD 200 mn"

Ring.... Ring.... Ring...

Varma let out an impatient wail of anger as the mobile phone broke his concentration. He had specifically advised Maggie, his secretary not to let anything escalate to him till the speech was done, not even the congratulatory calls. He swore to himself that he would make this the worst ever 10 seconds for whichever sorry son of a b***h was on the other end of the line.

He picked up the phone to see an unknown number which looked like was from India. He answered the call in a sentence which was just a bunch of choiciest swear words put together. Without even waiting for the caller to utter a word, he cut the line and went back to his couch.

"The bottom line has grown 1.5x to reach a sum of USD 200 mn. We now feel that it is time for us to share our profits with the public just as we share our food."

Ring.... Ring.... Ring…...

Shouting a rustic, countryside swear word from his native language Telugu, Varma reached out for his phone. It was the same person calling again. Varma was all set for a swear word marathon. As he answered the call, it was the lady at the other end of the phone who spoke first. Nothing but the shock of hearing that voice could have stopped Varma into silence.

"Good morning, Ravi. Oh, so sorry, I meant good evening, Ravi. This is Sharada speaking from Sivasamudram. Thanks for the previous call. I was slightly worried if I had the right number. But the swear words you shouted assuaged my fears. By the way, your poetry when you are in anger is still remembered by those of us here who knew you. I know this is your D-Day, so it is for me too. I won't take much of your time, rather I have called you to say that I am going to pick a time. A time for the wedding. Let's talk tomorrow once you are through with your ordeal. Oh, and by the way, I will subscribe to your IPO too. Take care."

The burning end of the cigar that sparked his finger brought him back this time. He looked up at himself in the mirror again. Gone was the smile. Gone was the pride too. All he could see was the reflection of a fat, old bucolic with grey whiskers on his head and sweat all over his face. He couldn't see himself wearing the suite's gown, rather he could only see a tattered half sleeve shirt and a checks lungi on himself. He was sweating, and yet he was shaking as if he was feeling freezing cold and stuffily sultry at the same time.

How could the damn woman still remember the deal they made or rather how could he forget? Did she mean what she said, about the wedding? No, she is only looking for the money, he said to himself. This calmed him up. And then the mask came back, he forced the prestige and demeanour upon himself again. The villager he just saw in the mirror was dead, long dead. He could not afford to bring him back, especially in front of all these bureaucrats waiting for him.

He looked at his watch, it was almost 23:30. He knew that Maggie knew better than to disturb him during his speech rehearsal. It would be his call when to come out of the room. In a hurry, he tried to memorize as much as he could from the rest of his speech and dressed up. Opening the door, he found Maggie waiting for him with a dozen staff members from the Plaza.

"Raj is almost done with his interview with the Vogue chief. Mr. Savaroy has just given the presiding note to the press and is taking the Q&A. So, there would be no questions asked to you as you instructed. All our staff from the city are in the lounge with their families. Just a pop of the champagne bottle after your speech is what the party is waiting for", recited Maggie in top speed as they walked towards the elevator. "Is everything OK chief?"

Varma didn't pay attention to much of what Maggie said earlier, but this last sentence jerked him from his thoughts. He just gave her a stern look and that was enough for her. As the elevator dinged open at the 12th floor and they entered the lounge, a cascade of people rose up, just like a Mexican wave in a cricket stadium. All eyes were on Varma. He could only assume they were clapping from their actions as the sound was not so audible to him for some reason.

"Must be the old age creeping in, should get myself checked up with an ENT specialist after this", thought Varma to himself. "Was it the call?" asked the voice of the villager in his head. "OF COURSE NOT !!!" he shouted back at himself in his head. "And you stay dead", he added in contempt to the villager. As he walked past towards the dias, he saw Sooraj Savaroy, his trusted CFO, Andrew Weinback, his CMO, the other board members and his son Ravi Raj Varma clapping back at him from the stage. They were the only 3 people who knew that "RV" in the name of his company stood for his son's initials and not his. As the company was not listed till date, they never published any annual report to the public and hence this stayed unknown.

Maggie stayed back as Varma climbed up the stage and took a seat beside his son. "Speech time dad", whispered Raj to Varma. "Oh shit", Varma walked sheepishly towards the podium. He started his rehearsed speech:

"It is an extremely prestigious moment for us at the RV family (as we love to call ourselves in our firm) as we complete 200 successful years this midnight."

Savaroy let out an audible cough. This was a cue to Varma that he had made a mistake in his speech. Varma was puzzled, what was it that he missed out? "Oh yeah sorry, I meant 25 successful years", he corrected himself.

"The years have been as delicious and fulfilling as the dishes we make. The company has expanded beyond boundaries and so has our cuisine. This year alone, we have ventured into the Chai, Varnish and Texas recipes with a great response from the customers."

The listeners began to murmur, Varma could hear a few sniggers too. But he carried on. He just needs to get this thing done with. Any corrections would be made before the morning prints he thought.

"At the expense of sounding toastful, I would like to add that we not only make good dishes but also make good profits. The bottom line has grown 1.5x to reach a sum of USD 25 mn"

Savaroy whispered back "200mn Varma". Varma shamefully corrected himself. Savaroy wondered what was wrong. It was normal for Varma to make pronunciation mistakes or miss out on jargons, but he never messed up on numbers before. Rest of the speech was just a slugfest for members on the dias and a laughing riot for the listeners below. With umpteen corrections, Varma finally concluded (omitting the last note of thanks altogether).

Savaroy tactfully took up the mantle by introducing Ravi Raj to the members of the media and asked him to speak a few words. Ravi, though born at Sivasamudram had most of his education done in Delhi and his graduation from states. He was a tall, fair handsome man with a slightly oval face and piercing sharp eyes. His voice was soothing, his English dialect posh, his manner poised and his attire simply top notch. As Vogue had come up to interview him just the very day, he was all likely to make it to the global list of the top 100 most eligible bachelors and by any luck, top 10 too.

He was hence more than capable to take over reigns from his father, just as he had taken up the podium from his father. Media was simply in awe of his speech. As everyone clapped encouragingly at the successor of the

RV empire, Ravikant Varma wondered what spoiled his D-Day so badly and the voice in his head said, "It was the call".

Chapter - 2

SHARADA DEVI'S D-DAY

It was around 9:30 AM in the morning of 17th December, and it was celebrations time in Maada Veedhi at Sivasamudram. People were celebrating the newly announced wedding ceremony of Gopala swamy's elder daughter. Gopala swamy was amongst the richest and most respected people in the village. He had salt and peppery facial hair which included his beard, mustache and shock of dirty unkempt hair. He was well built and too muscular for a rich man in a village. The physique was mainly because he loved to do his hunting and wrestling (which were the only major exercises he did). It was common knowledge that he was planning to get the marriages of his daughters done at the earliest, as he was entering the race for president of Sivasamudram that year and there was little doubt that he would win it.

That day Gopala swamy was all smiles as his wife Sharada Devi had finally given her consent for the marriage of her beloved elder daughter Suguna. The bride groom was from Gopala swamy's family as well, son of his first cousins. His name was Abhiram Kireeti. He was a well-bred, well-educated young chap (or at least in this part of the world where passing one's matriculation calls for celebrating the end of education, one can say so). Gopala Swamy was happy that he had found the right match for his daughter, one look at his face and any dumb witted villager could guess as much. Same could not however be said in Suguna's case. Her expression was closer to acceptance than joy. Abhiram was on cloud nine metaphysically, and physically on top of his jeep waving at people as though it was, he who was contesting for president.

But no one could guess how Sharada Devi felt, for the very simple reason that she was nowhere to be seen in the celebrations. She was watching the celebration convoy from her study room at the topmost floor in her house. She laughed at the people beneath her, they in her opinion were indeed beneath her.

Sharada Devi was tall and slender with a well tied and maintained long braid. She was beautiful but one would definitely guess that she would have been much more beautiful in her youth. Her face was pointed with sharp features and her jawline showed the rigidness of her character. Sharada Devi was the most educated person not just in Sivasamudram, but also considering a cluster of 32 villages in and around her village. She did her post-graduation in business administration from a renowned university in Hyderabad and this was in the late 1990s. One can say that this was in no sense a minor feat. However, destiny had other plans for her.

Her father had forced her into a marriage with Gopala swamy. She had to oblige as her father had put up with all her desires. He allowed her to pursue all her interests, all the while listening to uncomfortable taunts from his relatives and other villagers. She had to pay the price for that freedom she enjoyed. It was nothing short of a deal she entered into with her father. He would not stop her from her educational aspirations, he would finance them all, provided she married the man of his liking. That was how Sharada, a gold medalist from University of Hyderabad ended up marrying a 6th class dropout from Sivasamudram.

Sharada always hated her house at Sivasamudram. She saw it as an imprisonment of her intelligence. The only room she liked being in was this study. Funnily enough, no one from Gopala swamy's family understood why there had to be a room called "Study" in houses when there were schools outside. Sharada could find peace in all the study material she had gathered over the years, where she could remind herself who she was. And finally, today would be the day when the entire village would get to know who she is. Today was her D-Day. The day when her ideas would be termed as brain waves rather than stupid whims or weird tantrums by the villagers. Today, she would be able to shut down all the mouths that laughed at her, all the fingers that pointed at her more than two decades ago.

Her heart was thumping harder than the drumbeats from the celebrations downstairs. It was hard for her not to reach out to the telephone beside her. She had to wait for one final confirmation and then nothing would stop her.

Ring…. Ring….Ring…..

Sharada let out a whoop and picked up the phone. "The number is authentic, and he is available for the call now. But he hasn't much time, make it count", said the voice at the other end. Sharada didn't even reply, she quickly hung up the phone. Her moment has come. She was hammering the numbers on her cell at a lightning speed. She had rehearsed this moment a thousand times in her dreams before. She had it all planned, a mental speech prepared in her head.

Ring…. Ring….Ring…..

The call connected to the person, but before Sharada could utter a single word, there was an avalanche of swear words she got from the other end and the phone hung up. She smiled to herself. Strangely the swear words assuaged her. Any other woman or even a man perse, in her place would have felt disgusted, depressed or shell shocked to hear the words she had just heard. But for her, the voice plus the words were the only things that mattered. She had reached out to the right person. She dialed again. This was a mark of Sharada Devi's tenacity, she would not let anyone's stupidity or frustration, or feelings for that matter deter her. For her, she was the only living entity that mattered. This time, she had to be quick or else she might not be able to reach out for a third time.

Ring…. Ring….Ring…..

As soon as the dialler connected. Sharada greeted Ravikant Varma in her native Andhra telugu dialect which she was sure would disarm him. Little would Ravikant expect that a lady from his remote native village would remember him, let alone find him. She was right, she caught him unguarded and broke through his defense. She then delivered her well-rehearsed speech:

"Good morning, Ravi. Oh, so sorry, I meant good evening, Ravi. This is Sharada speaking from Sivasamudram. Thanks for the previous call. I was slightly worried if I had the right number. But the swear words you shouted assuaged my fears. By the way, your poetry when you are in anger is still remembered by those of us here who knew you. I know this is your D-Day, so it is for me too. I won't take much of your time, rather I have called you to say that I am going to pick a time. A time for the wedding. Let's talk tomorrow once you are through with your ordeal. Oh, and by the way, I will subscribe to your IPO too. Take care."

And then she hung up the phone. She knew that Ravi would not be capable of speech at the end of the call. Hence, she didn't wait for his reply. Her time was more precious. After all, even Ravikant Varma, the CEO of one of the most successful food chains in the west, was beneath her.

Chapter - 3

D+I-DAY

"What's all this T+1 thing they are writing in the papers?" asked Ravikant Varma to no one in particular, waving the morning copy of "The New York Times", who were one among the other papers that covered the company's celebrations the previous day. His room was usually filled up with a cluster of people which almost always included Maggie, Savaroy, his son Ravi Raj and few other trusted confederates. It was not very odd for Ravikant Varma to ask a few jargons he never understood. He would not ask someone in particular, as it would sound as if the answering person knew better. He would just pose the question to the room, as if he was thinking out loud and someone in the room would reply.

"It is a terminology they use for the transfer period of shares. T being the day the transaction for the shares is made. Once the transaction is successful, the process of transferring the ownership starts and goes on for like 2-3 days, give or take. So, if you buy a share on the Tth day, you become the actual owner on $T+3^{rd}$ day so as to say", answered Savaroy.

"Oh yeah of course, knew it would be something like that. These corporates have the knack of pushing in redundant terminology to complicate such simple stuff. It sounds as though they are talking about a great technicality or some super science stuff. When in reality, they are just fooling around pretending to be a smart-ass elite", scoffed Varma.

The room was slightly taken aback, Varma was never this touchy. Especially after a sound party. But they knew better than to question Varma when he was in this bad mood. Not even Savaroy had the guts to take on Varma. The only person who could do this was Ravi Raj Varma. But he would only ask in private.

"By the way, your idea of the food donation drive across 25 countries marking our 25th anniversary was bang on Varma. The press simply loved it. It is exactly the kind of publicity push we would need to drive in our IPO marketing campaign. And I am arranging the travel itinerary for you and Raj to go to India for the drive, which was also a brain wave from your mind", said Adam Wein back the CMO in an attempt to cheer up Varma.

"Where is Anand, I asked for him", replied Varma completely ignoring his CMO. This was directed towards Maggie.

She looked utterly dumbfounded. "I don't remember you asking for him chief", she sounded human on these rare mistakes.

"Oh, you don't, do you. Maybe you should stop enjoying yourself too much in these parties. When you know you need to work the next day", said Varma.

"Dad, I need a moment with you", said Raj before things got out of hand. The room looked relieved. And one by one, they all left giving some excuse or the other. "Should I ask Anand to join you chief?" enquired Maggie almost imploringly. Raj just lifted his hand to stop her from saying more, he nodded to assure her that he would take care of this.

"What's the matter pops?" asked Raj.

"I am fine. I feel great", replied Varma.

But Raj continued, he didn't want to let his father wriggle out of this, "Not just about today, about last night too. You were very edgy, your speech was, well what can I say, a stand up comedy performance. And today, you feel like you had a vat of, what do they call it "Kallu?" (a local palm wine found in Andhra Pradesh)"

"Well, we need to try it again someday. It's been so long", said a voice in Varma's head. "SHUT UP!!!" Varma shouted back, both at the villager and his son. Raj's tactic had worked. He knew that the best way to get his father talking was to make him angry. "One more Andhra reference from you and I swear I shall send you back there, never to return here. An interview with Vogue and you feel you have reached the top of the cliff don't you. Questioning me on my mood, you think yourself the CEO now huh!!!" snapped back Varma. He added a few telugu curse words here and there which Raj didn't fully understand. This was a jargon that no one in the company except Varma understood.

"When did you ask for Anand, and why did you ask for him? He is not such a good lawyer. I can talk to Bradley if you want some legal advice…", Raj treaded more carefully.

"Stop acting as if you are the CEO!!!" shouted Varma.

"Then why have you introduced me as the next in the line yesterday", shouted back Raj. The angrier Varma got, the more likely Raj is going to get his information.

"Bradley is a scoundrel, he deliberately speaks in jargon I don't understand, to make himself look smart", said Varma trying to calm himself down.

"No, he does that to make you look stupid", retorted Raj.

"Out of here, now!" Varma was at the top of his voice today.

"And looks like you don't need Bradley to make yourself look stupid today", smiled Raj wryly. He knew that the bubble would burst soon and he would get all he needed to hear.

"OUUUUUUTTTT", it sounded more like a plead than a retort from Varma. "This is exactly what I am asking you to do", said Raj. "Get out with it. Tell me what's wrong".

"Don't think you are smart alright, you know nothing. All you bureaucrats think you have seen the world, and all you guys have seen is the bloody sunrise and sunset from the windows of your coveted cabins. You never felt the heat yourself, you never laid down a drop of sweat except when you are shit scared in a horror movie. You raise money from these VCs or BCs or whoever the hell they are, as though you are pulling out a genie from the lamp. Things don't work that way. It's not like sitting across a business table, giving some stupid presentation, having some scotch, cracking a few punchlines, and getting your millions. You never begged for money as I had to. You'll never know desperate. You will never know how heavy you feel your stomach is, surprisingly so when it is empty. You will never know how it feels when a few trinkets would seem more valuable to you than your own life. People sell their own organs for a few thousand rupees, rupees mind you, not your fancy dollars. I was once prepared to sell my own life for a petty sum. I did that too. I sold a life for an amount you would wipe your drool with.

You come here, questioning me as though I am caught doing a crime. You think I am keeping my mouth shut to save myself from something. No, you fool, I am saving you from the pain. I am trying to save you without you ever knowing it. That's why I wanted Anand and not your white monkey who can sing in his jargons. Are you happy now you handsome sucker? You got what you wanted", Varma pushed away the contents of his desk onto the adjacent wall as though he hit a boundary.

"Wow, what a speech! And you didn't have to prepare for this. Cause this is who you actually are Varma. Don't fool yourself", said the villager in Varma's head. Varma just took a gulp and sat down crestfallen. He had finally become what he dreaded, what he once was, a rude rusty villager who was known for "his poetry" when he was angry.

Raj sat by his side and put a hand on his quivering shoulder. "You sold what?" he asked.

Varma looked at Raj and a tiny teardrop left his eye as he said in a croaky voice, "You".

Chapter - 4

THE DEAL

It was nearing sunset on the shores of Sivasamudram. There was a young man with a 10-year-old kid by his side, looking towards the horizon. It was hard to tell whether the man was enjoying the view or contemplating suicide. He just had a vacant look on his face, as though there was just this last hope he was clinging on to.

The young Ravikant Varma, or as the people of Sivasamudram called him "Vantala Varma" (which meant Dishes Varma) was dressed in a tattered half sleeve shirt and a checks lungi. He was trying to prepare a speech but was unable to find words for it. All he could think of was his previous attempts of raising a fund for his restaurant. The words kept echoing in his head:

"Hey, aren't you the man with a female soul who wants to cook?" "Why don't you think of changing your gender?" "Look at him, doesn't have food to eat, but wants to prepare food to sell", "You have a son you idiot, start masonry and feed him at least before you think of feeding half the world"

Tut tut, he forced himself back to the current predicament. He had a chance to get some money now. But he was not sure if he was happy about it. He hasn't heard a lot of good stuff about his potential lender. Her name was Sharada Devi. The only thing she had in common with Varma was that villagers called her a lot of things too. She too had endured a lot of jeers and taunts from the residents of Sivasamudram.

She was supposed to be a headstrong, stubborn, capricious and an unpredictable woman. Many believed this was the exact reason her father had "undersold'' her to a 6th class dropout in this village. He has heard that in spite of her being a gold medalist somewhere, she was stuck here and hence has gone mad. But God knows why such a woman took an interest in his proposal.

The kid by his side now stopped watching his clueless father and started running back and forth aimlessly himself, just like the tides of the sea. He was going far and returning from time to time to check if his dad said anything about leaving or staying. With no word from his father, he started running again. It was after his 12th marathon finish, no 13th, no maybe 14th or... (the kid didn't know any numbers higher than this) that he saw his father taking out what looked like milk which he often drank. But this milk was in a different bottle, which was taller than his and didn't have the sipper.

Varma started emptying the bottle so as to gradually empty his brain from all the meandering thoughts. The kid was shouting, "Dad! Give me some too. I haven't had anything since morning. Why didn't you tell me you bought an entire bottle of milk? Daaadddddd!!!!" But Varma was stopping his kid with one hand and strainfully holding the emptying bottle with the other.

This was good, some more drinks and then, he would lie down here thinking of Sridevi (famous actress at that time) taking him to her heaven. He would dance with her there and then return to Earth and (who was this little dung kid hitting him; or rather massaging him from besides, calling him Dad. Must be someone's lost kid). Where was he? Yes, after returning to Earth, he would get dressed up in his Superhero costume and think of....... think of....... thinnnnkkkkk

After some time, or after a long time rather (Varma didn't remember exactly), he was aware of some hitting he was receiving.

How has the kid's hitting become much harder? **"Hey Va....ala Varmaaaa! Get your......up. You're .... in my fa....rm!!!"** *What language was this new strong kid speaking? And why was that kid's voice distorted? Maybe the kid was drunk? Hahahahaha.* **"You craaaaapppy......of shiiii......tttt."** *Let's silence him by hitting. What was happening? How was that strong kid miraculously moving here and there? How was Varma's strong arm missing him?*

Jeezzz this strong kid has a white beard, he has become so tall! **"Waaa...k....e up!!! It's ti.... me to go!"** *Go where? Who was the toddler beside this strong guy? Hey there he was, the dung lost kid and why was he looking at him angrily? Maybe this new strong kid was his younger brother. He must have hit the kid, making him cry. Need to silence this dumb strong one. Where was his magical glass wand? Here it was. Aaaannndddd WHACK!!!!*

"AAAAAAGH!" *That's better. You're welcome dung kid.* **"You Prat! I came...... tell...... she....... waiting....... how dare......hit me....... bottle"** *Maybe he needed another shot.* **"Sharada ma'am! Here he is"** *What Sharada? Is he speaking of Sharada Devi? Now why is that name sounding familiar? Hmmmm. God! The deal!!!!*

Varma tried getting up but fell back in vain and was trying to bring some sense back to his senseless brain. His son, on the other hand, was standing beside him, wiping tears and clutching his stomach once in a while which was emitting burps frequently. Ovulayya (The dumb strong kid. Or to put it better, the owner of the farm where Ravikant was now lying) was catching his head (which was hit with the bottle held by Ravikant) writhing in pain.

Beside him was a handsome, not so dark and not so fair, middle aged village landlord looking in a *when-would-this-guy-change* sort of manner and ahead of them both stood Sharada Devi, who unlike the other pair, stood calm and was watching (rather scrutinizing) Varma patiently.

Varma was dazzled with the sudden sunlight dashing into his eyes. It was morning now. He didn't understand. He was supposed to be on the seashore and that was in the evening. Where was he now; and what was the time?

Taking his kid's head as a support, Ravikant got up and walked straight (according to him) to reach Sharada Devi. But he was going farther aside and then coming back to the same spot trying hard to get towards her.

"Let me make it easy for you" said Sharada Devi tiringly. She seemed to walk in a zigzag way towards him but eventually reached him. "Ovulayya! Get some milk for both the father and the son, I would say. And two Satyam Canteen's special coffee to me and my husb…., I mean, to Mr. Gopala Swamy"

In that 10 mins which seemed like 10 hrs for Varma, everything was silent. It looked as though everyone there were speaking with each other through their eyes. Ravikant kept shifting gaze from his son to Mr. Gopala Swamy and was somehow deliberately missing the gaze of Sharada Devi. He was embarrassed.

Mr. Gopala Swamy (whom Sharada Devi hesitated to introduce as her husband) was looking at the farm as if calculating its area and rate; thinking what could be harvested here to double its value. He then looked at the kid in a sorry kind of way, wondering how unlucky that kid was to lose a nice mother and gain a worse father. He then looked at Varma in a way he thought Varma's father should have looked upon him as and when his son got to such stupid things. He finally looked at his wife expecting her to look back at him, but this didn't happen.

Sharada Devi stood like a hawk that fixed its eyes upon its prey, or a leopard fixing its gaze on the exact deer in the herd so as to not let it escape its vision. She was staring only at Varma who was trying to say something, but was just letting out some burps or strange errrrrrrs or hmmms.

Finally, when Ovulayya brought 4 glasses in a glass holder, the kid was the first to gratefully reach out to the milk. He immediately started drinking it, not minding the heat, which Ovulayya constantly kept reminding. Gopala Swamy took the coffee with a smile, knowing its specialty. He was drinking it in a way, as if to show this was how it should be drunk to savor the full taste. Sharada Devi was just holding the glass, sometimes bringing it close to her mouth for the sake of it. Varma had to be forced to his drink by Ovulayya as he wasn't even able to hold the glass properly.

Once Varma emptied his glass, his senses returned to him rather painfully. He caught his head making *oooohhhh* sounds as if all his worries and thoughts came back racing to his mind. His mind seemed unable to hold all the thoughts that came back.

What should he say? What should he do? Gone was his last chance. SPIT!!! How comical must he have behaved? He was unable to recollect. Why did he have that Naatu Kallu (Local Wine in their language) knowing it was the D-1 day?

"Say something Ravi " asked Sharada Devi. "Tut!!! What Ravi? Call him Vantala Varma or should I now say, Thagubothu (drunkard) Varma!" said Gopala Swamy. Sharada half looked at her husband as though asking him to stay silent.

"Ma'am. I had waited and prepared a lot for this moment. But……", Varma, though sane now, was devoid of any words to say. No matter how hard he asked his brain to think, the response came in the form of tears ready to flow out from his eyes. He tried hard to stem the flow of tears.

"Why are you stopping? Bring it out!" jeered Gopala Swamy. "Bring out the routine sentimental actor hidden inside you. You so conveniently brought your son along, to get an emotional drama. Start begging".

"No", said Varma. "I was carrying him as he was scared to be left alone in the house and..". "I'll thrash your face with my slipper if you lie, you careless clown!" said Gopala Swamy in his village dialect. "You just took your son out for a walk and then, instead of buying something for him, you used that money to buy Naatu Kallu right? And from whom? That Malligaadi kottu (Malli's shop) right?" taunted Gopala Swamy.

How was Gopala Swamy getting everything out so right, like a detective? Varma's insides kept praying. *Oh God! Please do something to silence this village brute.* The answer had come, not from God, but from Sharada Devi. "Gopal, stay calm. It's supposed to be a business discussion, not a *Panchaayathi* discussion which you are so fond of."

It might have been sheer shock or repressed anger inside Gopala Swamy that silenced him, but the instruction had worked. He gave one last glance towards his wife, and then just kept giving Varma some tough looks, as though daring him to blurt out everything and then just run away from there.

With trust and hope in God, Varma started uttering out whatever struck his mind. He was just desperate to get it done with now. "Ma'am, you being a well-educated and brought up lady, must be aware how it is like in cities that food businesses are booming." Sharada Devi kept gazing at him.

"This Satyam special coffee for instance, or Malligaadi famous kallu (Ovulayya let out a grunt of laughter), Paanigaadi Kodi biryani (Paani's Chicken Biryani) are all so localized. They are just wasting their talent, wasting their opportunity", continued Varma.

"So, what's so special about you? Drinking an entire bottle of Naatu kallu in one gulp?" mocked Ovulayya. Sharada Devi just gave Ovulayya a look and that was enough to silence him.

Varma continued fast to avoid any further interruptions, "Yes. I agree I don't have anything special in the making, like them. But, my specialty is that I know them. I know these talented people and I know how to help them expand further. I can be the assembler of the car which has the best engine, the best wheels, the best chassis and I know how to fit them into one piece. Not just that, I also know where to take this car to and how fast to go. The only problem is...."

"Your car doesn't have the fuel to start", completed Sharada Devi with a Queen's smile. Varma gasped not knowing whether to praise her or deny her words. He just gave her a blank face for some time. She beat him in his own game.

He then said, "As you know ma'am, the costliest item in a heavy vehicle is always the fuel. It also is the most important. But, the brilliance is of the other parts designed so perfectly by the designer that just a small input of fuel will make the car run, the flight fly and the fire spread" finished Varma.

Even to this day in the distant future, Varma didn't know why he thought of saying nothing else, no business proposition, no numbers, no "great business jargon". He just gave out his proposal in a village slang, with him rising from his drunk state, as though rising from the dead. He just said all that came to his mind and had become normal.

After listening to all this, Sharada Devi at last shifted her gaze from Varma and he felt as relieved as though a gun pointed at his head was now lowered. She was immersed in her thoughts. Varma wondered if she was now going to use her weapons of knowledge and education on him, maybe ask him some "complicated English terminology". He is going to look like a village side good-for-nothing stargazer then. Even Gopala Swamy seemed to be expecting a similar reaction. However, Sharada Devi looked at Varma after a long time and just shot one arrow of a question.

"What will you keep as security?" Gopala Swamy looked aghast and tried to say something. Sharada Devi just raised her hand to silence him this time. Ovulayya, who was silently listening to the conversation, but acting as if he was feeding the cattle, also stopped dead and was looking at them. The cow was now directly eating away the grass he was holding in his hand. The kid had finished his milk and was looking at his father in a *shall-we-go-now* fashion. Varma was the only one who looked expressionless.

He was confused about his own feelings. He knew not whether to feel happy or sad. He never reached this point of discussion in any of his previous attempts. He was habituated to hearing taunts with cynical laughters or comments like "Po ra Vantaloda, velli oka manchi Mr. Pellam ni vethukko" (meaning "Get lost and search for a nice working tomboy girl as wife"). But now that the discussion had gone ahead, he was confused as to what he could keep as security. He never thought of this before. He then put on a look which Gopala Swamy aptly described as the "Sentimental Actor".

"What worth could I be holding ma'am? If I had anything with me, I would have tried consulting a bank long back. My dumb father was more interested in farming and gambling. He did both the things so well that they balanced each other out exactly. Neither my father-in-law nor my mother-in-law had done anything useful too, except giving their daughter. They lost their wealth to their health by taking medicines which ironically took their lives eventually, as though seeking a revenge for them taking it" chuckled Varma, expecting someone to laugh at this attempted joke.

But Sharada Devi again threw a Queen's smile. Gopala Swamy and Ovulayya however cast a look of "what sort of a man Varma was", now poking fun at his dead parents and in-laws. Sharada Devi replied, "There are things more expensive than land, property, currency and even life Ravi". "Which is?" asked Varma in a puzzled way. "Word" replied Sharada Devi "Everlasting, never dying, once given, can't be taken back or transferred" Varma remained silent.

"I know speaking about materialistic wealth with you is of no use. It is like trying to educate these bucolics". To this, only Sharada Devi laughed while Varma let out a small laugh just for the sake of it. Gopala Swamy and Ovulayya looked at each other first, and then looked down. "But look Ravi, if you're giving your word to me, don't you forget that I am not a bucolic. I won't take your word on its face value. We will be entering into a deal with it, an official and proper legal contract. So, think about it"

Varma was not expecting this type of conversation but was building it with whatever was coming to his hand, hoping it would stand. "May I know what word I am to give? Is it... any... partnership or share?" asked Varma hesitantly. "No" Sharada replied instantly. Everyone was taken aback by this.

"Then?" asked, not just Varma, but all of them except the kid. Ironically, that was where Sharada Devi pointed out. As if he was called, the kid looked up at the finger pointing at him, not knowing what was happening.

"You need to give your word that if I give you the money you asked for, (mind you, I am not asking how much it is); but if I give you the amount and you're unable to repay it on time, you should agree to either betroth your son to my daughter; or pay me how much ever I would demand at that time (mind you again, I am not mentioning how much it is going to be). Failing to do so could lead you to a life of imprisonment or any other punishment that I deem fit", finished Sharada Devi now looking as though she concluded a wartime address to an army.

"This is the deal Ravi".

Chapter - 5

THE ACTUAL DEBT

Varma blinked his eyes twice, rubbing them thoroughly with his hands. The images of his son Ravi Raj Varma (who now went back to looking young and a handsome man in his late twenties) and his beloved lawyer Ananda Raju came back to his irises. He was back in his living room in his house in New York.

He was scared for a second, as the images of Sharada Devi, Gopala Swamy, Ovulayya and his son's ten-year-old self in his mind looked so real. He was confused if he had just narrated the incident or re-lived it all over again. "What a day that was!" said the villager in his head. Varma just ignored this comment. He had adopted this tactic of ignoring the villager in his head so that he wouldn't drive the image of a crazy man in front of all the "bureaucrats".

"So, you say she made you sign a legal contract for this deal?" enquired Anand the lawyer. "Yeah, she did", replied Varma with a slight note of shame.

"The deadline to repay her has passed?" enquired Anand.

"I am guessing it has passed years ago", Varma scoffed.

"And when did she say she will call you back?" asked Anand

"She said tomorrow, as in today for us and tomorrow for her. As she called around midnight yesterday, I am assuming she will call me sometime tonight. As in when I say tonight, I mean night for us and morning, or afternoon for her, as in …", Varma was going on.

Anand stopped Varma before he started explaining latitude and longitudinal differences between US and India, "Woah woah ok, I get the drift. You mean to say we have around 4-5 hours from now before she calls right. That should give me enough time to give the contract an initial reading, just to grab the essentials."

"All that won't be necessary. Just tell me this, as the contract was signed in India, I am way outside the jurisdiction right. As in she can't get me here in US right. The contract won't be valid, she can't imprison me here, I am in a haven right here", Varma's worries started coming out like air out of an inflated balloon.

"Calm down Varma. As I said, let me have a look at the contract. I can't give you any assurance until and unless I look at the terms and conditions in its entirety", Anand replied irritably.

"And you also can't think of avoiding India dad. Remember what Adam said about the donation drive. We have planned out an entire host of marketing campaign activities including radio announcements, TV commercials. And you and I are supposed to do this all in India. It's all for the IPO", reminded Raj.

"What's the big deal in that, we can cancel that thing. How can it hurt, it's just some fancy showing off. It's just Adam trying to prove to me that marketing is a real thing, and if you remember right, all this was my idea. So, I own it, I cancel it immediately", replied Varma with a tone of audacity.

"No, you can't. As both Adam and Savaroy told you, IPO is something which is hugely driven by market sentiments dad. There is no logic there, people don't know if we do well or not, they just have to trust us. And only that which is visible is trusted, and only that which is trusted will be sold. We told you this umpteen times", fought back Raj.

"Why do I always have to remind you that you are not the CEO!!!", shouted back Varma.

"Okay, before you and your son have a shouting contest, please give me the contract. We are running short of time or rather I am. I got to explain you the implications before your call with Shantha", pleaded Anand.

"Her name is Sharada", replied Varma impatiently and looked back at his son.

"Okay, and what about my statement before that. Any comments?" asked Anand.

"As I said before, just tell me if the jurisdiction would work here. That's all I need before I call Sharada and tell her to….., well never mind that", Varma stopped himself forcefully from uttering an obscene phrase used in his native tongue. He was not going to become that "angry village poet" again.

"Oh my god, why is it so difficult to make you understand some things Varma. I cannot say anything unless you show me the contract. Please just let me have a look at it. I won't judge you by the way you signed on it", Anand's nerves were getting tested.

"As a matter of fact, I didn't sign on it, I put a thumb impression on it", replied Varma calmly.

"Devuda! Please show me the contract. Time is running like Usain Boult over here", Anand replied.

"Told you this guy's a quack", scoffed Raj pointing at Anand. "He's not even a pleader under the tree, he's a mugger on the footpath to be honest. Let me call Bradley".

"Don't speak of that white monkey again or I am going to test his legal skills by putting up a case of sexual harassment on him and seeing how he wriggles out of it. And I would make the LGBTQ community from our firm put that case on him", shouted back Varma.

"You guys are unbelievable. Varma, please show me the contract. I beg you. Not even a resurrected Mahatma Gandhi would be able to tell you if you are safe unless he is shown the contract", Anand was close to falling on his knees now.

"Is that so? What if I tell you I just signed a cheque of 2000 USD on your name for your consultation?" smiled Varma narcissistically. "Will a look at that paper give you a better idea?" he added.

"Yeah, I will charge 500 USD per hour of consultation if I have to visit my client in the Philadelphia prison. That's the idea that I get", replied Anand. "I will give you a 50% discount from that 2000 USD if you can just let me see the contract Varma, please".

"Okay just show him the contract pops. He has used up his quota of air conditioning in the room for the day", replied Raj sarcastically.

"The thing is I don't exactly remember where I kept that bloody thing actually. It was there in that big brown wooden cabinet in our house", started Varma.

"But we don't have any big brown wooden cabinet here pops", questioned Raj puzzlingly.

"I mean the house we lived in Delhi", said Varma.

"What! That's around 15 years ago dad", Raj said exasperatedly.

"Yeah, that was when I remember seeing it last", said Varma not looking at either Raj or Anand but fixing his gaze at the bird outside his window.

"You lost the contract!!!" exclaimed Anand. It was unsure if that was shock or incredulity.

"It's just that I don't remember seeing it again. It must be around somewhere. I will ask the housekeeping to just, you know, see if they can find the damn thing. I am not actually sure if I brought it to US, if I think about it", Varma was either talking to himself or with the bird outside the window.

Raj and Anand just looked at each other in disbelief. "Do you have a picture of the contract, or a photocopy would do too", asked Raj hopefully.

"I remember it was a 30 odd pager document, I don't think I have a picture of it. And there was certainly no photo copier in my village", Varma scoffed at the thought of the village.

"Then the 1st thing you need to ask Shanta is the copy of the contract Varma. We can't go any further without it", said Anand.

"Her name is Sharada, Anand. Are you actually as dumb witted as Raj thinks you are?" Varma added exhaustingly.

"Not quite. I was just making sure you heard me", answered Anand with a triumphant look.

Evening passed by and night fell in a couple of hours. Varma felt as though a century of waiting has passed. He and his son Raj were still trying to look for the contract document in the house along with all the housekeeping staff that worked for them.

Ring….Ring….Ring…..

A sudden shock of silence fell in the room. Everyone stopped rummaging or passing papers or whatever it was that they were doing. It was as though a bomb just blasted leaving the surroundings deafened. It was Varma's call and he knew only he had to attend it. With trembling hands, he picked up the cordless and answered.

"Who's this?" he said in a voice which was a bad attempt to hide his anxiety.

"Ready to pay back your actual debt Varma?" answered Sharada Devi.

Chapter - 6

THE BARGAIN

"Look Sharada, I am a very busy person and have no time to waste. So, I'll just get straight to the point. I know you are looking for money. So, cough up the amount you are looking at and we will close it soon", Varma said in a tone that indicated a mixture of fear and hope, but no authority whatsoever.

The housekeeping staff looked flabbergasted at this version of Varma. Raj ordered everyone to leave for the day.

"Some things don't change Varma. We are both included in that. You still remain the dim-witted emotional villager and I still am the brainy businesswoman. Funny how the world sees you as the businessman and me as the villager, but in reality, it is the reverse.

When I say debt, it is not the debt which appears in the financial statements of your company. It doesn't even show up in your bank statements. But it is the only debt that matters.

And if you think you can pay it in money, then it would be your son's net worth", Sharada spoke relentlessly as she knew that Varma would interfere otherwise.

"You are insane. How can I appraise my son?" Varma was shocked, it was just as he feared. Sharada was way too clever for his negotiation tactics.

"Well for starters, he is going to inherit your company. That should mean all the shares he is going to get, all the assets which would be transferred on to his name, all the money he is owed by people etc. This should help you in assessing your debt", Sharada mocked him.

"Utter nonsense, the amount I took from you was mere thousands of rupees. I will repay you in thousands of dollars now. That should settle it. You are going to get about 80 times your investment. This is a fair bargain Sharada", Varma knew this argument wouldn't hold even as he said it.

"Hahahaha. Your jokes have grown funnier Varma, they are getting better with age just like your son. You actually think I am that bad in maths. I know millions are greater than thousands Varma. And I really think that having RV chain headed by someone like me who actually knows what she is doing is much better for your shareholders too", replied Sharada.

Varma could think of no retort. His face was sweating badly. He wanted to shout at her, rage upon her, call her names no one knew existed in the swear word dictionary. But he would not become the villager again, not in Sharada's eyes at least or he would prove her point.

Sharada continued, "Look Varma. I am going to say it again. Some things don't change with time. The contract you signed 25 years ago too has not changed a single word. I have it in its entirety with me, not a single page or line or signature or thumb impression has gone astray".

Raj looked at his father holding the phone as though he held a gun at himself. He stood frozen, silent, not daring to move an inch and face sweating heavily.

"Hello! Varma, you there?" Sharada was afraid Varma cut the line. "Varma are you listening to me, my next call would go either to a lawyer or a priest. It is your response that is going to decide it. Speak up Vantala Varma", even Sharada knew that the best way to break Varma's silence was to make him angry.

But even this didn't work. Varma still stood like a life size statue of himself, holding the pose of speaking on a phone.

"If you are there at the other end, tell me this Varma. How was today? How was it waiting for my phone call?" asked Sharada. "Tell me that much and I will be ready to bargain."

"It was hell. Every minute felt like a year. It felt as though I spent a lifetime waiting", answered the villager in Varma's head, in a croaky childish voice out of Varma's mouth.

"And I waited for 25 years, Varma. Can you imagine that? I didn't wait for you to pay the debt. I waited for you not to pay it. Every day I read about your company, its expansions, its financials, I would just pray that you do not repay my debt.

Every call I got on my phone sounded like a train speeding to hit me. I would just hope before answering unknown calls, that it would not be you at the other end telling me you transferred the amount you owed. Imagine how it was. You said that a few hours felt like a lifetime of waiting. Imagine spending an actual lifetime waiting. That is what I went through Varma. And can you put a price to it?

I say that my wait is worth much more than your son or your lifetime of earnings. And I am settling for a much cheaper deal than I deserve. So, this is the bargain, either you give your son to my daughter or give your company to me. Or else prepare to spend an actual lifetime waiting to get out of the prison", and Sharada cut the line again. Calls with her always had to end on her terms.

Sharada was surprised at what all she had spoken. She never thought she could get so emotionally carried away.

It was as though she rediscovered herself today. Just for an instance, she too had behaved like "an emotional villager".

Back in the states, Varma still held the receiver and did not utter a word. It went on for a full 15 minutes before Raj realized that the call had actually ended. And he realized it just because there came another call on the phone.

"Dad, answer it", Raj said in a matter-of-fact manner. But his father remained frozen and the phone continued buzzing. Raj had to pry open his father's fingers to take the phone from him. For a moment, he was worried if his father actually died but pushed away the absurd notion, just because of the fact that his father was still standing.

"Hello. Yes Anand, dad just spoke to Sharada", said Raj.

"Did he ask her for the contract?" enquired Anand.

"I don't know, he didn't speak to me yet", replied Raj.

"Is everything alright?" Anand sounded concerned.

"I think so, he is just shocked, I guess. Let me get back to him and then I'll get back to you", Raj said in an assuring tone. He never panicked.

"Pops, when did the call end? How long were you silent? What went on in the call? Did you ask her for a copy of the contract?" Raj knew not what to do. He could only think of one possible solution.

From the refrigerator, he brought a bottle of his father's favorite brand of liquor, poured it in a glass and put it in front of Varma.

"Sorry about this", saying so, Raj took a step back and gave his father a tight slap right across the ear.

Varma came out of his trance with a roar of pain. He let out all the curse words he couldn't speak out on the call with Sharada.

"Drink up the glass dad and we can talk", said Raj. Surprisingly, not a single curse that came out of Varma's mouth was directed towards Raj. It was as though he didn't notice that he was just slapped by his son.

And then Varma drank up the bottle placed beside the glass, ignoring the glass.

"Dad, I said glass, not bottle", said Raj.

"Oh sorry", saying so Varma emptied the glass at the side too. And then he crashed onto the settee. Now, he started trembling all over, in spite of the fact that he just emptied an entire bottle of brandy all by himself.

"What's the matter then, did that village woman say what she wanted?" asked Raj.

"Yes, she wanted to either get you married or get me arrested. That's about it", Varma hiccupped.

"Did you ask her about the contract, I didn't hear you asking it on the phone", Raj enquired.

"There was no need, she says she is going to get me arrested, haven't you heard. Now there is not a chance in the world of me going back to India. As a matter of fact,

I am no longer an Indian. I am from a native Red-Indian tribe born and brought up in the Caribbean. And you were born to me and a, uh let me think, yeah, a West Indian woman.

I am going to create false identities and credentials for the both of us so that we fly off to Switzerland. We will sell up all the shares we hold in RV chain to the IPO. That will give us enough money to set ourselves up, we can try an alternate career in Switzerland, say bee farming?" Varma started ranting.

"Yeah, I can see that the brandy got to your head", replied Raj sarcastically.

"Don't underestimate me kiddo. I could drink up a vat of kallu and get away with it. What do you think your brandy could do to me?" Varma hiccupped.

"Okay now, time to go to bed," ordered Raj.

"You are not my mother, I am your mother. And I won't go to bed with strangers. I will sleep right here", and Varma collapsed onto the floor from the settee.

Raj dragged him like the body of a man he just murdered and hoisted him onto his bed. Raj sat beside his father and just looked at the man he idolized. He always felt so proud that his father built himself up from ground zero. Back from a villager in Andhra to a tycoon in America. But now, he could only see an innocent villager in front of him.

Raj stayed awake the entire night, just looking at his dad waking up suddenly, trembling and muttering something meaningless (mostly in his Andhra dialect) and going back to sleep. Though Raj was keeping an eye on his father, his mind was somewhere else. He was thinking hard.

He thought to himself, "Brother, guess what. You are going to have to solve this yourself. Not for your pops, but for yourself. Because though the deal was made by your dad, the deal was made on you. Though this problem was made up by your dad, it is your problem. Now, you got to take the matter into your hands".

And he looked at the first ray of sunlight that hit him through the glass window. Dawn was approaching. It was time now, to put it in his father's words from the previous morning, "to go out and face the heat".

Chapter - 7
THE ESCAPE

"I won't!!! No, I won't!!! I won't face the heat. Why should I listen to whatever Papa has to say? Did he ever quit smoking when I asked him to (though he still smokes in hiding from me)? Or did he ever stop hunting and posing like Shikari Shambu before aunties (he looks funny doing that)?" cried Queen Gayathri to her trusty chambermaids (oh sorry, she meant her trusty friends).

"Aw, look at cute lil daddy's princess crying!" said Sravani, one of Queen Gayathri's principal maids.

"I am not a princess you silly Sravani, I am a queen", Gayathri tried imitating her mother. Funny though, how she loves her father more, but tries to behave more like her mother.

But to be fair, she was more like her father. Uneducated and daring, beautiful and headstrong. Her elder sister Suguna has gotten the better share of Sharada devi's genetics while Gopala swamy passed on a lion's share to his younger daughter Gayathri.

Gayathri resembled her mother more physically. She was slender just like her mother, and with a black rather mid sized braid, matching the night sky. She had twinkling eyes and a queensy attitude upon her face just like her mother. Same could not however be said about her brains. These, she got from her dad.

"As these low lying people in my kingdom say, I'm not like my mother. How could I be? So calm, so compressed, not raising a voice, behaving like a sad priestess who knows everything yet is not allowed to speak out anything. Urghhhhh!" even the very thought of being like her mother made her shimmer.

"And so", she continued as though she had laid out all the evidence to prove her point, "I, unlike my mother, should not succumb to the pressure from "old bed ridden kingly fathers" and marry a lower statured yet highly decorated commander of the legions. I, like my father, should seek something beyond my reach. I should seek out the charming King from the neighboring lands who comes to beat my suitors at my swayamvara and claim my hand."

"Then, why is my Highness deciding to abandon her kingdom and flee like a Shepherdess? Is that the cleverest solution she could think of?" laughed Parvati, one of the lesser liked maids of the Queen.

"And to be fair, Suguna hasn't got that bad a guy for a match. That Kireeti is just like your father. Dumb and brave, strong and a slave. All in all, a perfect guy to become a henpecked husband. And knowing your sister, she is more than capable of making Kireeti squeeze her legs after having been lifted up the stairs, just because her legs touched the railings", said Subbalakshmi (a new joinee in the "maid" community).

"Yeah, that's a fair point. If you marry someone above your league, you would have to serve him. If you marry someone below your league, he would then serve you.

Think of it like you would have to become a queen bearing golden handcuffs, like that Jodha in Jodha Akbar movie (which we saw secretly) if you choose an Akbar", pitched in Radhika (just one other maid).

"Your thoughts are much appreciated Radhika. Remind me to tip you before I leave", scoffed her highness.

"Now, instead of giving useless pieces of advice like all the opposition parties do, why not give me ideas to get out of here, which I might eventually use in case they are better than my plot", yawned Gayathri.

"Alright then, where shall you go? And how would you go? What things should you pack? How much money (I mean gold) from the treasury would you have to steal ("HUH!!!" replied her highness) ok borrow!!!", came all questions like arrows from each of the maids, as if everyone wanted to contribute something to the royal discussion.

"Correct me if I am wrong. But isn't a plan supposed to be the answer to all these questions?" asked Gayathri.

"One last question if I may. Before we think of how you are gonna escape, shouldn't you think about why you want to escape? I mean tomorrow is your sister's engagement, not yours right?" asked the new joinee rather fearfully.

"Good question. And a good lesson for you all, my not so beautiful ladies. This shows the difference between an actual Queen and a two penny artist who dresses up as a queen in a 22nd hand me down oversized angel costume. It's not just about the beauties, it's about the brains too. And I am lucky I got my father's beauty and brain, and my mother's beauty and brain too.

Tomorrow won't just be an engagement ceremony but also a matchmaking ceremony. Matchmaking ceremony for me!!! And those invited would be those fat, ugly, free food sucking feudal kings (landlords) of the village who just know one thing, to chew up the chicken to the bone. And I am not going to be that chicken in their hands. I would be the one to place her legs upon their heads, which inturn would be considered a big blessing bestowed upon them." said Gayathri with a Queen's smile (just like her mother).

"Now that you've got the "Why" part of it, can we concentrate on the "How" part of it? Or should I answer that for you all too?" bored down Gayathri.

"We can try getting you a bullock cart and a whip, you can disguise as a farmer and get away?" suggested Sravani.

"Wow Sravani, I should seriously consider getting you married to one of those farmers", countered Gayathri. "You seem to fancy them. Once you get married to them, they would teach you, or should I say, give you the actual farmer's look. Next?"

"We can steal the dress of your sister and get you dressed as her", said Parvati, already thinking and blabbering the next part of the scheme.

"And do what?" asked Gayathri in a how-are-you-so-stupid look. "Get me engaged to that Kireeti instead? Next !!!" this time her retort was angrier.

"Maybe, we can try asking your father for help?" suggested Radhika.

"Oh wow, ask him to help us run away from him. Masterplan Radhika, you want your tip right now?" mocked Gayathri

"Let's get anyone of the servants into believing that you fell for him, and make him escort you dressed up as a maid. Later on, we can say, *sorry bro, I loved you as a brother, hope you get a good wife in future*?" suggested Subbalakshmi, appreciating herself on her brilliance

"Let's do one thing. I'll actually marry that servant before my dad gets me married to anybody else. In that case, I need not run away. I just have to live life like a servant dusting up my own castle. None of you have as much a brain as an ant!!!", raged Gayathri, stopping herself midway from waking the house

"Alright. It's upon the Queen herself now. I have lived like a Queen and I shall run away like a Queen too." announced Gayathri. "You guys keep a watch from various parts of the house and keep giving me running commentary of what is happening. I shall get my bag ready.

Get me in contact with Padavala Paidithaatha (Boat keeper Paidithaatha) and ask him how much he would charge for a one-way trip from Sivasamudram to Dubai on his boat. It might so happen that he would faint imagining the high price he would be getting for it, but we shall manage with him. The shortest route to Dubai without passport would be through the sea and then through the desert. That's where I will lay low for a while. Then, I shall go and watch the FIFA world cup and visit the Burj Khalifa and stay there for a year, or until I find a worthy King. BINGO!!!

Sravani, to the kitchen! Parvati, to the wash area! Radhika, to the Goshala (cattleshed)! Hey kiddo, Subbu, you might be afraid of such a high-risk mission. Hence am granting you the smallest task. Keep a lookout on my parents' room for any noise

I shall go pack my bags and call Paidithaatha to inform him of his big fortune"

And the girls dispersed.

Gayathri packed up her bags with toys, her favorite salwars, queen's gown, duplicate jewelry (as the expensive original ones were in the locker in her mother's room), imported perfumes and some cash (she stashed as much as she could find from underneath her mattress, her father's diwali givings and some more taken from her sister's purse). On the other hand, her friends were keeping watch on the other inmates of the house all the while yawning quite frequently. After zipping up her 5th bag, Gayathri was ready to go.

As she was just about to get out from her sanctum, her heart skipped a beat as she forgot her most important possession. It felt foolish how she forgot the most essential part of her daily routine, her bubble gum flavored pepsodent toothpaste with real stars in it. Her friends kept stopping her from going back but nothing could change her will. She had to go get her prize however dangerous the vigil might be.

Perhaps she got this from her father. He too had to turn a deaf ear to the villagers' warnings while going on his dangerous bird huntings across the lake. Removing her royal sandals, praying to God in the entrance, she crept back to her room silently. While going, she had to walk past several dangerous rooms such as the dragon room (family dog Tommy's room), Giant troll's room (snoring grandpa's room), Dungeon (visitor's room), Pricky Imps' room (Suguna's room). Now there was just one final room she had to pass. The BATHROOM.

Proud of her achievement, yet mindful that she had to walk past the dangerous rooms again on the return journey, Gayathri quietly opened the bathroom door to clinch the diamond of the holy……wait…..who was that dark devil sized pig standing near the commode (whistling to the song "Oo antaava… oo oo antaava")?

"Ammayigaaru (Madam), I'm already on my private job here. You can use the…..", stopped Murugayya who was staring at the bags carried by Gayathri (who shut her eyes unable to see the unbearable sight).

"Why have you brought bags to the bathroom Ammayigaaru?" asked Murugayya and before he could think of a follow up question, Gayathri clinched the toothpaste and ran for it.

Murugayya, unaware of his untied lungi, came out of bathroom slipping and shouting (reminding everyone of some strange half dressed Archimedes) "Ayyagaaru (Sir!!!)!!! Gayathri ma'am is running with her bags!!!!!"

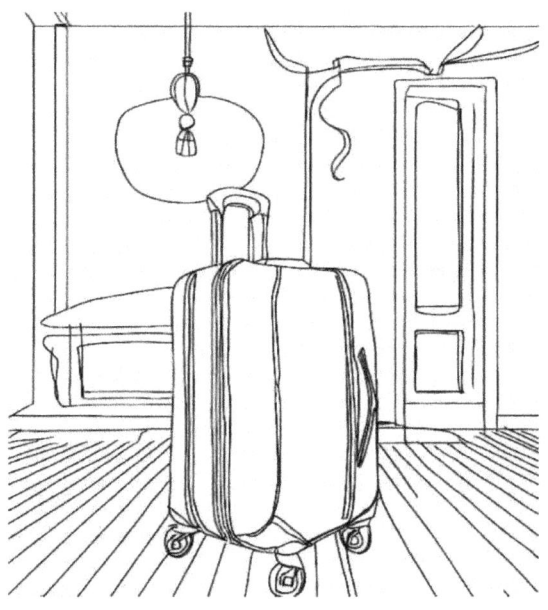

Chapter - 8

THE JOURNEY

Varma woke up to the sound. He rubbed his eyes to clear the blur, only to find his son packing his bags.

"Going somewhere Raj?" hiccuped Varma.

"Need to", replied Raj who was now packing his favorite sports shoes.

"Some sort of a trek?", enquired Varma, though he could guess from Raj's expression of seriousness that this was not some funky tour.

"Nope, but I daresay it will be nothing short of an adventure", said Raj smiling at himself.

"Huh, good for you. I will need your passport though, I think I will have to work a few extra hours, seeing that you would be on vacation. Hey Mathews, get me some coffee", Varma said, nursing his forehead which was battling a hangover.

"Coffee? Are you mad? Let's have some more of Kallu to become completely me", yawned the villager Varma who had also woken up. Varma just ignored this (he was not sure how long he could keep up with this though. He should go see a psychiatrist soon).

"Oh no, I am taking my passport with me", replied Raj without looking at his father and just thinking what else he would be needing to pack.

"You are going abroad!" exclaimed Varma. "After all that I told you yesterday, your first reaction is to go party?"

"Look who's talking, Pops. Who has been drinking a lot these days as though he was born for it? I bet the whole of our office is under the impression that you are partying hard after entering into an IPO, though that should have been the case", said Raj now looking directly at Varma.

"So you are going to actually party, to materialize their false impressions?" Varma's temper was rising.

"Please don't behave like an abandoned circus monkey Dad, though you're good at it, now that I see you", mocked Raj deliberately, knowing that it would raise Varma's temper.

"Please don't test me this early in the morning. Tell me where you are heading to?" Varma pleaded.

"Yeah, if you consider 12 O'clock early in the morning. Do tell me which country you had in mind too", remarked Raj. "And as to where I am going, think of it as a business trip for a personal reason", answered Raj after thinking hard and satisfying himself with the statement he made.

"If you try making another fool out of me playing around just because you're born to me, I would be doing the worst thing ever", scolded Varma coughing in between.

"Like what, selling me off? I think you have already done that", mocked Raj.

"I will.... I will....", Varma kept thinking childishly. "I will get you hitched to that devil Sharada devi's daughter for real", said Varma as though nothing could be worse than that.

"Yup. That's where I'm going", remarked Raj in a triumphant manner. He thought he had performed the magnificent magic trick of getting his thoughts out of Varma's mouth.

"Yeah right", scoffed Varma, this was indeed a comical retort from his son, he didn't mean it.

"Yeah, that's right. Now can I continue packing? Any idea how hot it would be in that village of yours? Will I be needing my jackets?" asked Raj in a matter-of-fact manner.

"Yeah, though it is lying close to the sea, the village is extremely cold", smiled Varma adding to the satire, "And so are the people. Ooohhh!!! You would be wanting to know about the 5-star hotels there, right? There is that Sattigaadi lodge (Varma gave a cynical grin) where he gives thaaaat supply too", whispered Varma with raised brows, recollecting those days.

"Remember Savitri?" asked the villager adding onto the conversation. Varma shut his eyes close, he was close to exploding from the headache (contributed by the hangover, his son and his past self)

"Mathews!!!! You deaf son of a b***h, where's my kallu? I mean, coffee?" shouted Varma in telugu (slightly embarrassed after the mix up).

"He doesn't understand Telugu Pops", reminded Raj.

"Now I can't think of a bad enough word in English, please go get my coffee", asked Varma.

"Coffee? Not kallu?" smiled Raj.

"Either would do", added the villager, "Though I would prefer the latter".

"Get me an appointment with that white monkey who calls himself a doctor without wearing a stethoscope, will you?", Varma asked Raj.

"Who, Jefferson or Anderson, you mean?" quizzed Raj.

"Who cares whose son he is? Just get me his appointment. I just don't want to go insane", said Varma.

"Right, I'll tell Maggie to do that while I'm on my way out", replied Raj. "Just tell me this. Which is the best route to reach your village from Delhi? And please, tell me a means of transport, not a list of places."

"Hahahahaha. You idiot, Delhi and my village are so far. Have you even seen how India looks like", laughed Varma. He then stopped suddenly as if a school teacher had caught him laughing in the middle of a class. "Wait! Are you serious about going to India?"

"As serious as you're about listing our company", assured Raj.

"You want to go kiss your motherland and sing a patriotic song, is it?" replied Varma, but he was not in a comical mood, he was pissed off.

"Not there in my plan, my schedule is pretty tied up. Maybe I will just rent a car from Delhi and drive my way. I'll see if I could give a ride to a Hippie who would sing for me", said Raj zipping up his bags, who didn't get his father's joke and just thought of finishing it for his father's sake.

"Wait for a minute you son of a ……, a genius", shouted Varma pulling Raj's bag from his grasp rather too passionately. The bag flew and hit Mathew who was getting the coffee. The coffee reached Varma, though not how he intended it to.

"Aaargh, kallu would have been cold", shouted the villager. "Told you to go for the latter, not latte. Why is it called latte by the way? Oh sorry, I would have known if you knew it".

"Get out!" shouted Varma, to both the villager and Mathew.

"Should I get you another coffee sir?" asked Mathew.

"On my face, you mean? No thanks", said Varma. "Remind me of this on your payday Mathews. And if you don't, you won't get paid."

"I am going out. You need not shout for that. This is supposed to be Skybag's latest brand and you did Paalaabhishekam (pouring ceremony of milk) on it", retorted Raj. "Why did you pull my bag? Is this not an auspicious time to leave? Any Varjyam or something like that?"

"This leaving itself is a very bad sign! Did you have a quarter of what I had been drinking, when I was asleep? I told you you were not ready for it yet", scolded Varma in a fatherly manner.

"Ready for? Drinking or going?" replied Raj lifting his bag and cleaning the reminder of coffee.

"Tell me the truth!!! Where do you think you're going?" questioned Varma in a lawyerly fashion, retrieving the bag from Raj.

"I've told you a hundred times by now, Pops! You yourself said it too. I'm going to your village, our village, everyone's village", reassured Raj. "Haven't you come out of your trance yet?" he added.

"Not entirely, to be honest. Damn these foreign brands. Hangover is higher than the high you get out of it" moaned the villager.

"No....no....noooooo! Again no. What wrong have I done? Didn't I put it in a proper way to you while I was narrating (or to say, crying out) my past? Didn't I tell you exactly how Sharada devi is?" asked Varma.

"Maybe I might have been living it more than telling it. But, to put it right, she's just a thousand times more than what I narrated, in every aspect. Just because I have been narrating, you might have mistaken it to a nice whimsical night time poem", said Varma still shaking his head.

"It's…. it's all my fault. I've just toned everything down. Probably because the lawyer was also there and I didn't want to put myself in a bad light. It was worse, way way worse, all the way worse. Note it down wherever you can", said Varma.

"Mathews! Get some brandy. Dad's going into a fit", called Raj alarmingly.

"No! Listen to me", shouted Varma holding Raj's collar.

"Just for a second, when I woke up, I thought you were in a plan to escape after what I've said. Though I was worried you were abandoning me and saving yourself, I would have felt much happier if you would've done that, but not this!" trembled Varma slowly sliding down Raj's collar.

"Dad, calm down. I am not a kid anymore to get afraid of your night time stories" said Raj as if he was wanting his father to realize how brave he was. "I am not afraid of the devil under the bed anymore."

"And this is not a nighttime story. Hence, you need to be afraid. There you go. Sharada devi is a devil in the real sense. And I'm her victim or prey or to-be-meat or whatever is apt", feared Varma hoping his son would show some slight fear.

"She's a devil, I agree dad. But she's a known devil. And I am a force unknown to her. That's why I am going, and not asking you to come. She could manipulate you as easily as she had done all those years ago. But me, she won't see me coming. That's why there is a chance this will work", Raj tried explaining.

"Son, just think through what you are about to do. What will the board of directors think you are doing? How will the media take this, what if they find out that you have gone to India, and eventually why you have gone to India? You think our company needs this?" Varma tried changing his tactic.

But Raj was up for it.

"Don't worry pops. I have it all thought up. I would be announcing that I am going to India for setting up that donation drive and marketing campaign we have planned as part of the IPO publicity. And what's better, no one would question my decision of going to our own village to kickstart this campaign, it will be thought of as our RV company giving back to its motherland", Raj reassured.

Varma dropped all pretense.

"You don't know her Raj. GET IT THROUGH YOUR HEAD", he shouted. "If you go, you will not come back. She will get my grandson on ransom too, the first chance she gets. She is such a woman."

"Once you go, I will have to wait for a phone call from her, not from you, telling me she picked up a good time. Not for a wedding, because that would have already been done, but for a honeymoon. And she would say that the entire Gopala swamy clan is heading to the US, where you newly weds would go around the city while me and her will go around the company and its assets", Varma was sweating. The villager went quiet too, even he dreaded Sharada devi back in his life.

"No issues, no problem. Seeing that you've already packed your bags, maybe I'll just get mine packed. Suits, shirts, blazers, pants, nighties whatever I can get hold of ("What about my lungi? And my flowery shirts?" asked the villager). We'll fly to Switzerland tonight and have champagne in the Royal Oak resort enjoying the scenery" remarked Varma.

"And then, when we wake up tomorrow, we'll get into thinking of our new names and new business. Bee farming? Remember? We'll set it up", said Varma.

"Dad, as the dawn gets brighter, the night goes dimmer. I mean to say, as I kept growing young and strong, Sharada devi kept growing weak and old. I can tackle her quite easily. It's just the matter of you not trusting me and underestimating me", said Raj, sitting down beside his father.

On the other end, Mathew had just arrived, holding a bottle of brandy keeping a safe distance from the father and son.

"It's not a matter of me underestimating you, but you underestimating her!" countered Varma.

"Dad, but....", started Raj.

"The point is, you're not going!", decided Varma.

"Hey Mama (Pal)! Aren't we leaving? Can't wait to see those Indian chics in their barn", greeted Manoj.

And then Varma realized his son was not explaining about what he was about to do, but what he had already done!!!

Chapter - 9

GOTCHA

"Where did you think you were going?" chided Gopala swamy.

"Just to enjoy the midnight waves", replied daughter Gayathri with forced innocence, expecting her father to be drunk and accepting an answer she herself thought was foolish.

"Also, our family priest told me that if I go and offer my beloved belongings to the god of the seas, I will get a bride groom like Lord Rama", she added quickly as Gopala Swamy looked questioningly at the bags in her royal maids' (friends') hands.

"And what should that poor guy do to escape from the jaws of this Soorpanaka dressed as Sita", murmured Parvati to which Queen Gayathri gave a quick look of warning.

"The funny part is that the reason you gave me now makes more sense to me than your actual plan to escape", said Gopala Swamy rolling his eyes.

And before Gayathri could oppose this "plan to escape" idea, Gopala Swamy stopped her, "And don't think for a minute I stopped you fearing you will succeed in this dumb Dubai plan. I stopped you knowing that you would fail and a fisherman would come to our house telling us he caught you in an unknown island in the middle of Bay of Bengal weeping with your native tribal husband, and would demand a fortune from me in return for not leaking this!"

"Typical old king blabber!", mouthed Queen Gayathri now getting dejected that her brilliant plan had been shattered by that good for nothing sugar patient courtesan Murugayya, who couldn't hold onto his shit for a minute.

"For the record, we didn't catch you. You got yourself caught. And that boatman Paidi came to me half drunk, after waiting an hour for your arrival. He asked me for a ship to take "your highness" across the sea to Lanka where your "Lord Rama" is looking for you", scoffed the old king.

"Huuuuuuh, so my Dubai plan was leaked by the boatman then, I knew it was dumb to select him. I should have selected his grandson for this. It was just that I would have to endure his flirting for an hour by which time I would have reached Dubai", wondered her highness.

"Uncle, looks like you both are getting on well now. Shall we leave? We have to get ready for the function tomorrow and we will ensure to put our best", replied Subbalakshmi.

"Best in what you mean? Looks right? To hook those sons of my Panchayat guests", came an angry reply from Gopala Swamy, like an arrow.

"No uncle. She meant best foot forward", Radhika immediately corrected. *"As if those piglets were worth getting ready for. Yuck!"* she thought to herself

"And I am telling you it's your job, not theirs to look the best tomorrow", Gopala swamy pointed at his daughter. "Cause guess what, one of those boys will be your husband very soon" he added as he left.

"I knew it! I told you all this was bound to happen. Tomorrow is going to be my matchmaking, which is why I had to escape", cried Queen Gayathri thinking the gallows would have been a worthier punishment for her brave act. This was a lifetime imprisonment.

"My dumb highness. It is the converse, the matchmaking is going to happen because you tried to escape. A mad witch could get this much by now", laughed Radhika. "And thus ends the reign of my queen", she bowed as she too left with what Queen Gayathri had definitely sensed, some cunning joy and some sympathy.

As Gayathri was retiring to her room, she was stopped by the old queen. It was already dawn and Gayathri had to first get her sister ready and then get ready herself "for the grand holy sacrifice".

Her mother handed the very thing which got her highness caught, the bubble gum flavored pepsodent toothpaste with real stars in it. Now, Gayathri was really looking forward to squeezing it, rubbing it vigorously against her teeth and spitting it out, for failing her mistress.

How come Gayathri got up so early today? Without me asking, then scolding and finally threatening her of sending to clear her 12th class supplementary exams (which have been pending for the past five years). Huh! How could my daughter not even clear such basic exams? Where did I miss…anyways no time to think now, I should act happy.

"Looks like your beloved daughter is more excited than her sister for the marriage", Sharada asked her husband, who was trimming his beard.

"Yeah, she better be. Today's going to be her marriage proposal too. That bachelor, I mean Lord Hanuman's disciple Venkappa swamy informed that today is as auspicious as it can get", replied Gopala Swamy.

"If it is so auspicious, he himself would have got married today", mocked Sharada.

"He still might…", said Gopala Swamy. "Maybe an angel would descend today from heavens claiming that my daughter's engagement ring is her divine Angulikam (ring from heaven) and she might ask him to don her the ring and then, she would take him to heaven as her husband", he smirked.

"Jokes apart, I have just informed Gayathri about this too, and now I told you. So my job's done. I will now have to tell one of the Panchayat members, maybe Bommireddy or Nagireddy to give me Kanyasulkam (dowry gifted to the bride's father) for their precious sons to enter my house as a house husband", he added in a matter-of-fact manner.

"Why so, you can just send them an invitation card on the wedding day, telling them to bring their sons for their marriage. And why bother informing me, you can just show me the marriage video and I can bless them online", Sharada devi smiled wider than her husband (sarcastically of course).

"What now? Ok, it would be upon you to select from those Panchayat sons who would be the correct son-in-law who matches your ego. Happy?" said Gopala Swamy in a this-is-decided-now manner.

"How is it possible for you to remain exactly as dumb a person as you were, when I first met you? Please share your secret Gopal" replied Sharada, this time genuinely smiling.

Gopala Swamy, now realizing he had touched a nerve, stopped trimming and looked at her with a half bearded face.

"Wow, your looks match your wit now. Dhishti theeyalsindhe (an Indian custom to wash off evil forces that arise out of jealousy from watchers)", taunted Sharada.

"Hey, knock it off. I just told you that today is a very auspicious day for both our daughters and you want to start the day with a quarrel? I am sorry if I did something wrong, and for the life of me I can't understand what it is. Just forgive me of all the sins I committed from the moment I saw you to this day. Now please let me proceed, it is already getting late", Gopala Swamy begged.

"It is you who started this fight by taking your own decisions. Oh sorry, 'our own decisions'. Don't you think *we should take our decisions?* And you are actually right, it is getting late now that I realize. Oh wait, *you being right*, this is really an auspicious day then. Very rare." said Sharada and before her husband could interrupt or continue trimming, she informed him of her ordeal with Ravikant Varma.

"Woah, this is supposed to be *our decision* right?" demanded Gopala Swamy, sure that his wife had just made this out of thin air just to oppose his decision. "Okay, I learnt my lesson. If you'd really done that, I would have felt really angry. So, I understand your anger. But, don't take me wrong. Just meet those young lads and then we both will see who's the worthy one", assured Gopala Swamy.

"For what? President position? The most dumb and drunk one would be it then" snapped Sharada Devi, noticing her husband took her big decision to be a joke.

"Stop kidding", Gopala Swamy continued trimming.

"I never was", replied Sharada. Gopala swamy looked at his wife's image in the mirror in earnest. Did she really mean what she had said? He opened his mouth in shock (and now in pain too as he cut himself slightly with the trimmer).

"Who gets cut with a trimmer?" mocked Sharada.

"Hey, you didn't really speak to that Vantala Varma, did you?" enquired Gopala Swamy.

"What if you come to know I had?" retaliated Sharada, feeling relieved.

"Don't play with your daughter's life and that guy's time. That foolish cook would have been rejoiced by it, but when he comes to know that it was just a prank, he would jump into a boiling gas stove and cook himself to death", laughed Gopala Swamy, but just for a while. He stopped as he noticed Sharada Devi was still as cold as an ice gola.

"Don't you imagine for a second that I will get my daughter married to that woman + man's son. And this is your daughter, our daughter. What about her free will?" demanded Gopala Swamy.

"Please don't act intelligent Gopal, it only makes you look dumber than usual. What happened to 'your daughter's free will' when you were planning for the next President gaari alludu (President's son-in-law). When we are anyway getting her married against her will, why not give her a better life while doing it?" finished Sharada as if she setup a complicated trap from which Gopala Swamy couldn't escape now.

"Better I call a necromancer now, instead of a priest for marriage. How are you thinking of donating your daughter's hand to the one's whose hands are seeking alms in America? He is just getting alms in dollars. That's the only difference! He knows only one thing, how to cook, clean utensils and lick boots to make the white man whiter", scoffed Gopala Swamy, catching his breath.

"Don't even try to understand what he's doing there Gopal. He has hundreds of white people working under him. He's a millionaire now", Sharada argued.

"But he's still a cook, a maid, a slave, a monkey, a drunkard and what else can I add. Is he a President there? No, he's not. He will always be called a "Vantalodu" only", Gopala Swamy pleaded his wife.

"Oh God Gopal, I asked you not to try to understand. And let's be honest, when you say President, you had meant a village President right not the President of the US. You think that other country is just a country side, don't you? That's why I stopped trying to make you understand for all these years. Please leave this to me", now Sharada pleaded.

And before Gopala Swamy could retort, she said, "I haven't said a single word regarding our elder daughter's marriage. I allowed you to ruin her life with that villager

Kireeti, just like my father did to me. I will not allow you to do that with Gayathri. She has to get out of this place, see the world. My grandchildren, at least some of them need to be educated, need to be smart like me. This is un-arguable now".

"Is that so? Great! The next time you get in touch with that loser of a cook, tell him my husband is going to chop his son into pieces and serve him in my daughter's reception if he ever lands at my doorstep", shouted out Gopala Swamy.

"Ayyagaru, the bride groom's party is here", replied a shaking Murugayya who just arrived at the doorstep.

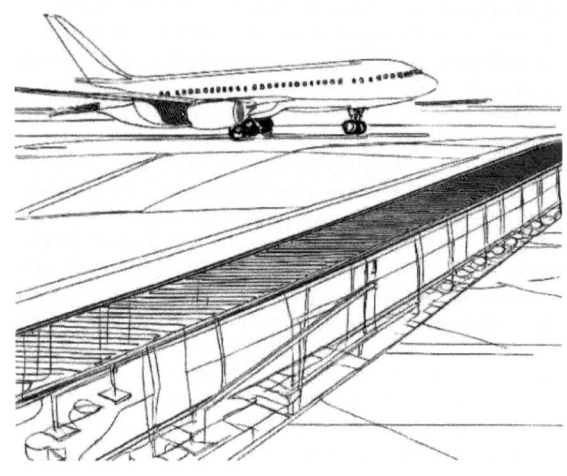

Chapter - 10
THE ARRIVAL

"VANDE MATARAM!!!" shouted Manoj as he stepped foot on the runway in Delhi.

People around him looked at him in surprise. There were instant murmurs like "Is he going to set off a bomb now?" "Is he a suicide bomber?" "I think this is that mentally challenged person they were kicking off from the states", "Children stay away from that psycho hairstyle uncle"

"Hello! Excuse me, Miss, or Mrs.... Savitramma... Pullamma.... whatever name", roared Manoj on the lady who was passing the remark of psycho uncle.

"Are you blind?" shouted back the lady, who was holding her son's hand who looked like he was just waiting for an opportunity to run. "Am having a son, how can you call me Miss? Is it because of my forever young looks that you got deceived?"

"So what if you have a son? Could still be a Miss. Isn't it quite common?" answered Manoj, ignoring the shocked expression from fellow passengers. "But, I wanted to ask another similar question *'Are you deaf?'* coz I shouted Vande Mataram, and how can I be a bomber? If I would have shouted words like *Jihaad*, it could have made sense!"

"There, there, now he's said Jihaad! Hubby, don't go near him, he might give a last cynical laugh when you touch him, and then BOOOMMM!", replied the lady who was now holding the hand of a fatter than tall, black hair coloured (with stains of white clearly visible) on both skin and head, waiting-for-an-opportunity-to-hit middle aged man, who according to Manoj, looked like that Bear God (what was his name?) Jambaavatha (if he's pronouncing correct) from Ramayana, his grandmother used to read.

"Let's run Darling. Don't waste time. At any moment, there would be his accomplices joining him"

"Why run when I can smack, squeeze and remove the bomb as well as brains out of him? Then we can hand over the leftovers to the cops for cleaning and taking photos", remarked the Bear man.

"I know babes, that you have always had the zeal to do something for this country. That's one of the qualities I found way back in you, and I liked it very much. And believe me baby, your running of wine shops is making this country better. You're a true patriot! Don't die fighting such worthless people. Think about our son and step back", pleaded the lady.

"Oho! So, him getting into a senseless fight with me sounds patriotic to you, while me chanting the divine line of Vande Mataram sounds militant?" mocked Manoj. "See Mr…. Jumbo…vathaa. If you really care about your son, marry her and inform your family members about both the good news (about the marriage and son)."

"Wait! Wait!" interrupted Raj, who came just in the nick of time to see the fat bear-like man ready to pounce on a stupid, brave looking proud-to-be-fish prey Manoj. "Sorry sir. My friend is a little, I mean very much new to India and he is over exhausted and excited due to the flight journey. Hence, he was making some stupid remarks. I'll handle him. Sorry once again."

Raj again had to try stopping the bear man with all his might, who didn't care what Raj was saying, and was only looking at his would-be prey Manoj, who was not even changing his look of confidence by a fickle.

"I've overheard from your beloved wife that you're a very successful entrepreneur in the alcoholic beverages business. That's a wonderful and very rare achievement.

As a token of appreciation, will you be obliged to receive this imported whisky from the U.S? Though I know it wouldn't be upto the standards of your wine quality sir", remarked Raj who was used to giving such statements to his partners and guests.

Looking at the bottle, the bear man grabbed it so fast from Raj's hands that he thought he was about to strike Manoj's head with it. But, instead, he immediately unleashed it and started drinking, as if he changed plans to strike the bottle as a prey, instead of Manoj.

"OMG! You disgusting accomplice. Now look at what you've done. Babe, please stop it. This is the 1421st time I'm asking you and is the 324th time that you agreed to stop and started again", cried the lady.

Her son and Manoj, on the other hand looked astonishingly at the drunkard's capacity while Raj silently kicked Manoj and indicated to him to start moving.

"What Manoj? Are you going to get us handed over to the cops as soon as we step on India. Are you so excited to see Indian jails?" whispered Raj, while in background there were hearing some shouts between the drinking husband and weeping wife with some remarks like *"Listen to me honey"*.... *"Customs would be charging for this bottle honey, if we come out of the airport with it. That's why"* .... *"You promised to stop"* ......*"It was your brother who provoked me to show my drinking capacity, during the 301 or 310th time"*.

"What did I do mama? Can't I even express my feelings of happiness and joy of entering my motherland? What dumb people did we run into, man! Let's hope they were just the once and for all bad, we had to endure to remove Dishti (an Indian tradition followed to remove any bad thoughts of other persons on one) from us while we enter India" answered Manoj.

"Ok. Let's get to the luggage belt and collect our belongings. Then we'll head to the enquiry counter and ask for any cab or bus which can take us to that place of my father's", decided Raj.

"We'll also find out how far is Taj Mahal from here. I heard from my jealous Indian neighbors in USA, that it's nearby Delhi only. Then will see how far and accessible is Kasi village from there. My granny told to do some Pooja for my grandfather's soul in Kasi. If it's nearby to Taj Mahal, we'll go from there. But if it's too far, will find out at Taj Mahal itself, if I can offer the prayers", added Manoj.

"What? Taj Mahal is a historical place bro made as a mark for love. How will it be having prayers and all there?" quashed Raj.

"Why not? Though it's known for looovveeee, it is also a sort of graveyard, right? So, will ask if I can add my grandpa's name in that list. It's also lying on the banks of a river. So, I can bath there and offer my grandpa's remainings there as well, similar to what I would have done at Ganga River in Kasi", replied Manoj.

"Will do one thing. You wait at the luggage belt and get our belongings. I will go and enquire at the enquiry desk, so that we can save time", thought Raj.

"Why should *I* take the luggage? You can do that while I will go and enquire", revolted Manoj.

"Oh, is it? Do you know the name of my father's village for asking at the counter? Or do you have the access or network to get things and arrangements done in India. Seems like I have both of them. So, go and get our luggage", finalized Raj with a triumphant look.

"You just wait till I find a dark and gorgeous Indian model here and will keep taking her wherever we go. You'll then realize the cost of this tiny laziness you've shown in waiting and collecting luggage", cried Manoj going towards the belts area.

Raj kept shaking his head, laughing, and went to the enquiry counter where his laugh drained instantly. There was already a big queue of 20-25 members. He only saw such a queue earlier in the USA when he was a teenager, when he went to a concert of one of his favorite pop singers without informing his dad.

There were complaints being told, rather than enquiries being asked, as Raj could hear. One such was *"Why didn't you inform earlier that my flight got delayed?"* to which the enquiry desk girl gave the only possible answer, *"How could we have informed you earlier sir, that your flight will be delayed? For that, the flight should actually get delayed for us to inform right?"* To that, the person replied *"I have to be there by tonight 7:35pm for a marriage. You know whose? MINE!!!!! And do you know the meaning of muhurath (auspicious time for marriage)? Our families are so particular to do the marriage on that time. Now if I am still in airport by that time, whom should I marry? You? Or should I tie an online knot with the bride and all you airport staff shower us with flowers and blessings. Stupid, idiotic, useless management!"*

Then, there came an immediate shout from behind, *"Elope with a girl you find interesting here and marry on that auspicious time. Happy now? Now move!!!"*

Raj had to endure all those shouts, complaints for an hour. The only good thing was that there was no sight of Manoj returning with the luggage looking happy that Raj had to wait longer. Now, there were only 3 people ahead of him. An old short plump lady in the front, wearing a blue saree with huge round spectacles, already swearing inside her as if rehearsing to release them on the enquiry desk. And then there was an average height girl, seemingly young (judging by her voice as she was shouting at the old lady to move quickly). Her face was hidden by her extra long hat and face mask, her neck hidden by big round earphones and hands covered by what looked like an elongated sweater. Only a part of her hair slightly falling out from her hat, and her eyes were visible. It looked to Raj as if she was a scarred witch or a ninja hidden behind her disguise who was going to suddenly reveal herself once her turn came, and do a mind boggling stunt or spell.

The person in front of Raj looked like a foreigner who could be in his 50s. He was wearing a hunter's hat with a matching color shirt bearing a lion on it and torn lined jeans, which looked as if the lion on the shirt had torn it. Raj imagined he must be some sort of a famous wild animal shooter or an adventure video shooter who was on his way to the next hunt. By the looks of it, the man was also new to India, and might be having a small enquiry to ask. Raj thought if he could solve the foreigner's issue himself, it would save some time. So he patted the man on his shoulder and greeted. The other man replied back with a "hello".

"Sir, which country are you coming from?" asked Raj.

"Am just now coming from Argentina", replied the passenger.

"Oh wow, I've been there frequently and love the forests and natural habitat there. Which place are you visiting now then?"asked Raj in an excited tone, hoping the foreigner would just give the place's name, instead of getting over excited and start explaining all his plans.

By the time the foreigner could reply, to Raj's surprise and luck, the old lady who was being deaf to the young girl's taunts had somehow heard the young lady's F word and returned with a *WHACK* on her face, so that the lady's mask and hat got askew in a dramatic manner. It revealed a completely normal human face (contrary to Raj's imagination). She now started shouting swear words even louder and both got involved in a verbal, followed by a physical tussle. The enquiry lady called for guards to take them off.

When the foreigner turned to the desk, the lady immediately replied, "Flight to Congo has been delayed, and we'll update you the timings shortly. Kindly wait with the other passengers over there."

Foreigner replied, "I'm not travelling to Congo. I have booked for Delhi only and have landed successfully as well, I presume."

"Yes sir", replied the enquiry girl with a puzzled look.

"I wanted to know if there was any helicopter to land tourists near the temple of Dwaraka", enquired the foreigner.

"Sorry sir, but we don't have any such helicopter arrangements, but you can go by a cab or train", replied the lady.

"No, no. I don't have time to navigate all through the forest, escape the booby traps and visit the tribes there, dance with them, and then visit the temple. I want a direct helicopter to avoid these complications and visit the temple", remarked the foreigner in a serious business like tone.

"As far as I recollect, you need not go through a forest to Dwaraka from Delhi sir", answered the lady this time in an undertone.

"How come? Is the temple of Dwaraka any unconventional temple of India?" foreigner enquired as if to note this point down.

"It's a normal temple, like all other temples in India, though not much renovated as others I think", she said.

"Then why isn't it like the Temple of Doom? If it's not in the forest, then this must be in the middle of an Ocean", thought the foreigner.

"Though you're partially correct on it, we have most of our temples in normal cities only sir", remarked the lady hiding a laugh now that she understood what the foreigner thought.

"Ok, then tell me where I can get a jeep car to go till the ocean. I would even be wanting a hunter with me by my side, in case there is a wild animal attack", demanded the foreigner.

"You'll get one as you go to the exit and ask for a Black and Yellow cab sir. Those are the uniform codes for hunters. You need not worry about the vehicle not being a jeep, as the driver, I mean, hunter is well-trained to drive at any condition and speed. Happy journey or a happy adventure sir", giggled the lady.

As the foreigner left the enquiry, the enquiry lady immediately started giggling with her colleagues saying they could have recorded this and posted on social media. Raj had to come and call her twice when she reappeared and asked, "How may I help you sir?"

"Can I know about the best transport possible from here to.... what is that place's name.... *Raj checked his mobile......*Siva.... samudram?"

"Sorry, what did you say the name of the place was?" enquired the lady.

"It is called Sivasamudram", repeated Raj.

"Am sorry I don't know about any such place nearby. Why don't you check in Google maps? Why do you need to enquire about it offline? My God, what a day!", saying this, the lady closed the desk now relieved that it was lunchtime and left.

Dejected, Raj returned to the luggage section and looked around for Manoj. He wasn't there in the luggage section. When Raj checked for his flight's luggage, it was showing that the last luggage had already come out and the next flight luggage was being loaded. After looking at the shopping section and in-transit section, with last hope, Raj went to the lounge and beverages section, wherein he found Manoj eating Idly (South Indian dish) with many other items such as Idiyappam, Dosa, Pickle, Poori - all placed before him with dozen water bottles. With every single dip of Idly in chutney, sambar and having a bite, Manoj gasped and emptied half a bottle of water and again started eating. Frustrated, Raj came and pushed Manoj aside.

"I had been standing long for an enquiry without getting any result, and you, you just wait for some luggage, get so hungry and start eating...what is this.... a devil's appetite?" he shouted.

"This is my place, my network and power! I will take decisions here", Manoj imitated Raj and then raised one of his eyebrows, "You might be the one taking decisions. But I need to follow them, right? Otherwise, they won't be of any proper execution. Did you see how luck favored me by not making me stand for an enquiry?"

Tired, unable to argue, Raj replied,"Ok man. Think whatever you want to think. But, hear this. The enquiry people said they never heard of any place called

Sivasamudram. Now, I am not able to understand how dad managed to do it."

"That is because uncle never trusted these people to get his job done. We are doing a mistake. Why ask them when we can figure it out ourselves?" boasted Manoj. "As soon as I experienced these people firsthand, I understood they won't even look out, let alone bother to come out of their comfort zone. They are in a tremendous state of self-pride. Let's figure it out ourselves. Here, have a seat and some water".

Saying this, Manoj opened his mobile and started looking in Google maps. "Oh shit! Our international sim doesn't work here. Excuse me, what is the Wifi password of this airport?" he asked a nearby retail outlet person.

"I don't think there is a common Wifi here sir. Every private outlet has its own Wifi and is chargeable", the outlet person replied.

"Huh! Take this", said Manoj, showing an obscene sign. "Now, what to do?"

"Don't worry, there is a mobile showroom there. Let's open maps from one of the model phones there and see", replied Raj who, after drinking water, gained back some energy.

"Yes sir, what phone would you like to see?" asked the employee inside.

"Not phones, apps", replied Manoj, pushing aside the bewildered employee.

"Nice, these are connected to the local Wifi inside the shop. Let's check in gmaps", sighed Manoj.

After opening gmaps and searching Sivasamudram in it, both of them looked at the maps and after a second, looked at each other.

"Is this the right place it's showing?" asked Manoj.

"Well, it didn't ask for any other place when we typed", replied Raj looking as if he was questioned about how much his total valuation was, in an interview.

"Dude, we could be traveling to many states within the US in such a distance", said Manoj. "Better we confirm with someone who knows this place."

"Well, there's only one person who can say", said Raj, taking out his phone.

"But, how are you going to call him when our network isn't working here?" asked Manoj.

"Switch on the hotspot in the model phone, Mr. Rip Van Winkle", commanded Raj.

"Hello?" answered (or rather questioned) Varma who was sitting miles away in his office, wondering what he will have to hear.

"Hi Dad. We landed a few hours back in Delhi. When we tried looking for a nice transport to your village, we were searching for our village in gmaps. Now when we searched, it showed a place which is 1,000 km away from here in a state called Andhra Pradesh. Is this village situated so far away?" asked Raj.

"Hahahahaha. Look at your son Varma, I mean our son. Doesn't even know where his birthplace is. Went and landed in Delhi, hahaha! Now he is asking us", laughed the villager in Varma's head.

"Huh! That's why I've told you not to take any stupid decision. Why did you go to Delhi in the first place?" asked Varma.

"Because it is the first place to start with, right? You said our house was at Delhi, after you left the village", replied Raj.

"Not left, absconded", retorted the villager. Varma banged the villager in his head with an ice pack and replied. "Get a return flight from Delhi to here immediately."

"Dad, if you're not going to say, I would have to find out the hard way, and believe me, I already have a hard way to get us out from the trouble. Don't make it tougher", replied Raj with slight worry in his tone.

"Yes, it is the place. But, son, please!!! Listen to me. You're following a trap", pleaded Varma. "Huh, Varma! Let him enjoy. After all, it's his place and his palace. He needs to fight and protect right", said the villager repairing his wound where Varma had hit.

"Thanks Dad! I am not following a trap, I am setting one actually. Will call you later. Take care but don't take wine." cut Raj.

"Sir, what have you done? How could you have used our mobile hotspot without informing", questioned the employee, again reappearing.

"Oh, is it? Then how come you've come exactly after he finished the call, not when he started?" enquired Manoj. "You did it because you expected some payment for using hotspot. Why is it that every person I meet in India is turning out like this? And of course, I have learnt to handle you guys so fast. Here, keep this." said Manoj taking a blank cheque out of his pocket, and signing it. "Write how much ever you want in it. Mind you, the account balance is just 1 Million USD."

"Thank you, sir! I will take utmost care", greeted the employee with a satisfied and cunning smile.

"We both know that there is no amount in your account, right?" remarked Raj, as they were walking away.

"Yeah, and to be on the safer side, I signed, imagining how Brad Pitt must be signing his autographs. So, no worries", assured Manoj, this time he gave a satisfied but cunning smile.

"Fine, I'll call our marketing team once and ask them to arrange for a transport to that village", replied Raj.

"What? I thought this was a personal trip, not a professional one?" asked Manoj.

"It is kind of both actually. How will we be traveling to such a far place without any help?" questioned Raj.

"Rahadhaari (The Highway)!" replied Manoj, mimicking Rajnikanth (Superstar in Kollywood film industry).

This time, Raj showed a bad sign to Manoj, which the latter ignored and started pleading, "Come on bro, it will be fun. Let's keep singing patriotic and romantic songs on the way. We'll keep stopping at some places and drinking water. And then, some native young women will look at me and smile. Then, I will go join them and start dancing, and you, you will be singing with the adult people there. It'll be soo fun!"

"I'll drop you in an asylum nearby and you'll grow old there, trying to dig a hole in the tunnel until your hole in the brain gets filled. I'll inform your family that you were too drunk and took a fight with the local cops and landed in a prison", remarked Raj.

"Why do you do this mama? You were the one who said we would be going back to India, and you said we would be going on a personal vacation and trip. How will we justify our trip if you don't let me participate?" Manoj replied with a childish face.

"It will take months if we go by road coz we don't even know the route properly and will get lost. What if we get stolen by prowlers on the highway?" asked Raj in a get-back-to-reality tone.

"I know Martial arts mama!" Manoj assured, already starting to show some moves. "We will be rewarded, not the prowlers, if ever we face one. Because I'll smack them and loot their stolen money."

Raj hesitated, but thought for a moment. Manoj couldn't understand what Raj must be thinking. But finally, Raj replied, "Ok, but on one condition. You won't ask me whatever I might do in the middle of the journey. Of course, you're free to do whatever you want."

"Fine mama, whatever happens in India stays in India. Zip…Zip…" replied Manoj naughtily indicating closure of a zip to his lip.

Raj started going towards the telephone booth, still giving Manoj a suspicious glance as though wondering if it was safe to leave him alone. He dialed.

"Bastard!!! I don't want any credit card or loan. Now just go and eat someone else's head", barked Surya.

"But you do want your job right? To repay those credit card bills and loans you already have, Surya?" asked Raj in an already-tired-of-this-place tone.

"Ugh? Hello? Who is it? This is Suryadev speaking, the CMO of Indian arm of the RV Restaurants chain. How may I help you?" replied Surya in a sort of dignified tone.

"You can start by not asking anymore questions or revealing your true nature or your grip on the english swear word poetry. I am your boss's boss's and so on so forth's boss. By that I mean I am your boss too. Arrange for a ….." replied Raj.

"Hold on, hold on! Is this Narendra Modi by any chance? Is this regarding the municipality complaint regarding the Nala near my street?" asked Surya now expecting to get a yes and a sudden cascade of presspeople in front of him.

"If by Narendra Modi, you mean the newly appointed CEO of your company who has just landed in India, then yes", remarked Raj with a little bossy attitude.

"Is this a prank call?' asked Surya.

"Do you want a letter of suspension as a proof of authenticity? I can get it faxed to you in 10 minutes? And on a serious note, don't get me started on my swear word dictionary. Believe me, having been brought up in America, I know lots of unique words with some added nuance. Now, I don't know how I can prove to you that I am who I am. If you want it tested, then send a car with a wiser person (than you) who reads the newspapers and identifies his boss. Or else, I will send the fax to the one who is above you whom you would instantly recognize because of the swear words he gifts you everyday", saying this, Raj disconnected the phone.

"Let me guess, it's your Indian girlfriend whom you are angry with. And you are angry because she is angry that you have not told her you were landing", asked Manoj, practicing Martial arts with his now useless airplane ticket as though it was his sword.

"Have you suffered an electric shock with a memory loss in these 5 minutes? I told you not to ask me any questions right?" wondered Raj.

"My guess is that a car is going to arrive soon, along with an apology letter and a bouquet and my guesses usually come true", replied Raj.

"Right, let's go for a ride", shrugged Manoj, throwing his ticket like a chakra into the dustbin (which innocently obeyed) and kicked his bag onto his hand.

Chapter - 11
PLAN OF ACTION

Abhiram (Sharada's elder daughter Suguna's fiance) was dancing with his hands on his horse ride as he was afraid the horse might mistake his leg shake to some other command (maybe like a king's order to race into the battlefield) and sprint ahead in an uncontrollable speed. His friends, Gopala Swamy's supporters, students from nearby college, villagers who were just too drunk to stay still were all dancing as his horse marched towards Gopala Swamy's house.

"Who is this guy? Why is he having Baarat for engagement instead of a marriage? Seems like he is more drunk than I am", laughed a random dancing drunkard, offering some of his wine to the horse.

"Hey! Hey! Get lost. What are you doing, you mid-sized buffoon? Ramesh? Giri? Guys, get this half-baked idiot out of here!", shooed off Abhiram, trying whatever he could with the ropes, to take his horse away from the drunkard, and more importantly from the drink, as the horse started sniffing.

But his friends could neither listen to Abhiram's rants through the loud music nor care less for what was happening with him behind. They were too busy losing their minds drinking and dancing.

"Soori, what the heck! I know you're looking at the girls out there. I also know you're able to hear me. Listen, I am trying to…..hey? HEYY!!! What is that sound?" paused Abhiram, with fright in his eyes now.

A loud reverberating sound filled Abhiram's ears and he wasn't sure if anybody else could hear it. He was getting random dreadful thoughts with that sound. *Was it his time to go?*

With a sense of panic, he kept looking everywhere expecting a stranger to land from heaven or hell on a bull calling him with a pitiful look that he had to die a bachelor at this moment. But, to his relief, some of the dancers and less drunk people stopped and started searching.

Atlast, one of them pointed to Abhiram's left, and he saw an old saint blowing a shell with full energy and with a sense of responsibility.

"Hey! You old permanent beggar cum bachelor", shouted Abhiram, removing his garland and throwing at the saint who smiled and placed his neck on time to receive the flying garland gracefully around him. "Have you taken a stronger drag than you normally do from your pipe? Can't you see the difference between a wedding and a funeral? I can see that you missed your wedding and the only event where anyone is going to dance for you now is your funeral."

"Aren't you the one entering the Gopala Swamy cum Sharada Devi household as a house husband?" asked the beggar (or saint) dramatically as though asking him to choose his pill (red or blue).

Abhiram looked around for help. No one came to his rescue. So he replied, "What if I am?"

"Then I see no difference", laughed the beggar to himself and he blew the conch once again with a renewed energy.

Some of the sober guests from Gopala Swamy's house came out and chased away the chuckling saint and came back smiling at the oncoming procession. "Pack your stuff my youthful son, your countdown has begun!!!" came a distant voice from the beggar. The horse gave a kneighing leap standing up on its hindlegs as though ready for the battle. Abhiram hugged the horse's neck, befuddled whether the horse had shown its agreement or disobedience to the beggar's words.

The caterers were packing the remaining dishes, the servants from the tent house were gathering the chairs, some of the guests were still gossiping with empty plates in their hands. It was almost sunset as the exorbitant engagement came to an end.

There were some feeble tantrums being heard like *Our guy is a Naughty Krishna, dude. Gopala Swamy is a man above his word, see how he got his daughter a house husband. Don't forget! He got himself a free slave with this. Sister, you know the necklace worn by Suguna is not so expensive. I wore such an ornament for my brother's divorce hearing. What food man? What a food man!*

Sharada Devi was again missing from all this humdrum while Gopala Swamy was in the thick of it. Sharada Devi was sitting in her study watching television. This was of course the hot topic in the female section's gossip. But Sharada Devi wasn't watching a daily serial or a *star mahila* show which the village women approve of. She was watching the NDTV business news for some reason. She was looking at the young man on her television screen. Some women were of the opinion that Sharada was admiring the guy's looks and didn't waste any time in spreading this rumor. Their rumor had a reason after all, Sharada was smiling as she looked at the guy, and her gaze was so intense as though a leopard had spotted its prey.

"Now this is a surprise", she thought to herself. She usually hated surprises too, as it would mean she was unable to anticipate the predicament. But she liked this surprise, this meant she was more than successful in shaking Ravikant Varma. She had shaken his son too. However, the news said the son was here for a marketing campaign ahead of his soon-to-be firm's IPO. But

Sharada didn't seem to buy it. Somehow, for a moment, she felt as though there was no T.V. barrier; she and Raj were directly looking into each other's eyes.

"Aunty?" came a voice behind her. She turned back to see her foolish worthless son-in-law. "We, I mean, not we both, but we all need to take a photoshoot. That priest says the auspicious time for the shoot is running out."

"Huh? Oh. Ok, am coming. You go ahead and start the ritual", replied Sharada with a tone that suggested *what else are you capable of anyway.*

After the formal guests (who had come more to eat than to greet) had left, Gopala Swamy took his tiny panchayat team players to his study room (or so to say an in-house bar). He switched on the gramophone where old 90s song "Raavoyi chandamama, maa vintha gaadha vinuma" started to play, and he lit himself a big stuffed cigar as he sat down.

"What Gopalam? A panchayat meeting just after the engagement? We expected a private party from you, not a panchayat meet", "Yeah, and it's the groom who's got to drink now, thinking of his future, not us". Some of them laughed at this remark.

Gopala Swamy gestured the guests to sit down. "This is not regarding Suguna's engagement. This is about Gayathri's marriage", he said.

"Hey, will you stop calling a panchayat meet every time you have a fight with your wife", remarked an angry panchayat member (who had lost to Gopala Swamy in the latest cock fight).

"Gopal, Suguna's marriage is not done yet and you've started to worry about Gayathri's?" asked another panchayat member who was pouring himself a vintage brand of wine, without asking for.

"If this was indeed my daughter's wedding alone, I wouldn't have trusted you half hearted, half witted dumbos with it. This is also regarding one of your sons' wedding, which is why I am bringing this up with you", Gopala Swamy was talking to the room at large.

"Has your wife taught you this?" laughed a fellow panchayat member.

"You ask for my son to be your daughter's house husband too?" asked the cocky panchayat cock fight loser.

"Hey, give him a quarter of his favorite. That will ease the egg inside him", retorted Gopala Swamy with literal smoke of fire emitting out of his mouth.

"What? You mean our sons?" asked the current drunk panchayat person (his mind took some time to process the information he got, which led to a delayed response).

"Yes, my dear little soldiers. Now start bidding your princes and your prices. I hope you guys have already found how much that Abhigaadu has got. So, be reasonable considering your sons' true colors", puffed Gopala Swamy.

"As you all know that my son is about to get close to 100 acres of my fields as his inheritance, I would consider another century from your end as a price. And that century would be my retirement plan, as in the land would have to be on my name", remarked the richest of the lot (of course lower than Gopala Swamy himself)

"You mean that Jack of all trades, who can't get a Jack in the card pack to save his life, that "Pekata Babji"? I prefer to call him Joker of all trades, though Joker is a valuable card. And also, regarding his farming activities, I have only seen him peeing and playing in the fields. He knows only one use of land, betting on it. If you give him a wife, he will use her as a bet too. Then I would have to give the bastard who won over your son another century to free my daughter. I guess one day he will just bet on himself and lose himself to a camel dealer and settle as a camel dung lifter in Rajasthan", spitted Gopala Swamy.

"Think about my one. He owns the famous Sattigaadi canteen and is also planning to launch a Kallu compound in competition to that Malligaadu", replied a fatty panchayat colleague, lighting his own cigarette.

"No thanks, I don't want to see my daughter's name and photo on that Kallu compound. Every stupid drunk dumbass would be looking and imagining a duet with her. And your son will be cashing it by offering one to the premium customers", scoffed Gopala Swamy.

"I am not selling my son to you", said the cocky guy.

"You think your son is worth a penny. I will take him with a payment from you in case you offer him. Can't select a proper cock for the fight, I don't expect him to select a proper girl for his life. And coming to fights, I heard he got into a fight with the women's society (mahila mandali) demanding a membership for him too, similar to how there are reserved seats for women in panchayat and public buses. I wish him luck for that", smirked Gopala Swamy, accidentally dropping his cigar laughing.

Before the taunted panchayat people could get up and revolt, the closer Panchayat member to Gopala Swamy (both in position and relation) rose and replied, "Gopalam! Calm down. Firstly, I feel it is too early to decide on a proper groom for Gayathri. Secondly, don't you think it should be Gayathri's choice first?"

"Subbu, will you give your son to my daughter?" Gopala Swamy asked quickly.

All other panchayat members broke into a fit of laughter on hearing this.

"Hey Subbu, congratulate your son on behalf of us, for getting promoted to a watchman for Gopalam's house and his wife. Anyhow, he is a confused soul within himself. Maybe a few beatings from his wife would bring out the man inside him."

"I…. I don't know. Are you sure Gopalam? Why don't you ask Sharada or Gayathri first?" blinked Subrahmanyam.

"Just a disclaimer, all this should happen without Sharada or Gayathri's knowledge. We will need a plan", started Gopala Swamy shaking his cigar to puff out the dregs.

"Wow, now this is news. We were under the impression that Gayathri or Sharada loved what you did with your first born and were really on the edge for a second function in the house. It is you who is unable to hold your horses, is it?" laughed the others.

"What would you say to the ownership of my poultry farms and two ambassadors Subbu? Is your son worth it?" Gopala Swamy meant business. "And yeah, a guaranteed spot of Upasarpanch to you or your son once I become the sarpanch" he added.

"But what about Abhiram then?" asked Subbu.

"He is already trapped. Why would your 'Gopalam' give him the bait. He is showing you the worm now. Will you bite?" asked the cocky panchayat guy.

"He will be the next Sarpanch, you jealous seagull", Gopala Swamy gave back.

"Hey! Hey! Wait, where did that come from? Then we will set our sons to follow and trap your daughter, come to your house wearing stylish glasses like Rajnikanth from Narasimha movie, and ask for half of your wealth in acceptance." said the drunk panchayat guy, now angry on losing the high as well as Gopala Swamy's offer.

"For that, your son needs to be an Abbas, Murthy. Get that in your mind. Or else, I will show you and the village your son's photo again. Let's see if we don't get a 'Beware of Thieves' posters in the village by tomorrow", mocked Gopala Swamy.

"It is decided then I guess, it will be Subbu's son Phalguna for my younger daughter. All of you need to help me with a plan of action now. We have until Suguna's marriage for this. We should plan to make an announcement of the next wedding right at the marriage hall. And I should not hear a word of protest from Sharada or Gayathri", Gopala Swamy put it bluntly.

"Then there's just one way to do that. You threaten to jump into the holy fire if anyone protests against this proposal. Then Gayathri would up the ante by threatening to do just the same if you don't call it off. Then you need to take out your revolver and put it on your head. Sharada would run towards you and squeeze the trigger herself to everyone's surprise (not us of course) and enact a small "OOPS" as though it were an accident. And this is not a plan Gopala Swamy, this is actual action", called out the drunkard.

On the floor just below, Sharada Devi kept checking google maps in her phone. She kept noting down the distance and time it would take to reach Sivasamudram from Delhi by all transports, wondering how this time even luck seemed to favour her (which didn't happen for so many years). In front of her stood a shivering priest, pleading to leave. He requested for his payment for the engagement ceremony while Sharada Devi took out Gayathri's birth certificate and uttered,"Start".

"Ma'am?" replied the priest not understanding if she was asking him to abscond.

"Come on, I don't have time to praise you. Show us your gifted skills", replied Sharada.

The priest kept thinking, slightly blushing about what skills might Sharada Devi be referring to. Noticing this, Sharada Devi gave a look which could only have meant that if he was not going to do whatever she was thinking, his funeral will be performed in that very spot with his son taking payment for performing the last rites.

"You want me to prepare a horoscope?" asked the priest praying the Gods for it to be true.

"No, I want you to adopt her and get her admitted in the Singapore massage center for her to earn a living", it seemed like Sharada was interviewing the priest on his prowess in all the four Vedas.

"Was that a joke ma'am?" the priest could never guess when Sharada was being sarcastic or serious.

"Of course, I actually want you to marry her, you braided priest. And I want you to recite your own mantras for the marriage, put up an auspicious time for the kid's naming ceremony, cradle ceremony, his marriage, his honeymoon. And if you ask me if I am joking now, you will only see people laughing at your face for the rest of your life", she put it as sarcastically as she could.

The priest realized he put her in the exact spot he shouldn't have. He needs to run out of this place as soon as possible.

"I will need three days ma'am", he pleaded.

"To marry her? Wasn't that five days?" Sharada looked at the priest with forced innocence.

"Please don't misunderstand me. Because Gayathri papa has never had her palm read by me, I need to.... I need to.... Yeah, I need to find her birth star, her.... zodiac sign, chakravakam, kaundinyam, praptham and so many other complex parameters. Just three days please", he was already starting to leave.

"In three days, I will have your horoscope with me. Remember that. Everything from your financials, your customers, clients, cases filed against you, your potential inheritors, your mistress (married or otherwise as applicable), your daily routine, your eating habits, your medical status, your insurance policies down to your clothing sizes. I will have everything. This is how I gauge your future. Oh sorry, telling the future is your job right? I will tell you your past, present and decide your future and make you read it. Now get lost and get going. I need to know an auspicious date for Gayathri's marriage in 3 days from now", and she just turned away.

The priest just took a split second to reach the exit and another second to a toilet to let off the pressurized fluids he had to hold (thinking *to hell with the payment he didn't get for the engagement ceremony, let's ask for it during the marriage function*).

"All this would be for the family's well being. After all, the family's well being was always my responsibility.

They might not have understood this for so many years, but they will, in the coming years. Once they realize what was in store, there would be no more misgivings. Everything is falling and will fall into place. My god, what a decision it was", thought Gopala Swamy… and Sharada Devi too.

Chapter - 12

THE UNEXPECTED

"There you go sir, these are your Indian numbers, we have got you an unlimited free calling sim with a high data pack. And this is the uh.... google maps installed car you asked for if I am not mistaken", explained the man in black suit with black spectacles wearing a black watch and standing on black shoes.

"Thanks M. By the way, has someone in your family passed away? What's with all this black and black?" asked Manoj grabbing only the car keys, leaving Raj to collect the sim.

"Yeah! Cool! A BMW, not bad", remarked Manoj as he sat down. He immediately changed the gear, released the handbrake.

"Not just any BMW sir, it is a 2019 BMW 8 series convertible. Maximum speed upto 225 kmph. People died driving these cars at those speeds in these roads", said the "M"an in black proudly.

"What the…...? Hey where is the… wheel?" asked Manoj in shock.

"There are six wheels actually, including the spares in the trunk. Four are under the car I think sir, fully air blown. I don't know about America, but here in India, the wheels are usually under the car", remarked "M"an in black.

"I meant the steering w…." continued Manoj but before he could complete, Raj sat to his right where the wheel was. As he looked for the gear and brake, he saw it was already done and good to go.

"Thanks a lot mama, you didn't have to do it actually. So the coordinates to our office are fed in this?" asked Raj.

"No sir, the location pin has been set actually", replied M shamefully. "Coordinates are set in flights currently", he added.

"Is he an AI robot your company designed?" asked Manoj doubtfully.

"No idea, see you soon M bro", saying so Raj drove to his company's Delhi office (all the near accidents caused en route either due to Raj's ignorance of Indian traffic rules or due to lack of importance assigned to the Indian traffic rules by the fellow drivers are being omitted here for the sake of brevity).

"Phew, finally we reached. Why were all the nut case car drivers driving to the right mama?" came an agitated grunt from Manoj to which Raj gave a shrug.

That evening in the board room, the marketing campaign schedule was just getting done as the "no-nonsene but full-on nuisance" Mr. Rajagopala Chary entered the room.

"And then as Deepika Padukone opens the platter…. shock…..there is no food on it. The camera cuts to the director of the shoot (actually an actor who would pretend to be the director) looking clueless and angry. And cut to Deepika who gives a guilty smile and says *Sorry guys, couldn't help it.* The scene would then rewind to show the sizzling hot Indian variant of the Mexican Taco placed in front of Deepika and she looks at it with a helpless longing look and grabs the plate. The screen would blur out and a message says "Sorry guys, you can't help it"...." concluded a pony tailed Vijju who was the creative head at RV India.

"Hey, I was told this meet would start at 6", entered Rajagopal.

"Yeah, you are right. We told you so", said Vijju closing the presentation. "We didn't want you to waste time."

"But this is my job", argued Rajagopal.

"Not your time, our time", saying so Vijju sat down to a cascade of claps and some jeers of appreciation for his counter to Rajagopal. Vijju just smiled and batted an eyelid at Manoj, who drew back in his seat uncomfortably.

"So, you're done with your grand scheme of conning millions of people showing as if the celebrity eats our shit daily for breakfast, lunch, snacks, dinner, timepass and what not? Well, in reality, she eats up all our budgets and has, what shall I say, half boiled leafy vegetables to keep her so-called beauty drive. I swear if the pictures of these current heroines were shown 20 years back, people would have thought it were the pictures of some Vietnamese ladies who starved to death due to the war", Rajagopal sat grudgingly.

"Did you ask or just answer your own question?" asked Vijju once again to amazing applause from the board room. Raj and Manoj looked confused at the ongoing turmoil.

"Oh I am so sorry Mr.Varma. This here is Rajagopal, a marketing team lead who never works with the team", added Vijju, "He works against the team, works without informing the team, takes all the team decisions alone and without consultation but finally scolds the team as a whole when things start making sense and he realizes the situation spitting at his plans", introduced Vijju, all the while withholding a smile from turning into laughter.

"Good evening Mr.Varma. Now that you yourself have come all the way, I hope the team realizes how critical the situation has become as a result of your stupid planning and execution. Let's all, as usual, leave the decision to me once it gets out of hands. I am now proposing to neatly wrap this well made senseless presentation and throw it as far and fast as we can. Let's face the reality and actually show it. Oh, and by the way the next time you talk to your father, please ask him on my behalf to share his secret of sleeping peacefully besides being fully aware that he is responsible directly or indirectly for the bankruptcy of over 200,000 people in the globe in the past 6 years alone" finished Rajagopal looking at the room as a whole and giving a fake cough.

"So, what do you actually wish to say Raja?" asked Vijju.

"I say we make a clean and plain ad, as how we project ourselves to be from outside. We show them all, our restaurant, the entire items in the menu along with their pricelist, and a small video of our administration and cooking room. Oh, and we also show them that we intend to ban a few foods for children as they might be addictive with added artificial flavoring; and as parents you should not let your kids eat this grass you decided to punish yourselves with." completed Rajagopal sounding bored.

"And? Shall we also give a disclaimer saying Smoking and Drinking are injurious to health? Show the stats of how many people die smoking, drinking and eating junk food, and take interviews of some Mukesh or Vimal or Sunitha?" bashed Vijju.

"Are you aware we intend to make an ad, not a documentary or a hopeless warcry", asked another team member. Rajagopal was just looking at Raj as the latter stared back interestingly.

"Come on, prove yourself worthier than your father. For once, think about the people at the bottom and not the bottom line. I have a daughter who lost her appetite to the traditional gongura pickle because of your father's stupid spanish fancy dish I can't even name. Your decision is going to affect the global food chain, prove you are not an animal and actually think about the food you eat." Rajagopal almost spoke as if he was interrogating Raj for a confession.

"Hey chill uncle," replied Manoj. "Don't worry. I can see you're a fan of Megastar, inspired from his movie "Tagore". We are not Lex Luther, creating some ecological or biological weapon of war. And as to your daughter, I think she lost an appetite for a pickle because her mother/father doesn't know how to make it properly. And I completely understand you not being able to afford the food she likes. Why not send her to me? I will take her outside for a few days and open her up to this romantic world. And you need not worry, I won't reveal that you had fixed it all along." reassured Manoj. But he was unable to understand the look he got in return.

"I think the meet is over", and saying so Rajagopal left the room.

Everyone else raised and started congratulating each other.

"Hey, what did we do? Why are we shaking hands?" asked Manoj.

"Oh, we could never successfully drive him out in 10 minutes. You did a great job buddy. Just make sure he doesn't get your number and reach out. Cause if you get so much as a missed call from him once, then you are out of our help. Best of luck", patted Vijju.

"Actually, can you give me his number?" asked Raj.

The atmosphere in the room felt like Raj had just died of a heart attack. Everyone was looking at him, as though waiting for some indication of lunacy.

Finally, Vijju broke the ice, "Uh, you want to like donate something to his family? You can use the donation bin right at the entrance to the office. We will make sure his family gets it, discreetly of course."

"Not exactly, but can I know if he is a tech savvy person? Like how often does he check his netbanking or do online investment and stuff?" remarked Raj.

To his and Manoj surprise, the silence was broken instantly and unexpectedly by a burst of laughter.

One of the guys came out of the laughing gas spell and replied, "Leave alone netbanking. He doesn't even get his cheques to his bank account. What was that? Let me remember.... *All these banks are just massive chit fund swindlers. They show how much money they looted just to attract us to foolishly offer ours as well. They take money from 10 and give it to 20, assuring the original 10 that their money is safe in the bank by showing them a number on the screen. There is no money physically in the account behind that number. But if I keep my money in the "Popula Dabba" (a box of spices in Indian kitchens), I am rest assured that my money is real".*

"Oh my god Raghava, you must start starring in our ads", applauded Vijju for Raghava's imitation of Rajagopal.

"No problem Mr. Varma. One day, we'll arrange a virtual meet with him and you can get the full blast and still be safe and sane. But, please don't blame us later", continued Raghava but he was instantly stopped by a hand raise from Raj.

"You definitely sound entertaining. We'll surely plan a mimicry show starring you as a part of the marketing campaign. But, please sound useful. Give me his number, or I'll have ya'll report to him for 5yrs from now", warned Raj now sure that he would get his number within seconds.

Sure, enough Raj had his number from everyone's whatsapp. While Manoj got a picture of Rajagopal's daughter (just as an added incentive). Everyone left the room with surprised and suppressed looks.

"Now tell the truth mama. You took his number just to scare the team so that they won't get on to you right?" enquired Manoj, now scanning Rajagopal's daughter.

"You need not worry bro. You can focus on his daughter while I have a small work with her father", taunted Raj as they left the board room.

"Where to now?" asked Manoj.

"Let's drive to Sivasamudram now", announced Raj.

"What? Are you mad? All this time, we spoke shit and I didn't even get Deepika's number. Now you want us to leave? And why couldn't you ask these clowns who wear suits in India when it's shit hot outside?" questioned or rather bursted Manoj.

"That was a professional gig. To make the world believe that I've started being a part of the marketing campaign here. We'll be now going to deal with this personal one and I don't want any flight tickets or traces of any travel destinations which these board members would use to trace me", said Raj.

"What mama? You're sounding as if each one of these board members are plotting to kill us for your wealth? Is there some sort of Game of Thrones going on? Is this why you had brought me into this? To have a stupid handsome bodyguard who knows martial arts, as a human shield", weeped Manoj with the innocent childish look he generally gives to girls.

"Though it would have been much more fun, it's not as cruel or creative as you put it. It's just a trip to my native place and I don't want anyone knowing about it. That's all", said Raj as they reached the car in the cellar.

The topless 2019 BMW 8 series convertible vroomed to life as Raj turned on the engine. He set the location to Sivasamudram, Andhra Pradesh and looked ahead as Manoj gently touched Raj's shoulder.

Raj looked at the naughty expression on Manoj's face as he asked, "Who's that chick mama? I knew all along there was some Indian girl involved in all this. Sounds like Ramaayan story my granny used to say. We are the Rama and Laxmana here who crossed an ocean to find the Sita you loovveed. So, will there be any monkeyman or a bearman who will help us fight the ten-headed Raavana (who is it here…. yeah, the girl's brother or father)?"

"The Sita's name is Sharada and I think she must be some fifty years old now", replied Raj as he drove outside the gates having "RV" etched on them, leaving behind a puff of smoke and a huge skyscraper named after him.

Chapter - 13

AND SO, IT BEGINS

The BMW was parked outside the Lucky's Famous Family dhaba on the outskirts of Agra, early in the morning. Raj just freshened up with some listerine as he came towards the table where a distraught Manoj sat silently.

"Have you ordered anything mama?" asked Raj as he patted Manoj on the shoulder.

Manoj jerked off Raj's hand irritably and said, "Now I am going to order and you should follow it. Just shut up for the rest of our journey back to US, as I am going to find the nearest internet cafe and book us our return tickets."

"Did you drink any local stuff here?" asked Raj alarmed.

"I think it was you who drank some shit in New York, fell in love with a 50 year old granny on an online dating app and brought me into this. And you tell me just yesterday night that you have done all this for that old chic who will surely have at least 10 daughters of her own!!!", Manoj just shouted as the nearby waiter came and yawned.

"Who said I am marrying that girl, you lazy joker?" asked Raj indignantly.

"Mama!!! This is too much now. I might be an American by colour and glamour, but am an Indian at heart. And I can't accept you entering the life of an Indian girl.... I mean....woman (they are stopped being called a girl after half her age) and just dating her and abandoning." Manoj retorted by hitting hard on the table.

"Are you going to order something or should I order you to get out?" asked the waiter.

"Alright, one pancake with maple syrup, and an omelet for me. Also, get me a musk melon juice with no added sugars, with a pinch of lemon and a dose of glucose in it", asked Manoj.

"A bagel for me, and maybe some chocolate waffles", added Raj.

The waiter looked at both of them and said, "1 paneer curry, 1 malai kofta, 1 omelet for you, with one water melon juice without sugar, one lemon juice (the lemon will be pinched) with glucose in it. And for you, 1 baigan bartha and chocolate wafers. Anything else?"

"Better to order an ear machine for you first, mate. What's the matter? Did your wife shout a lot yesterday night or hit you right in the ear? Can't sympathize more", said Manoj, casually hitting the waiter's stomach, who looked at them both as if he was going to take his last order and run away.

"A lassi is complimentary, so have fun", saying so he left.

"Oy!!! Am I looking like I've drunk? Then, why is lassi complimentary? Do one thing. If you're giving lassi complimentary, how about you give a complimentary whisky or rum with it, so that it will get complimentary", winked Manoj, playing with the fork.

The waiter yawned and shouted, "Arey ek kudi dha gaana lagao oye!!!" and a loud punjabi disco song was played.

"I am sure this guy is deaf or has become deaf after listening to this loud music", complained Manoj.

"What a country man! A deaf waiter, a mindless marketing manager. No wonder your pops is weird. I always thought US made him weird, now I know he was born weird", sighed Manoj, "Oh and on the topic of being weird, will you atleast tell me what is it that you liked in this aunty that made you fly back home? And you are enroute to featuring in Vogue's Top 10 most eligible bachelors too."

"Mama, now am feeling it's you who might have become either deaf or mindless or both. It's for the umpteenth plus oneth time I said not to ask me anything on the way. Though I'm explaining again so that your childish soul gets satisfied. I'm not interested in either loving her or dating her or marrying her, or so much as winking at her. You can think of it like…. my dad has got some deal with her in the past…. yeah, that's the closest I can say", replied Raj.

"Wheew…wheeew, so your father dealt with her in the past and she has some love letter with her, which your father fears would come out in the public. In order to avoid this, she might have asked for some cash or help which you're planning to sort out secretly right?" asked Manoj with a wolfish glare."Or….don't say…..is there another unofficial heir? Whoa…wait!!!"

Raj was about to drain the entire water from the bottle he was holding, onto Manoj.

"You ask me one more question, and I will leave you here. Then you would become the deaf waiter around here and take orders from NRIs like us who would come to visit Taj Mahal. And you would keep begging them to tip in dollars, so that you could cherish your old days", roared Raj. "How is it that your brain has got so much cringy stuff mama? I've hardly seen 1% of it in others. Looks like you've set a self-record in it which you would break the very next second."

"Then, what is it we're doing here mama?" asked Manoj.

"And that's a question", saying so, Raj got up, about to leave.

"Whoa, Ok, Ok I am sorry. No more questions from my end", Manoj imitated zipping his mouth.

"No questions about my stuff would do", remarked Raj.

And then they were served food. Surprisingly, not a single item matched with what they had ordered. They were so confused with what they got and more so, trying to match each item with its name (as in what did they get for ordering bagel etc.,). However, they just ate whatever was given to them and left with some odd stares from the adjacent tables (as they ate the paneer curry and malai kofta directly, without any rotis or side dishes)

"Maybe this is the specialty of India" they both thought. "We would be asked to order for formality but would eventually be given what they had in stock or wished to serve".

They took turns in driving for a stretch of 2-3 hours each. There were countless instances when they almost got themselves or the others on the road killed. It was either a truck (which horned musically as manoj gave a thumbs up to it and eventually danced wondering if that's what the driver was expecting) dashing past or them getting confused on which lane to drive because, as and when they tried to switch, some fast bike or a car would dash past them in a whiff of a second as though chasing or being chased by a cheetah.

Once or twice, Manoj tried stopping the car whenever he noticed girls at the side, and tried asking if there was any traditional village dance they did. So that he can join them with Raj shooting the video. But, to his grief, they were either receiving giggles from the girls or sweet words from the local people carrying sticks with them, and chasing them for atleast 2-3 kms.

They drove past country sides, bypassed cities, valleys, rivers and pitted roads. As night approached, maps showed a 100 km stretch more. They decided to stay back in some nearest town they would find. But unfortunately, they were just driving past villages now, with not so much as an airbnb nearby. So they parked by a beach (the maps showed the place as some Visakhapatnam) nearby. Raj slept in the backseat as Manoj setup a camping sleeping bag (he used this in Amazon rainforests earlier) on the sand.

They woke up to a dog pissing on Manoj's sleeping bag early in the morning. Manoj initially wondered if the waves had hit him on the cheek to wake him up. People stared confused as Manoj went full shirtless and dived into the beach. Somehow, he came back much more dirty, stinking and covered in some soap and shampoo covers as he came back from the water.

"Whoa. I thought you said you were going for a bath in the beach mama? How come you ended up cleaning it?" wondered Raj, looking at Manoj who, as per Raj, perfectly resembled a handsome muscular drainage cleaner who just completed his work and tried coming out pretending to be stylish doing it.

They continued driving along the coastline as the name Sivasamudram and his father's story suggested that the village was on the seashore. Manoj wondered why there was no one on the beach lying down for a sun tan. Maybe it was because they already had a sun tan.

Now they had to drive up and down a few cliffs and a seashore again. Here, Manoj tried his hand at fishing as they were really hungry and wanted some breakfast. However the local fishermen there took up a fight with Manoj, broke his fishing rod, threatened to use him as a bait in a net as they fish for sharks nearby and chased him away. He came back exhausted to see Raj buying some fish from the same fishermen on the roadside.

It then took 30-40 mins for Raj to separate Manoj from the fishermen who kept throwing nets on him as they were trying to flee, after Manoj had taken a fish from the fisherman's cart and shoved it up the fisherman's mouth. Finally, they drove again to a place called Yarada and then further until the car came to a stop suddenly.

"Wow, I only thought this happened in movies. I think the car recognizes this as its owner's native place. Will you get down and kiss the land?" asked Manoj as Raj got down the car.

Raj ignored his silly cousin and checked what was wrong. The car had no problem whatsoever, it was the road which had stones all over it that punctured the car.

"It's a puncture, need to get it replaced", said Raj kicking the tyre.

"Oh, I will search for BMW showrooms nearby", said Manoj scanning the phone, "Oh no, the nearest one is 100 kms behind us, in that crazy Visakhapatnam we came here from".

"Yeah, why not I just go look for a mechanic and get this filled?" suggested Raj sarcastically, "or would that be considered barbaric", he added scathingly.

"Oh ok, go ahead. I will just wait here", replied Manoj.

As Raj left to find a mechanic, a bored Manoj took out his guitar and started playing it. A shower of coins landed at his side as he stopped playing his favorite band. He looked around to see a bunch of dhoti cladded old men walking past him.

"Hey oldie! You think this amount would be accepted by any beggar? Not that I am a beggar, but the amount you threw suggests you might be close to becoming one", Manoj shouted at the guy who looked like he was the leader of the pack.

"Aey aey, beware how you talk to Gopala Swamy", shouted another oldie from the pack.

"Oh, why? Is he mentally challenged? Or is he deaf, should I try sign language?" saying so, he showed the obscene finger to them.

As Raj returned after a while with the mechanic, he found the car to be empty, looking back at him innocently. To his shock, he could neither find Manoj nor their luggage. He went around asking the villagers for them. There were some odd stories shared by villagers as he described some features of Manoj, like

"Who? Do you mean that guy who looked like a hen pecked on his head and left his hair standing?" "Is it that guy you're talking about, the one who was speaking something rude language which we immediately understood as he showed the finger?"

With each story, Raj's feeling of *"Why can't this Manoj stay still for 5 minutes. It was always these short gaps that got them into trouble, Once in the airport, once in states (when Manoj almost got himself forcefully married to a gang of homosexuals), once in the office and now again"* kept aggravating.

"Any idea where he is please? He is a kid by brain, I mean he is under developed in the inside, like that film Koi Mil Gaya. Please don't mind his language, he always gets yanky without his bournvita supply", Raj attempted some wild story hoping it would gather some sympathy.

"Oh, I am sorry. We didn't know. And now we don't know what must have happened to him. Gopala Swamy took him to his house", Raj was told.

He ran (as the car was getting repaired by the mechanic) towards Gopala Swamy's house guided by the passers by. He found himself outside a 3 storeyed house which was decorated as though some very auspicious or a very sad occasion has just taken place. Hoping it was not the latter, and especially not with Manoj involved in it, he opened the gate and knocked on the door.

As it opened, to a mix of shock and surprise, he found Manoj laughing and entertaining a crowd of audience who sat in a circle around him (with an unnaturally silent atmosphere). Raj wondered whether the audience was listening intently or else not listening at all, and just waiting for Manoj to finish, so that they could finish him.

As Manoj turned around laughing and clutching his stomach, he found Raj walking slowly towards him with a *What have you done now?* expression on his face.

"Hey mama, it seems this GoPaul Swamy here is a would be sirpunch in this village. I guessed he can help us find this 50 year old mad woman love interest of yours. I was just telling them her features like the entire village considers her mad, eccentric, irritable etc., and she had a bad past dealing with your father. They call him some Onetala Varma it seems, funny right? Maybe it is to say No.1 Varma I think. This guy here (he pointed towards GoPaul Swamy who was completely still, except for the smoke coming out of his cigar. It looked as though the fumes were of anger rather than of the cigar) is very interested in the story. But for the life of me, I can't seem to remember that cranky granny's name. Was it Shady, Shardy, Shraddha, Sh…. Shanti? What was that mama?" Manoj gave an essay.

"Her name is Sharada Devi and she is crankier than you can guess", came a woman's voice from behind (the only voice apart from Manoj's in the room), "If I were you, I would tread more carefully knowing I entered her province now".

Manoj snapped his fingers pointing at the woman, "That's it, Sharad Devi".

Raj looked towards the source of the voice and noticed a fairly tall, loose haired but definitely sharp minded, defiant looking and seemingly 30-40 year old.... "Hello Raj Varma. You look nothing like your old man, lucky I saw you in the T.V. or else no one would have recognized you" the woman broke his thoughts.

Though he neither saw her nor knew her or heard her voice before, oddly he recognized her instantly. This could be no one else but *her*.

"Have you gotten acclimatized to India's weather yet? It might be hotter than you must have thought, right?" asked the woman, Raj didn't reply.

"With all the discussions with your father and his usual foolish villager responses, I thought it would take a lot more time to meet you and get things going. But, looks like, for the very first time, destiny has done something unusual with me, though I must say it's something positive this time", replied the woman.

But, with no response from either Raj or any of the members in the room, the woman stopped talking as though she just realized something.

"Oh, by the way, I'm...." she continued. "Nice to meet you Sharada" replied the most eligible bachelor.

Chapter - 14
THE ELEPHANT IN THE ROOM

"Thankfully, it was just a few of my panchayat batch in the room today. I can't imagine how disgraceful it must have looked if these jokers had arrived during the engagement. Did you call them here?" Gopala Swamy was still fuming, just without a cigar this time.

He was in his least favorite room in the house, Sharada Devi's study and not to mention in his least favorite mood. The two foreigners were asked to appreciate the store room till Gopala Swamy's "panchayat" comes up with a suitable verdict for them. If choice be given, Gopala Swamy was all in for a public hunt where he would hunt them both down on his jeep along with his party.

"In a way", Sharada replied calmly. "To put it in your rustic lingo, I smoked the hole in the wall and the mice came out. And mind you, they are my guests and I will take care of them", she added.

"Oh, your guests! Then they will be guests for four occasions in total: My elder's marriage, younger's engagement, her marriage and their funeral", Gopala Swamy spoke to his wife, however his voice seemed like he wanted the "mice" in the store room to get the message.

"And then what? Get arrested for the murder of the most successful food chain's CEO, not to mention an American citizen. You would be deported to America for your prison time dear. Though I will cover it up to the relatives saying my husband is in the states not mentioning where exactly, the arrest will still jeopardize your run for the sarpanch slightly", Sharada sounded as though she was irking off a fly.

"That is if their bodies are ever found", Gopala Swamy looked mutinous.

"Oh, shut up Gopal, please let me handle this. And in the meanwhile, if anything happens to either of them, I will help Gayathri in her plan to escape the house next time. And you know the plan would work and work so well that not a single soul in the village (Gayathri included) would know exactly where she is, except me" neither

Sharada's voice nor her body language suggested aggression, but her words marked her tenacity. Only she could silence Gopala Swamy when he was in such a rage and still stand her ground.

As she was about to leave for the store room, Gopala Swamy caught her on the shoulder and whispered, "Tell your mice in the store room that I am the elephant here and I can squash them anytime".

"Elephants fear mice Gopal", smiled Sharada as she pushed his hand away and walked off.

As Sharada Devi opened the store room door, she found the spiked hair guy clutching Raj Varma's collar and sobbing all over him. As they saw Sharada, the spiked guy rubbed his eyes hurriedly and spoke in a slightly high pitched voice.

"Don't you Indians know how doors work? You knock on them before opening them", said Manoj.

"Had I knocked, the door would have fallen down. It's slightly fragile and no one cares about repairing the door to a store room", smiled Sharada as she guessed what must have happened in her absence.

"I hope the voices from the study haven't carried over here", she asked even though she knew the answer.

"Oh no they didn't "carry", they echoed all over this place, and vibrated a few vessels too might I add", sobbed Manoj.

"My husband's a fool", replied Sharada.

"But we are not", answered Manoj, "we are leaving here right away."

"I need to talk to you alone for a while", Sharada thought of saying this, however Raj said it first. Sharada let out a fit of laughter which "echoed all over the place and vibrated a few vessels too".

Manoj recoiled a bit. He could suddenly remember with painful ease all the Indian horror movies he had watched. He laughed at the usage of women wearing classical dance wear and whimsical laughter to frighten people, it usually amused him. But now, he understood exactly why people feared those characters.

"We can talk over on the terrace", Sharada suggested.

"Why not here, I don't want someone eavesdropping", asked Raj.

"Which is exactly why I asked you to come to the terrace. If you could hear what we were talking in the study from here, then someone in the study (if they stay silent) can hear what is being discussed in this room equally well", Sharada replied.

"Fair enough", Raj stepped out of the room.

"Mama, please don't leave me alone in this roo…", Sharada closed the door before Manoj could finish.

As they reached the terrace, few of Gayathri's courtesans were asked to get lost from there. All of them looked strangely at Raj, his dress and not to mention his looks. They started murmuring immediately as they descended the stairs.

"Firstly, let's address the elephant in the room", started Sharada "Why have you co..."

"I am ready to marry your daughter athayya (mother in law in Telugu)" answered Raj with a wide smile on his face.

For the first time in her life, Sharada was completely taken aback. She felt as though she was slapped shut. What the heck happened to her birth star? How did her fate turn 180 degrees? How come luck started favouring her and favouring her big time? Was she dreaming? Did she hear him right?

"Hello? Athayya? Are you dreaming?" smiled Raj.

"Huh, I was just wondering the same", blurted out Sharada. She immediately cursed herself, she shouldn't have said that. She has just shown her nemesis a sign of weakness.

"Hahaha, you are not", saying so, he pinched her arm to prove it.

CLANG…. CLANG…. CLANG

One of Gayathri's courtesans, Sravani dropped the coffee serving tray and the steel glasses on them dripping all the coffee everywhere.

"What are you doing here silly girl, didn't I tell you all to get lost", shouted Sharada.

"I…. I…. thought of getting some coffee to this…this….guy here", Sravani blushed "oh, and you too", she quickly added.

"Out", whispered Sharada.

Sravani ran without picking up the tray and glasses, shouting back to her associates downstairs, "He pinched her".

"Never mind her. Did you just say you are ready.... to....to....", started Sharada.

"Of course, athayya, why do you think I am calling you 'athayya'?" Raj tried proving.

"Wow, that's really.... really .... great to hear. But you haven't seen Gayathri yet right?" Sharada looked sharp.

"Oh, her name's Gayathri, is it?" smiled Raj.

"What a joke! Don't try fooling me, you'll never get me. Tell me what you are playing at", demanded Sharada.

"You mean you don't want me to marry your daughter, or is there something wrong with her?" Raj questioned back.

"No no no, it's just that I .... I .... didn't expect you to ..., just forget it. So you are ready to marry Gayathri then?" Sharada asked with a shade of smile (she will get him now). "So why not I call our priest to set up an auspicious time for the marriage, and then you can call your doting dad to his motherland", she added with a genuine smile as she thought of her foolish village partner.

"That's the problem actually athayya", Raj's face dropped in concern.

Aha got him now, thought he could outwit Sharada Devi, she thought.

"I personally think all these auspicious times and all are farce athayya. Shall we plan the wedding sometime next week? And regarding dad, he won't be able to make it to India. I can't reveal much but he is, how do I put it, not allowed to leave New York for now. So, we need not wait for him. And we can have the engagement tomorrow. The house looks ready for the occasion too", Raj as good as shot a bullet through Sharada's head.

Sharada was completely lost for words. *What is this guy playing at? Is he for real? Am I just overthinking it? He might genuinely want to marry my daughter. No, he hasn't even seen her, he didn't know her name till now. There is surely something fishy.*

Downstairs, Gopala Swamy was in a deep discussion with his private panchayat group. Each of them had their own viewpoints on the occurrences of the day:

"You mean your wife wants that spiky guy to be your son in law?"

"But isn't America the sponsor for that terrorist group which bombed them back?"

"Do you think Gayathri will be able to compete with the masterchef contestants there?"

"But if Gayathri goes to America, does that mean you have to go as a house father-in-law to America?"

Gopala Swamy was tired of shouting at them, trying to tell them he wants them to stop the proposal etc., and so, he just let them blabber. Out of the blabber, he overheard some girls giggling and discussing by the corridor window.

"Oh god, that guy is so good looking. Anyone knows why he has come here, is he Kireeti's friend?" asked a girl.

"What? You really think that Kireeti is worth that much, he is a slob", said another.

"But I am telling you I just saw him pinch Sharada Devi on the terrace, it looks like he fancies her", said a girl.

Gopala Swamy sprang out of his chair and made some excuse to get out of the room. He lit himself a cigar and just shooed off the notion he heard from that girl. No one in their right mind could take a fancy to that nut case he has made his wife. He smiled to himself and looked out of the balcony to see the side of the terrace opposite to his wing. He could see that the foreigner and Sharada were talking about something, but the voices didn't carry.

On the terrace, Sharada was forcing herself to buy Raj's story but she just couldn't.

"So, you are going to take Gayathri along with you to New York after the marriage right?" she asked.

"Actually, there is a catch there too. I don't intend to go to New York anytime soon", replied Raj in a shy manner.

"What? What are you saying? I just don't get it, what's wrong?" now Sharada was growing restless.

"It has nothing to do with the marriage athayya, just get us married as soon as possible and I will stay here along with all of you", Raj said.

"Please be honest, I am about to give my daughter's hand to you", pleaded Sharada.

"You won't if I be honest, that's the catch here athayya", Raj tried explaining.

"I will give you my daughter if you are honest with me, totally honest I mean. And I promise you whatever you say won't go beyond me", Sharada Devi just wanted to know. It didn't mean she trusted him but whatever Raj would say would give her a clue as to what Raj was upto.

"You must promise me that you will give me your daughter's hand no matter what and also promise me that whatever I say would not go beyond you. Is that a promise?" Raj asked.

"Do you want me to make a contract with you now?" Sharada replied impatiently.

"That's not necessary, I trust your word", Raj replied.

Sharada hesitated for a moment and then said, "Fine then, I give you my word".

Raj was elated, he went ahead and hugged Sharada. She was shocked and confused as to why Raj was behaving the exact opposite of what she expected. Gopala Swamy burnt his finger holding the cigar as he was not paying attention to it, he was just livid with what he just saw.

And then Raj whispered into Sharada Devi's ear, "I have abandoned my father and absconded from New York. I am completely…..bankrupt".

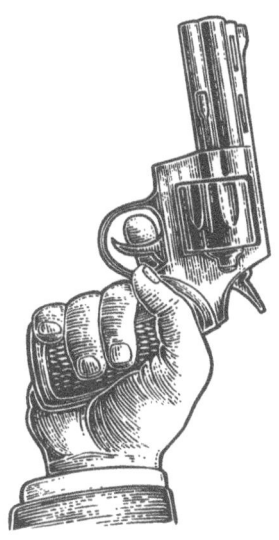

Chapter - 15
MARRIAGE FIXED

If he wanted to marry my daughter (whom he hopefully hasn't met or talked to yet), he should have shown that he was ultra-rich and can take her not just to the United States of America, but even to the Split countries of Europe Union in his private jet. Or.... if he didn't want to marry her, he should have said that he was bankrupt and hence can't be marrying her. But what is this? I mean.... seriously.... what is this? What are you playing at, Jr. Varma? kept thinking Sharada Devi on the roof, unaware of Kireeti, who must have called her a dozen times till then.

"Athayya (Aunt)! Are you ok? Please don't scare me. It's my first marriage and I don't want it to be stopped because the bride's mother got stuck between on and off button. Athayya!!!" saying which Kireeti tried pushing Sharada who got woken up recognizing similar action of Raj.

"What…..who…..you! What were you trying to do you idiot? With your everlasting foolishness? You could have killed me pushing!" blasted Sharada which made Kireeti slip, trying to run back.

"Actually, it was to save you Athayya. You went into some kind of trance. My grandmother used to say that it would happen when Ammavaaru (Goddess) gets into a woman to bless the luckiest person in front of her, called Poonakam. So, I waited to listen if you're going to tell me about my future. But there was some connectivity issue, I think, and you got stuck in that position, for 30 whole mins. So, to get you back, I tried pushing you", concluded Kireeti, again waiting, maybe expecting Sharada to feel proud about him.

Thinking not to waste time arguing with him, Sharada Devi asked "Why did you come here firstly?"

"To marry your daughter Athayya. Believe me. Seriously, I don't have any other intentions. Am not trying to loot your money or Mavayya's (Father-in-law) position. I really like Suguna, right from the time I saw her that day at the Jaathara. She was wearing that Venkatagiri pattu, aakupacha (green colour) saree with diamond embroidery and....", continued Kireeti diving into his memories and imagination.

"Hey, keep that rubbish waste of a time story to yourself! I was asking why have you come to the roof? Was anyone asking for me?" replied Sharada, her rage was now turning into restlessness.

"Oh, about that.... actually, my friends had come to see you right from the town Athayya," blushed Kireeti.

"Huh? Am I a museum girl to come and visit from places far away?" asked Sharada Devi confused.

"No, they actually came to see me. I mean, see me getting married" again blushed Kireeti.

"Tell them they're pretty early and that your marriage date isn't fixed. If they wanted to see you getting engaged, then tell them they're pretty late, as you already exchanged rings. Have you come to ask me about this?" remarked Sharada now wondering why hasn't she kept silent and just hear out what Kireeti would have blabbered, and said OK to whatever it was. Instead, she was now having to face the complete blast of her would be son-in-law's stupidity.

"No no Athayya. Actually, they wanted to see and ask you something", again Kireeti started to.... "STOP! Please don't blush again. Complete the sentence for God's sake", pleaded Sharada Devi.

"Yeah. It's that we're planning....no no.... actually, they're planning to organize a kacheri for me", replied Kireeti, about to blush, but looking at his would-be mother-in-law's angry eyes, immediately continued.

"Not here in this house Athayya, I mean....in the village jaathara site. Actually, they're my college friends and have come a long way, and wanted to see how village kacheri gets organized. I refused, but they've been insisting on it just once before I get married."

"So? Have you come to take my blessings for the act?" fired Sharada, who generally gets agitated with any unintelligent conversation, but this discussion was not a spark to her fuel, it was just bombing the fuel altogether.

"Not blessings, permission", pleaded Kireeti this time. "I've already informed Mavayya. He showed signs of giving company, but when I asked if I should inform you as well, he backed out and asked to take your permission. Also, he wanted me to add that he always takes decisions collectively, unlike some others who wish to decide everything on their own and then say it's because they care for the family and it's their duty to do so."

Sharada Devi looked aside ignoring Kireeti. She decided she would deal with this matter with her husband later. For now, she turned again to Kireeti and said, "Ok. Even Suguna had come to me yesterday requesting to allow her to complete some small wishes before getting married."

"Yeah Athayya, true. Tell Suguna she need not worry or ask me if she wants to roam around some places with her friends. I'll arrange for her security and she can happily visit any place she wants, before marriage. But, also tell her not to visit all the places and to leave some for our honey....um.... I mean.... family trips", replied Kireeti rejoicing that Sharada Devi approved so fast.

"No no you innocent Kireeti, she doesn't have such minute wishes", replied Sharada Devi with the most fake smile she could ever make. "She expressed her wish to dance in a Kacheri, as she once accidentally saw her father and panchayat people coming from a kacheri and praising the girl there, mentioning about her dance moves and they gifting her gold watch, money, flowers and all. Now that you are also planning to do one, why don't we combine them both? She'll dance before your friends and you. But, mind you...you need to throw those watches, bangles, necklaces and money which she's expecting. See! Both desires match. You both are truly made for each other"

"Stop it! How the heck did you leave her without slapping her a dozen times? Do you even remember you're a mother? And how come Suguna has such stupid wishes? I'll want to speak with her on this", raged Kireeti like a perfect village husband in a Gopala Swamy's son-in-law style, and was about to walk back in Rajnikanth's style, when Sharada Devi called him.

"Oh, so you mean it's my daughter's fault for thinking of dancing in a kacheri. Hmm.... yeah.... then let's do one thing. Whenever you guys are planning to do that destination kacheri (similar to destination wedding), I'll invite my friends as well. They're S.I Ramchandar, C.I. Manohar and few others. I tell you Kireeti, these are all bad cop friends of mine. They won't directly do their duty. They will first join you guys in the kacheri, enjoy with you all, and then reveal their identity. Let's see then, if they'll arrest the girl who was dancing, or the people who were enjoying it", smiled Sharada Devi, feeling a little proud that she had defeated Kireeti with just two moves in the mind chess game.

Kireeti, unable to speak anything, facing a bit of Sharada Devi's anger, retreated shaking his head murmuring, "These foreign people.... get excited…. just asked for a small thing…. can't even fulfill that wish"

"What foreign? Are some of your friends from foreign as well? Well, Kireeti….am surprised seeing the network of…. I would say…. native villager like you", replied Sharada Devi.

"Not that Athayya. That foreign guy…. some Mohan or Manohar. He was very excited and had asked me and my friends about village girls and if they dance here. Then, my friends also asked me *Yes mama, it's been long since we attended a kacheri and it would be my last one,* and since our India is famous for *Athidhi Devo Bhava* (Guest is our God), I felt we should not depress our guest friends and your foreign relatives," finished Kireeti closing his eyes, expecting to hear another roar from Sharada Devi but got even more scared when he heard silence and saw his Athayya going back to the previous thinking state once more, and ran away.

Mohan…. Manohar? But, the foreigner in the house was Raj Verma. Then who is this…. oh, the joker cum associate. Why didn't I think of it earlier? Let's speak with him. He would be giving me some update as to what he was told, when Raj brought him along from the US.

Thinking so, Sharada Devi climbed down the stairs from the roof, stopped at the top floor and stared at the ground floor audience.

To the farther end of Sharada and right were the foolish gang girls of Suguna and Gayathri who were murmuring more than breathing, and giggling pointing to their right. Looking to their right were the probable friends of Kireeti who were knocking each other's shoulders while looking at (or to say flirting at) the young girls, fighting as to who would try first, speaking with the girls. To their right and at the closer end was the usual Pekaata (Cards game) team of panchayat members already smoking half packet of newly brought town brand cigars by Gopala Swamy, along with them, the priest of the wedding was not smoking but playing vigorously. And then to their right was the prey Mohan (or) Manohar, who was holding a useless guitar and whenever a stupid friend of Gayathri peeped at him, was letting out a stroke from it.

Kireeti just descended the stairs and his friends along with the guitarist went towards him. With each of Kireeti's replies, the brightness on their faces reduced and each of them looked at Sharada slowly (not a direct eye contact but a slight glance). When Mohan (or) Manohar turned to look at her, Sharada grabbed the opportunity with a smile and signaled him to come up, to which he immediately looked down as if to enact that he never gazed up. Sharada Devi widened her smile, happy that she caught the fish, called Murugayya (the servant who ruined Queen Gayathri's great escape plan) to get that foreign musician cum street beggar to her study as she needed to study him.

As she was preparing the room for the subject, she heard shrill cries coupled with Murugayya's words *Ammagaaru (Madam) called you……. She won't do anything………Understand, am not allowed in that room……. Only special people like you Abbayigaaru (Boy) are allowed.* And then, Murugayya came holding the foreign guy, who was weeping like a child forcibly taken to school by his dad. Once he looked at the headmistress Sharada Devi, the foreigner stopped crying and stood in attention, not looking into her eyes.

"See ma'am, th...this is an offense in the US. You…. you can't bring a person forcibly and ho…house arrest anywhere in US, even if it is the family members there. I don't know if India is much advanced, but I will call the cops. I am leaving now. Tell your darling (or) lover if not married, or to your husband if you guys are married, that he can't threaten us. Do you know how big a person Raj is over there?" said (or to say cried) Manoj in a tone which was more requesting than threatening.

Seizing the opportunity, Sharada Devi immediately pounced, "Exactly, that's what I was wondering, Mr…Mohan right?" "No, I'm Manoj, and am also called Man of Justice in my place. I've a..a..arrested numerous old neighbor aunties and uncles in my vicinity because they caught me with their daughters. I've complained that they were intruding on our privacy. In the States, the younger generation has the rights and freedom to do whatever they want. Get this…straight," replied Manoj.

"I haven't asked all that. Let's get back from these jokes to a little serious discussion. I know it's difficult for you to get serious, whether in your life or in your position or even in this situation, but I am sure we can try. You told me everything about you, without even asking for it. But now, I am asking. Tell me about your friend Mr. Raj Varma," asked Sharada Devi as gently as possible, respecting her prey before eating.

"Why? How does that matter to you? I know about you Indian parents, right from when I saw a similar lady villain character of yours from *Nuvvu Nenu (yesteryear 2000's Telugu movie), Gundamma Katha (90's yesteryear Telugu movie)* and many more. So, please respect the love birds and get them hitched", answered Manoj feeling scared as to what might happen after finishing every word of his. That was the usual courage Manoj had, which as per Raj, was like proudly saying *am not afraid of fire as it can't do anything to me* in front of an impending Lava.

"See Mr. Manoj, I don't know what you know about me, and what you don't know about me. Believe me, both those parts are equally dangerous. And the question I asked is very simple. Now, let's try again. Tell me about your friend Mr. Raj Verma." asked Sharada.

Thinking he could boast about his friend, and get his marriage done, Manoj started, "Have you ever heard of RV restaurant? It's not like these Sattigaadi canteen (Satti's canteen), Mallesh anna's mess (Mallesh bro's mess) and all those idiotic places in a village. It recruits the annual winner of the US Master Chef for a yearly package of $1Mn USD. Do you know how much that is?

Hmm....Rs.8 crores here. Now, for all of them, my friend is the King chef. Now, you can estimate how much he is worth, and how much is your daughter who can barely cook 1% of the entire recipe there, not even to 10 members. Now get going." remarked Manoj, only to find something metallic touching his neck from the back. Turning back, he saw a long hunting gun being pointed now at his throat (as he turned back) and the trigger being held by the rough and rustic hand of Gopala Swamy who looked more dangerous than Sharada Devi now.

"What did you say to my wife, you escaping squirrel!!!" thundered Gopala Swamy. "Gopal, leave him. He's not even aware of his own situation in this house", said Sharada. "Then he better be", said Gopala Swamy in a threatening fashion, this time loading the gun instead of lowering it.

"Ayee! You can't kill a US person. I will.... I know martial arts.... you don't know. I have an instagram page followed by many celebrity sons. If I don't post for one day, they will interrogate and catch you", cried Manoj, clearly every part of his face wet with sweat.

"Then, post your last post there saying 'Who so ever tries finding out how I died are welcome to come to Sivasamudram and experience it first hand. YOUR VISIT WOULD BE AT YOUR OWN PERSONAL RISK!!!' ", shouted Gopala Swamy.

And then, before he could proceed, a voice came from inside the study, not locating the source. "Any tragic incident inside the house before the wedding is a bad omen Mavayya. Leave aside the omen, it will attract police and be subject to enquiry. What about the elections? OMG, won't you lose all the good publicity?"

As if obeying nature's voice, Gopala Swamy lowered the gun now looking around at the study room. Then, from behind Sharada Devi, adjacent to the back door of the study, turned in Raj, wearing Checks shirt and a dhoti. All of them turned towards him looking half surprised with the appearance and the other half with his statement.

"Who is it that you call mavayya? You.... *censored word.... censored word.....,*" continued Gopala Swamy. "Stop it Gopal, what he said is correct, though you might not understand. But, believe me. Don't risk Suguna's life and yours by such a foolish act", said Sharada Devi in a casual tone.

Gopala Swamy shouted and threw the gun onto Manoj who caught it athletically but quite unknowingly, and threw it away scared that it might explode. Gopala Swamy stormed out of the room.

"What is this Athayya? What happened? Didn't you inform Mavayya about the deal, my marriage, our marriage? I heard from my father that even Mavayya was there at the time of making the deal?" asked Raj.

Manoj looked scared and confused but Sharada Devi became restless and replied, "Please don't go about telling everyone. Give me time till my elder daughter's marriage is done. We can discuss then."

"But it would take time, right? As it's still the engagement that's finished. It might be months before her marriage. How can I control myself? Oh God, what a beautiful village, what a beautiful house, such a gorgeous Athayya, and hot hot Mavayya! Who cares about the remaining bride? Please make it done Athayya," replied Raj romantically.

"Will discuss with the priest and get it fixed. Until then….", but Sharada Devi's voice was cut by Gopala Swamy who called her.

When three of them came out of the study looking down, Gopala Swamy and his panchayat members were dancing and shouting (as if drunk) along with Kireeti's friends, forcibly making the priest also to dance, and lifting Kireeti who was also looking confused but overjoyed.

"Listen everyone! Especially those who are worried about Suguna's marriage. I've just spoken with the priest now and to our goodness, the marriage date has been FIXED!!! It's going to be the same date as the elections which is half a month from now. WHOOOO!!! This is called God's plan and destiny. Everyone who attends the marriage will show their inked finger as an entry and will be allowed only if he/she says he voted for me. We'll celebrate my victory and the marriage for the whole 5 days".

Suddenly his voice became a little serious, and he looked straight up, not towards Manoj but towards Raj and said, "It's also going to be a bad day for my competitors and ill wishers as I am going to set scores with them one by one. If they wish to stay unharmed, flee from this village before the elections are done with. Coz it'll be a Death sentence for them in my very first panchayat session!"

His speech was received by a tumult of applause from the people downstairs and then, he fired 3 bullets into the air with a hand pistol.

Manoj looked dumb scared at Raj while Sharada Devi looked calm, but raised a hand onto her head thinking, and went downstairs.

"Excuse me, the Queen has sent orders for you to visit her in her room. By the way, you look so handsome in the Dhoti", remarked a young village girl, coming towards Raj and then ran away blushing.

Chapter - 16

THE QUEEN STEPS IN

What's this that she's hearing from the people in her kingdom? The people in her kingdom were discussing about a charming hippie entering her kingdom and all girls shifting gaze towards him. And then…. the other news which her useless maids were saying; that the handsome prince fell for the mad old Witch and her prophecies? YUCK!!! That was why Queen Gayathri invited the man to meet her, not for her to see him but for him to see her and realize who the Snow White of the village was. After that, she would decide whether he should be sent to the Grand Dinner or the Gallows.

"M...my highness" faltered Subbalakshmi.

"Huh? When did you get so high?" enquired Gayathri.

"Sorry, I meant your highness. Could you not just think once again before calling him here? Remember what happened when you were rash last time, I mean you are about to get married for that" asked Subbalakshmi cautiously this time.

"Think about what? How to look? For that, am already gifted with everlasting charms and beauty Subbu, unlike y'all. But don't worry, I understand your intention. You wish to get yourself ready to atleast look presentful right? At the very least expecting that he might fall for you. Hahaha Oh My God, I can't even imagine that, just quit thinking about it altogether. No worries, he won't be dejected looking at the Queen's low lying maids, his attention would undividedly be on the Queen. Heard that he's got a clown servant for himself too. Why not try your luck with him?" played on her highness.

"Excuse me, I have been asked to meet a...a...Queer Gayathri here", asked an odd lungi clad chap.

He wore a rugged jeans shirt which was definitely a branded one, but at the bottom was a checks lungi. It looked as though he won the shirt in a lottery somehow or lost the pant on a bet.

"It's not Queer Gayathri you....you....Queer guy", blushed Sravani. "It's Queen Gayathri and by the way by queer I mean oddly cute", she added.

"Oh so sorry about that, just didn't think India still had a Queen", smiled that young chap.

"When America still has a queen, why not India?" asked Sravani.

"America has no queen, England does", laughed the young man.

"Oh, then I guess they left one Queen behind while they quit India", somehow Sravani didn't want to look stupid.

"Oh right, then why didn't you all fight for abolishing her to England too?" asked the guy.

"Uh coz she's still immature and mentally delicate. Her parents requested us to act in such a way until she is sent to her actual kingdom…you know…near Erragadda." whispered and giggled Sravani.

"Okay…never heard of that place. Must be beautiful" replied the guy looking puzzled but accepting nonetheless.

"Yeah. It's the only place in India where there is 24hrs power supply", laughed Sravani this time.

"Ahem…ahem Sravani? Sraaavaniii. Look! Your dad has called for you. It seems a black moon…I mean…man is waiting for you, claiming you ran away with him and now from him. Do you mind handling that issue and leaving the actual matter to your Queen?" wondered Queen Gayathri who suddenly appeared behind Sravani and before the chap.

"Huh? Oh ma'am. We were just talking about you, and I have been explaining this uh…who are you?" enquired Sravani slightly falling to her left.

"Can't you tell from his attire? He is the one whom we call *Lungi Rayudu* here. Are you the NRI joker or his assistant?" asked Gayathri raising herself to her fullest height, trying to reach out to atleast an inch below the chap.

"Actually, the assistant *is* the Joker, the joker himself. Were y'all asking for him? He's just in a meeting with your...landlady. He'll just enchant her and comeback to you'all. He is equally excited to meet and speak to you village girls. And if he comes to know that you called for him, the joker will get transformed to cupid." finished the *Lungi Rayudu* with a decent smile in the end as if he just finished a proposal to his clients.

"No no no, we wanted to meet you, the one who my mother is so interested in. Are you really an NRI or are you just masquerading as one to impress her. I will most likely put you as a panchayat guy from the nearby *Kodiguddu gramam*", conversed her highness.

"It was definitely this guy, he ahem ahem hugged your mom", replied Parvati, "and not to mention, he.... he.... pinched her. Oh my god, do I have to say this?"

"Oh then you have the right guy. I am Ravi Raj Varma. And I have brought this as a small getting to know present", replied Raj as he handed a bottle of champagne.

The room was filled with a huge "Huuuuuh".

"Yeah, it's a vintage one. You girls seemed to have recognized it so soon. Is it the same here or do you have the…. what was it that pops said, yeah naatu kallu?" asked Raj innocently.

"How dare you present this to the Queen? Don't you boys have any other pastime except for drinking and then crying out that the girl hasn't fallen for you, or that the girl fell for someone else and all?" bashed Gayathri.

"No no, I don't have such issues. Coz there isn't any girl who hasn't fallen for me or any girl whom I fell for. So…all going great for me. How about you?" clarified Raj.

"Yeah, she's actually about to get married soon, to a guy whom she didn't fall for, or rather a guy she doesn't know yet (and thankfully the guy doesn't know about her too). So, going really well for her too", mocked Parvati.

"What? Is it so? I didn't know that. Why wasn't I told about it? And how come people like you all (I mean friends who work for her for some petty daily salary) were informed about it way before?" revolted Raj which gave a small smile on Gayathri's face while her maids took it to be their time to revolt.

"Hey! Hey! Watch your tongue buddy. Who do you think we are? Her servants?" cried Parvati.

"Are you not? I just tried to put that delicately. Should I say Slave queens then? You know in Telugu we say *Saamantha Raanulu*?"

"Am actually the immediate cousin of hers. My mom and her dad are siblings. And for the record, my dad always wins in the card game with her dad. Got that?" informed Parvati.

"And my mother is the sister-in-law of her father. Was almost going to marry him, and I would have been the would be Sarpanch's daughter" remarked Sravani, already imagining how different it would have been in the alternate reality.

"All of us are related to her", summarized Radhika with a tiny whisper of *Our Karma*.

"Oh, so sorry to hear you are not getting paid for this. Maybe you girls are paying for something else and that's why you are where you are. *Karma* as you rightly pointed out. I'll make a move then", saying so, Raj was about to leave.

"Hey wait, where do you think you are going? Do you think I called you to admire your lungi? Tell me what is it with you and mom. Mind you my dad is a hunter. So tell me straight, I heard things which can't be explained by anything other than a possible extra marital affair. I don't know if you are capable enough for mom, but I sure can tell you, you are nothing in comparison to dad", shouted Gayathri.

"Oh that...that...why are you making me blush unnecessarily? I get redder and girls like it even more. Ok, the answer I would give is *Ask your mom*. I think both you and her are mature enough to discuss and understand this. I would end by saying that it is not an extra marital affair rather a marital affair between me and her. Cheers!" departed Raj with a fair imitation of the Rajnikanth salute.

"My father will hear about this", shouted Gayathri with a fair imitation of malfoy.

"What else do you want from me? You scary woman from the 90's horrors. Please let me go. I came here to see the village, not my cousin's death and certainly not mine. Now, we already got our death dates registered by your even scarier and dumber husband. Didn't it satisfy your soul, your ego, oh almighty witch?" cried Manoj like a child who was resisting going to school.

"Do you want me to call my husband again?" Sharada silently replied, checking her finger nails.

Manoj just gave a teary terrified nod of denial.

"That's nice. Now then, will you be a good boy and start talking with your guardian angel and your only savior present here?" Sharada asked her nails.

Manoj gave a teary but angry nod of approval this time.

"Great, firstly why did you, I mean, why did you both come here?" threw Sharada.

"To...to...*see the Indian chics in their barn*", Manoj replied, closing his eyes.

"Huh? Come again", asked Sharada Devi, confused.

"No! Never. This is the last time I am coming to India. And...that doesn't mean these will be my last days. We will leave and never return. And regarding your daughter, I will show Raj hundreds of much more beautiful girls and he will forget your daughter. So, please tell me your Wifi password so that I can book the flight tickets.... huh...please", Manoj let out a monologue.

"Listen, listen. Before you start showing your true colours, understand what I meant. I asked you to repeat what you just said about the reason for coming to India?" asked Sharada. "And if you start telling your previous dialogue, you will get to know that I am much scarier than my dumber husband."

"To see some Indian girls and survey on who dances the best. Happy?" replied Manoj.

"Raj has come to see some Indian girls you mean to say?" Sharada tried to make sense out of this.

"I don't know exactly why he has come. I ask him once he says let's go see some girls, I ask him twice, he says there is some marketing campaign, I ask him thrice he says he wants to see a 50 year old woman, I ask him for the fourth time, he says shut up", Manoj was close to running away now.

"Ok, leave your brains aside. You know what your friend told me was his reason for visiting India? He said he has absconded from the US and from his bankrupt company. Hence, he decided to marry my daughter and stay here with us forever", Sharada replied, closing the door and with clear authority on the cornered cat.

"Whaaaaat the shit!!! Does that mean I stay here forever too!!!" shouted Manoj with a mixed expression of whether to laugh at Sharada Devi's rare joke, or fear the dreadful truth she puts in such a comical way.

"You're asking *me* this? Go ask your friend you silly cat. And mind you, in case I get a feeling you or your friend are planning on leaving the village without my consent, I will make sure my husband's life long goal of a human hunt followed by a human sacrifice to Ammoru is fulfilled", Sharada opened the door.

Manoj ran or rather disapparated from the room. He heard some feeble sound of *And tell me what he says* from behind. Firstly, he ran into the kitchen where a servant was filling water into a jar, and started emptying it into his mouth.

"Ayyagaaru! That is for feeding Tommy! It's mixed with veterinary medicine for its digestion issues." completed Murugayya.

"Will this affect me?" asked Manoj, stopping in between, not noticing the jar emptying on his face now.

"Uh…do you have digestion issues?" enquired Murugayya.

"No", replied Manoj.

"Are you a dog?" continued Murugayya.

"Obviously not, you pig", replied Manoj, shaking Murugayya.

"Then, I don't think it will affect you. But unnecessarily, the medicine got wasted. How can I bring it back now?" hesitated Murugayya.

"Do one thing. I will go and piss within 30mins. Ensure you collect the holy water and give it to the over-eating and lesser working piece of shit herself/himself" shouted Manoj and went away.

What would he do now? He promised Raj he would not ask him anything about the India trip? Whom should he talk to about this hallucination of Sharada Devi?

"Oh Jesus! Oh, mother Mary! Oh, father Joseph! What to do? Where do I go and meditate, in order to get a confirmation.... wait.... father??? Yes!!!" cried Manoj and attempted to perform a somersault which only worked half.

The girls behind him laughed so hard that Manoj acted as if he was possessed by chandramukhi (popular ghost) to make them flee.

He then picked up his phone (literally as *it fell* for and *fell due* to his somersault) and dialed.

"Hello Ravikant Varma is out of office, kindly leave a voice message in case you are from Sivasamudram" came an automatic reply in his phone followed by "Sir, your drink is ready" and a "Get out of here!!!" scream.

"Hello mavayya, it's me Manoj. How did the phone get picked up automatically in between?" asked Manoj sounding dejected.

"Hey hey hey, it's me Ravikant mama speaking you asshole. Now tell me what it is?" replied Ravikant Varma.

"Oh wow. Once you pick up the phone, please let me know how your phone is able to give customized AI enabled replies? Maybe you are given the privilege, being the CEO of such a big food chain. I will also install the same," replied Manoj now happy to hear his mavayya's voice.

"You ******* (a native Telugu swear word). You think your AI can generate this? How's that?" shouted Ravikant almost about to throw away his phone but refraining himself, in order to save whatever money, he will be left with now.

"Oh, when did you come in between Mavayya? Do you know your phone managed to speak with me until you came? Anyways, I wanted to ask you something mavayyaaaa", Manoj completed the last words in cries.

"Hey, stop crying like a new born baby's mother who has been trying to push that thing out without success" replied Ravikant sipping the bottle as usual leaving the glass aside. "Ask away now", he scoffed.

"Oh ok, I know it's a stupid question but are you bankrupt?" Manoj tried to put up a casual tone, "And has Raj abandoned you?" he added in a matter of fact manner.

But the reply was not as expected and came in the form of Mathew's face getting drenched with the wine spitted out by Ravikant Varma.

"You dumbass. Didn't I tell you not to try that *Naatu Kallu*? You novice foreigners don't know its intensity and value. *Speaking of it, can we try importing some here Ravi* (asked the villager)?" which Ravikant shook away like a fly which was inside his head.

"No, I didn't have any yet. It's just one of this Sharada Devi's tantrums. Oh, do you know who she is?" started Manoj.

"Why the hell did you go anywhere near that woman!!!!!", it sounded as loud as though Ravikant was just beside Manoj's ear.

"Forget about me going near her mavayya. She is behind us and ironically, Raj is going after her again and again," replied Manoj.

There you go, we lost a son now. Huh...he used to be a good boy. Only when he came to know of that ludicrous deal did he get overconfident and tried something which he shouldn't have. What now Ravi? Shall we run away to Switzerland and adopt a white man who knows bee farming there? Need to get all the money we have in the bank immediately...wait, are we really bankrupt? Did Sharada do something with the contract...with Raj?

Ravikant would have won the fastest fingers first at KBC, only if he had applied for it. Within seconds the homepage of their joint account (Raj and his, as Raj was soon to be CEO, he was given full control of the accounts) was loading, as Ravikant Varma re-loaded his drink.

"Hello?" asked Manoj.

And there was a sound from the other end as though a glass bottle was crushed with bare hands or rather hit against the skull.

"The…. the…. acc…. account shows zzzz…zzzeeerrooo balance", quivered a voice which was animated but surely not automated.

"Shit!!!" shouted Manoj.

"Yeah shit", shouted back Ravikant.

"No I mean real shit, the medicine has worked", and Manoj cut the line.

Chapter - 17
TAKE A CALL

Manoj was lying on a shaky bed in the store room. Raj had gone to get some medicine for the continuous outflow Manoj's stomach was sending. It felt as though his stomach fell in love with that wretched bathroom (which was an Indian one without either a Western Commode or tissues) and wanted him to spend some more time there every time he got out. He could hear some agitated voices coming closer to the door.

"Mother Mary! Has Gopala Swamy decided to murder me before Raj comes back and lie to Raj later that Manoj died of the continuous motions", Manoj thought to himself. And BANG.

It was Raj and Murugayya (who was carrying that stupid dog whose drink he shared).

"Ayyagaru, please be careful with the door, it will fall off if such force is applied on it. And regular opening and closing of the door is also not recommended. So please ask your servant to go to the fields and sleep there tonight, there he can use the sleeping place for shitting too", Murugayya was explaining Raj.

"Sure anna (brother), will keep it in mind. Mama, take a glass of this and everything's gonna be fine", Raj held out a glass of what looked like a glass of shit or maybe some local wine.

"What's this and why does this taste so dreadful?" Manoj asked as he took a gulp from the glass.

"It's Tommy's....", started Murugayya "Let, let me handle this please", Raj interrupted him.

"Don't you dare tell me this is from that dog", Manoj was ready to throw the glass at Raj.

"No, you silly sleepy mama, it's just the antidote for the earlier dog medicine", Raj answered but Manoj was not assured, "Could you be more specific?" he asked.

"Well see, we have asked a lot of doctors for a medicine to work on the laxative you have taken and none from the pharmacy stores, homeopathy store or a sadhu whom these villagers believe has powers could find some. And then we had this brainwave and we have asked the veterinary doctors. They immediately gave us a medicine which dogs need to take in case they.... well.... suffer from what you are currently going through", Raj finished the sentence looking at the wall clock behind Manoj.

"You mean to say this thing is for dogs and somehow it works for me too", Manoj asked sarcastically.

"See Murugayya, this is how you handle him", Raj said in a satisfied tone to Murugayya.

Manoj threw the glass aiming at Raj but it missed him and hit Murugayya who dropped the dog in pain. The dog launched itself onto Manoj. The resulting tussle resulted in Raj finding out what was there in each of the cupboards in the room as almost all of them were broken now.

"Lucky for you the dog is vaccinated", cried Murugayya holding his head in pain.

"Get lost and take your son (dog) out with you", shouted Manoj who could not hold all the hurting places in his body due to paucity of hands.

Murugayya and Tommy left as Raj sat on a sofa nearby and then the sofa sat on the floor.

"Thanks a lot for this mama", Raj howled at Manoj.

"Oh, in that case I need to thank you for this trip altogether. Cause I know now that we ain't going back. I will be killed by Gopala Swamy or his dog and hence can't go back and you, well I found out that this store room is the only room in India you can now afford.

Hence you will not go back", Manoj sounded close to crying now.

"Who told you this?" asked Raj suspiciously.

"I am not supposed to ask you anything but you can ask me everything right?" revolted Manoj.

"Should I just abandon you here?" threatened Raj.

"Like you abandoned your dad?" laughed Manoj.

"Did Sharada Devi tell you this?" asked Raj.

"What if she did?" Manoj let out a tear.

"And you believe her?" Raj asked.

"I spoke to your dad too you liar, he confirmed to me that your account shows zeerroooo balance", Manoj got up and looked at Raj.

"Do you need to go again, cause I need to take you to the fields in case you have to go?" Raj asked.

Manoj pulled Raj up holding his collar and shook him as he asked, "Just tell me the truth now Raj! Are you bankrupt? Is that why you are here? If that is so, then why am I here?"

"I have told you again and again, do not ask me anything regarding what I do here. One thing I assure you, nothing is going to harm you. You will be back to the states soon", Raj explained.

"Yeah nothing is going to harm me is really good except that I have already been harmed. Physically by that stupid dog, and mentally by Gopala Swamy and his wife. I promise you this is the very last time I will question you", pleaded Manoj.

"One last question then", Raj allowed.

"Are you bankrupt?" Manoj pulled Raj closer and looked him in the eye.

"In a way, yes and in another way, no", Raj pulled Manoj's hands off him "And that's all you are going to get from me. And if you want to leave, then you have to leave alone" he continued.

"I need to go", Manoj said.

"Then go for the fields", Raj replied.

"Got it", saying so, Manoj started to leave as Raj stopped him and handed him a piece of paper.

"What's this? Is there something you wrote on it cause you can't say it out loud?" Manoj asked.

"No, I thought you could use this as a toilet paper", Raj let go off Manoj who stormed angrily and kicked the store room door open, or rather down to his horror.

All the people having dinner downstairs looked up in surprise and shock as Manoj came out of the room sheepishly. He started looking for Sharada Devi downstairs at the dinner table, in the kitchen, near the lawn but couldn't find her. He found few girls giggling at him near the foot of the stairs as he attempted to climb back.

"Excuse me, is Sharada Devi upstairs?" he asked the group of girls at large.

"We think so", answered one of the girls.

Manoj pushed his way through and was about to climb the stairs.

"How's your stomach now Tommy?" asked a giggling girl.

"Mine is good but yours looks like you could be pregnant", Manoj gave it back to her.

All the other girls gave a huge gasp as a weeping Sravani slapped Manoj and ran away. As the other girls started chiding, cursing, twisting Manoj's ears, there was a voice from above.

"What's all this ruckus there!" shouted Gopala Swamy.

Before Manoj could say anything, "This Joker was asking for Sharada atta mavayya. And he called Sravani a…a…I can't even speak it out. He also kicked the door of the store room down", Parvati went first.

"He has also challenged you for a hand to hand wrestling match saying you would be on top of him but would be unconscious as he will throw you onto your panchayat friends", Radhika added.

"He also said Suguna looks pretty and should be marrying him instead of that good for nothing Kireeti", Subbalaskhmi whispered.

"And then he saw me and took back what he said about Suguna. He said he would rather have me and asked me if I was available", Gayathri finished.

"Oh, I see you like to play games", Gopala Swamy looked happy (in a somewhat cunning sense).

"What…I…no, not at all. These village girls are just making this stuff up", Manoj was getting down the two stairs he managed to climb before the girls attacked him as Gopala Swamy started climbing down.

"Let's just have a friendly contest then, what do you say? I remember you mentioning about your martial arts" lured Gopala Swamy.

"Oh, I am just an amateur sir. And martial arts and wrestling are not the same", Manoj gave a nervous giggle. "Oh and am unwell too, I need to go pee, and shit", he added.

The girls behind him laughed under their breaths.

"What's the matter tough American, losing your shit when you come face to face with me? Would you fight someone else on my behalf then?" Gopala Swamy didn't want to lose this chance. He knew the girls were lying to him (or atleast partly). But the stupid girls actually gave him a brilliant idea, a chance to play with his prey and this would not affect his elections too. It would just be considered a friendly contest at the beginning of his campaign.

"I am unwell sir, how can I fight. The doctor told I would not get cured till the marriage", Manoj bumped into the girls as he was walking behind, who pushed him back towards Gopala Swamy.

"Oh very well, maybe your friend can fight on your behalf just like someone else will fight on my behalf?" Gopala Swamy smiled as his beard contorted to a wild shape.

"He is not trained in martial arts like me sir", Manoj started praying for Sharada Devi to miraculously appear and save him.

"Either that or I will have a hunting match where you will be my hunt. You need not fight in that case, you just need to run", Gopala Swamy gave out a laugh and continued, "Your call American".

"Oh, I remember he is trained well in wrestling though not in martial arts. So yeah sir, good to go, he will be fighting on my behalf" Manoj lost his faith in God by now.

"That's done then. I am going to announce the marriage date and the beginning of my election campaign, the day after tomorrow. We can have the match on that day near the village center", Gopala Swamy pushed Manoj aside and left to get a smoke.

Manoj ran upstairs in a fright ignoring the tantrums of the girls behind him. As he turned a corner, he bumped into Suguna (he recognized her from the engagement banner he saw in the village).

"You blind idiot", Suguna shouted as she nursed her leg.

"So sorry, I wanted to meet Sharada", gasped Manoj.

"She is in the study, it's her favourite room. You will find her there most of the time", indicated Suguna who seemed to have just come from the study room herself.

Manoj ran into the room as he saw Sharada Devi closing for the day.

"What's wrong? You look like your indigestion got the better of you", Sharada asked.

"Lots of things have gone wrong. I spoke to Ravi's father who confirmed he got bankrupt but Raj wouldn't admit it. He says he is bankrupt in a way but not in another way, whatever the hell that means. And oh, he is about to have a fight the day after tomorrow with someone from Gopala Swamy Sivasamudram Champions team", gasped Manoj as he started nursing his ribs from the pain of running hard.

"What the shit! Raj challenged my husb…Gopal for a fight. He didn't seem so dumb when I spoke to him", Sharada Devi was taken aback. She could not get the hang of Varma's kid.

"Actually, it was me. Hey, wait a minute, it wasn't me. It was those stupid giggling imps who set this up", Manoj cried as he explained what happened.

"Let me go talk to Gopal", Sharada Devi left the study in a hurry.

Manoj was about to leave the study too when….

Ring….Ring….Ring…..

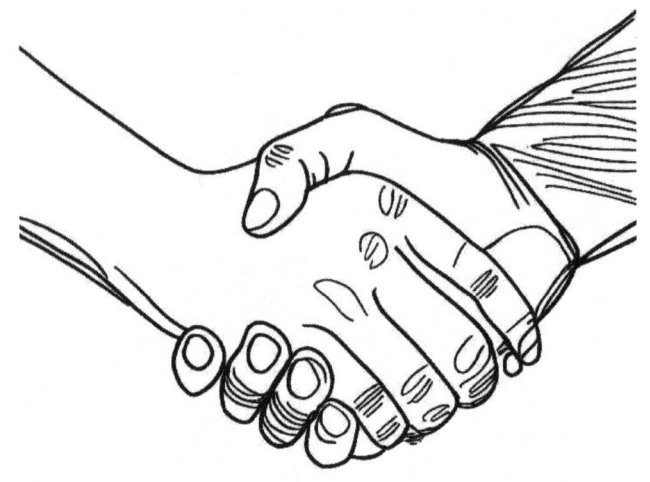

Chapter - 18
THE CHALLENGE

It was an unknown Indian number.

"Who the **** is this? What hour is this you are calling me at?" Manoj shouted at the phone.

"Hello, is this not Manoj I am speaking to? Ravi Raj Varma's secretary?" a dignified voice at the other end spoke.

"Yes it is Manoj, no it is not Raj's secretary. Who's this?" Manoj sounded doubtful, he could understand call centers getting his name from the registered number but how could they get Raj's name. And what made the caller think he was Raj's secretary.

"This is Rajagopal speaking, I work as a marketing team lead at RV food chain India. I called to give an update on my progress in the challenge", Rajagopal answered.

"The challenge? How did you know about the challenge?" Manoj asked stupidly.

"I know because I was challenged you stupid mongrel", Rajagopal was always irritated by the stupidity of people around him.

"Hey, now I remember you. You have a beautiful daughter, don't you?" Manoj asked childishly.

"And you have a monkey's face, don't you?" Rajagopal was reaching his boiling point.

"I am sorry…. I mean….that's just how I remember people. And what challenge are you talking about? Is that by any chance the wrestling contest at Sivasamudram the day after tomorrow? Please tell me you have a damn good fighter who looks like Raj", Manoj asked.

"Hellooo!!! Monkey Maharaaaaj!!! Please slap yourself awake. I am talking about the documentary which my team is developing under my leadership which will win us the challenge amount", Rajagopal sounded as though he was training a monkey to dance.

"Are you dreaming you old monk? Do you have a gay mistress with my name in your contacts? I do not understand a single word of what you say?" Manoj was in a testy mood too.

"I will call you later. Looks like you drank something you couldn't handle", and Rajagopal hung up.

"What in the name of God's green earth was that?" Manoj was confused as hell.

But, suddenly both his stomach and his half brain (the one which is taking the side of his friend) immediately rang the bell to rush. So, he started jogging and then realizing it wasn't helping, started sprinting towards the washroom via the store room. Hurtling past the study, where the giggling girls were outside trying to stop Sharada Devi who was also in an equal hurry, he set off searching for the first vacant washroom he could locate.

He remembered the one near the stairs where he could go, though the store room would be on the opposite side. Hoping that Raj would be visible from the other end, he was clinching to his stomach which was wrestling with him from inside to knock out the waste. Maybe because those were the only words his mind was filled with currently, he was murmuring "Wrestling", "Knock out", "Stomach" and "Shittttttt". Once he reached the washroom he planned, thankfully he saw Raj busy on his mobile phone. Without caring who else was listening or how Raj might react after hearing, he shouted.

"Mama!!! Don't ask how and please don't think why. But, know this. We've successfully booked a friendly wrestling match for you the day after tomorrow, which is definitely not going to end up friendly. Start watching *Warrior*, *Fighter* and ...what was that Indian movie..yeah *Dangal*. I'll just complete my wrestling here and come back and exp…AAARGH" THUD!!!

Before Manoj could complete the sentence, few things happened. He, without checking whether the washroom was free, rushed into the door which was unfortunately filled. Either because Manoj rushed with such brutal force, or because the door wasn't properly locked, the washroom opened and presented itself with an old rustic faced beedi smoking (a cheaper version of cigarette usually smoked by villagers) man having raw white beard and a white-turned-gray turban. Before both Manoj and the old guy could register, Manoj's hands did what his stomach ordered him to do.

"HEY, WHO THE F***K ARE YOU MAN! AM BUSY SHITTING AND SMOKING HERE. ISN'T YOUR SHIT STOPPING? GO FIND ANOTHER… HEY NO…NO…NO…STOP MY BOTTOM IS NAAAAKEEEED"

Manoj literally threw the old man out of the washroom and then locked the door with his leg still on it (to prevent anyone else from opening it). Once his brain took control of the body from his stomach, he slowly released his leg, took out a cigarette, smoked two puffs and came out, about to apologize to the old man.

To his…surprise or shock…, there was a big gathering outside the washroom as if it became a good tourist attraction with him using it. He and the old man (who was now crying and farting, like a molested woman) were the centre of attraction and the rest of the corridor was so crowded that there was hardly any place to stand.

Everyone was standing on toes to watch him and the old man who was…to Manoj's now conscious brain…half naked. He was being given a lungi to cover, and then to the front came…now to Manoj's horror…Gopala Swamy along with Sharada Devi at the back, and another young man who was not so handsome compared to him.

"Gopal!!! NO, Stop!!! Stop.... I said…please", Sharada Devi was trying to pull Gopala Swamy back whose hand was clutching Manoj's throat with both the ends almost intersecting. With Raj stepping forward and helping, and some of the servants getting braver now that one person stepped forward, had come for the rescue. Slowly, they brought the hand out of Manoj's neck who felt every inch of Gopala Swamy's hand slowly going back, he made weird noises in between and then choked, coughed and fell down as if he apparated for the first time.

The youngman who was at the side went to the old man. "Dad, are you ok? Did you complete the task or is it still pending? PHEW, ok…ok…stop farting. We understood. Hey you!!! Murugayya…Kodayya… whoever you are. Take dad inside the washroom."

"Kireeti, who is that young dog? Is he one of your useless town friends? After so many days, I was about to go to the washroom (has constipation issue) and was feeling happy. I even lit a beedi enjoying it. And then…this vulture of a relative came into the washroom and before I could realize…he…he.. aaah aaah aaah" wept the oldman who was carefully being lifted and taken by Murugayya who closed his nose with one hand and kept saying "Ayyagaaru…wait wait…not now. Let's finish the process in the washroom. Oh man, you've wetted the floor. Need to clean that."

"Also Murugayya, you need to clean my father's also, once he's done inside. He is in a shock and doesn't seem to be in sense", replied Kireeti to a facepalming Murugayya who was looking at Manoj in a *didn't-I-tell-you-to-go-to-farm* fashion.

"Ok, now that it's done, everyone let's leave. Come on Gopal. Let's go, I needed to talk to you", spoke Sharada breaking the ice and also trying to silence Gopala Swamy who was looking as if he was carrying an invisible gun in his hand ready to shoot one sharp bullet into Manoj's head who was writhing and resting at the same time.

As everyone started to leave, Kireeti entered into the scene again and shouted surprisingly at Sharada Devi, "Who are these parrots, Athayya? They're doing a lot of crazy stuff coming to my…I mean…our house. That guy who initially looked to be a decent city bullodu has suddenly become a *Lungi Rayudu* and was asking for kacheri and all" he said pointing at Raj to which Sharada Devi went into a small shock for a moment but immediately hid it and went into thought. "Then comes this…this…what do I call him…*circus Seenu*…who only knows two things, how to eat (both food and other's brains) and how to sh…"

"Shhhh", pointed Gopala Swamy this time. "Won't you ever say to, or point something at *my wife* who is later *your Athayya* Kireeti. And don't you worry about these petty, nasty, pricking parrots. I am going to handle them."

Saying so, he walked just two paces towards Manoj which was enough to make him get up and retreat a bit.

"My boy Manoj. Why don't we make a small alteration to the challenge?" he asked in an angry cum sarcastic way.

Manoj was only able to move his lips in the shape of *what*.

"If the contestant who is representing you or me gets knocked out in the midst of the...*friendly* match, you will step into the ring if yours is knocked down and I would do the same if mine is knocked down. Got it?" saying that Gopala Swamy started going away. Sharada Devi immediately intruded.

"Gopal. Please think for a while. The match, you said, is going to be conducted before the village. How will it be friendly when it will include wrestling, knock out and if anyone gets hurt, it might impact your..."

"RESULT!!! Now, I won't be falling for it, Sharada. That's why if you see I've decided I'll send a person as representative for me and not me directly. Hehehehe. And don't you worry. There won't be a necessity where I would need to step in", Gopalaswamy kept laughing in a way he never laughed for a while.

Gayathri looked triumphantly at her friends who were all standing there witnessing it saying, "That's how my dad is. He's like a knife kept on a moving wheel. When it gets hot, he becomes sharper and sharper. Just like me."

Now, both Manoj and Sharada Devi were left silent as there was nothing left to speak. Noticing this, everyone started to leave speaking and gossiping about the *friendly* match.

"My dear Mavayya. I mean uncle. Wow, what a speech and what an announcement!!! You really excel yourself day-by-day whenever you make announcements, be it your daughter's marriage date, your election date and your nominations date. Am becoming a fan of it."

Everyone turned back to see who could speak in such a way, especially to an angry Gopala Swamy who generally becomes a hungry wild animal when provoked.

Raj stepped ahead, crossing Manoj and clapping gently. Leaving Sharada devi, Manoj, Gayathri, Kireeti and all others present dumbstruck, he continued "Was this the match you were saying about, mama? God, I like these challenges which are so native, village-like and so much different from a corporate one made in posh offices drinking wine."

This was turning Gopala Swamy redder and wilder than usual. "So, you're saying you've accepted it and are ready for it?" his voice was trembling as if he was about to shout. Both Manoj and Sharada Devi were ready. One to run and other to stop,

"I have taken many challenges and risks in life which I didn't share even with my family uncle. However, the most daring and difficult one was done with me many years ago (saying so, he saw those two people in the house who knew what it was). But, the point is, they were worthy of being challenged. But, this? This one is merely a nail which tried to scratch the surface."

"What did you say? WHAT DID YOU SAY!!!" Gopala Swamy got to 'boiled' from 'heated'.

"Mama, run!", "Gopal, stop". Both lines came at a time.

"I say why don't we make another small alteration to this 'friendly' match?" Raj made signs of quotes in the air with his hands.

"What…alteration…what is it?" asked Gopala Swamy, suddenly stopping.

"After all, when this friendly match involves knockdown and substitution, what fun will it be without a prize?" pointed Raj.

"Prize?" asked everyone in which Gopala Swamy's voice got carried away.

"Yeah. Like an offer no one can refuse to. So that there will be some fun and motivation in both the wrestlers and their…their…let me say their masters", said Raj sounding cheerful.

"What is that?" asked Gopala Swamy transfixed.

"As you said it is the auspicious day of nominations for Sarpanch, let's make it more auspicious. The one who wins in the friendly match shall be…hmmm…contesting for Upasarpanch along with you maybe?" finished Raj.

"Hey…hey…HEY" random people from the audience kept shouting. Some of them being Kireeti, the panchayat club members of Gopala Swamy. "How can a friendly match decide such serious results? Gopal, no…no… don't listen to that foreign brand fox."

"What's the matter tough villagers, losing your shit when you come face to face with me?" asked Raj which fired like an invisible bullet onto Gopala Swamy.

He reacted spontaneously, "Done."

"Shhhh. Everyone CALM DOWN!!! I said it's done. Let's meet on that day you egoistic squirrel!"

Saying so, Gopala Swamy left. Raj now looked at everyone, gave a wink and left.

Everyone forgot to leave or even to move.

One of the friends of Gayathri whispered to her "Never seen someone who could make your dad think or silence him other than your mother. If your dad is the knife on the wheel, he looks like the one wielding it."

Chapter -19
THE THREATS

Sharada Devi's study room was never this crowded and never with the current crowd. The crowd consisted of the least likely villagers Sharada would have predicted to be in her study. It was the Queen along with her chamber maids and Sharada (the old priestess) could neither care nor conjecture their purpose.

"If you girls need a place to chit chat or gossip about the challenge the day after, then march to the terrace of the castle", said the priestess.

"No, it's not that. We had a few questions for you and honest replies would be much appreciated", the queen corresponded.

All the chamber maids were standing there in silence as though they were witnessing a verbatim duel of the century in the colosseum.

"Is it about the dress you girls get to wear for the contest? You want my permission for some stupid dress you girls bought so that the village folk admire you and you admonish them?" the priestess asked exhaustingly.

"It is nothing related to the contest", the queen replied.

"In that case it can wait because I have something to say regarding the contest", the priestess continued.

"Oh, then speak it out", the queen was puzzled.

"Not to you Gayathri, to 'him' ", saying so the priestess was about to leave when the chambermaids blocked the door shamefully.

"What a coincidence, I needed to ask you about 'him' and so you would be allowed to join 'him' only after you have answered my questions", the queen ordered.

"Do you want to study for your supplementary exams Gayathri?" the priestess questioned to which all the chambermaids laughed out.

"You can't wriggle out of this amma or I would have to speak to dad", queen…. Gayathri tried to stand her ground.

"And do what exactly?" Sharada stared at Gayathri intently.

"Don't test or underestimate me amma, it was the same mistake that brought the challenge upon the foreigner", Gayathri tried hard not to blink or stare away bringing tears to her eyes.

"You brought this challenge upon him?" the priestess was confused.

"Oh yes, and serves him right too for having a (and I am quoting him here, oh my god do I really have to say this out loud) 'marital affair' with you. Now daddy can set score with him properly and you would see for yourself who the boss is", said a teary eyed Queen.

"Don't you dare speak to me like that Gayathri or I will have you sent to a boarding school with hostel facility for you to do an MBBS which would take 5 years of studying and with your brains, I will say 10 years give or take", shouted Sharada Devi.

Out of the corner of her eyes, Gayathri saw her chambermaids just vanish.

"Why does it anger you, who is he to you? Who is he to me?" squealed Gayathri and this time the tears were not due to the strain of keeping her eyes open.

"He is just the son of a friend or rather someone I once knew. He has come to see Suguna's wedding and that's all there is to it", Sharada said.

Gayathri, though not completely convinced, didn't want to test her luck any further. She would have much better luck with her father (as she did earlier in the night). She could manipulate him through his love or a tear or two. She will ask him straight.

"What is this Gopalam", asked Subbaraju (whose son Phalguna was meant to marry Gayathri according to Gopala Swamy's plan).

"It's a chance Subbu, for your son to show who he truly is. It's his chance to make an impression on me and on my daughter Gayathri and on the entire village too. It's a chance for him to become upasarpanch", smoked Gopalam.

"Bullshit! He was supposed to become upasarpanch no matter what remember. He was supposed to marry Gayathri and come to your house and in return you would make him upasarpanch. This was your word, our deal", Subbu was outraged.

"I told you this 'Gopalam' of yours can't be trusted", hiccupped the cocky panchayat guy. "Now your son will not just be a house husband but a big bland buffoon in front of the entire village. Fighting a foreigner over Gopala Swamy's challenge. And if he loses..." he continued.

"He will wear a half saree and roam around the entire village on a donkey if he has an ounce of dignity", laughed another panchayat member.

"That is not the point. The point is my son will not even participate in this nonsense challenge", Subbu was about to leave.

"So does that mean you are no longer interested in my daughter or your son Subbu?" shouted Gopala Swamy. "In that case, I announce now that if any of your sons fight the challenge on my behalf tomorrow and win, he will not just contest for upasarpanch but will marry Gayathri and inherit half of my wealth from my will", he spoke to the entire panchayat in his room.

"Is that a threat, Gopalam?" Subbu just turned half a circle and whispered back.

"Again it's a chance Subbu", smiled Gopalam.

The entire room was filled with random "Oh my son is ready", "I am calling him right now", "Can my son-in-law participate in this?" "I have a wrestler with me, if he wins, can my son still be eligible, he will deliver the last punch once the wrestler is done with that foreigner".

Amidst all this, Subbu's voice alone mattered to Gopalam. Finally, there was a shout from the fag end of the room, "Phalguna becomes the upasarpanch but I get half your wealth Gopalam".

"Why did you accept the challenge without having a word with me?" Manoj shouted.

"Oh, why then did you bring the challenge up without having a letter with me?" Raj gave it back without sparing a look towards Manoj.

"Haven't you seen how that Gopala Swamy looks like? Can't you guess how his builders or what do they say 'palewaans' will be like? Though they are called 'pale'waans they are really strong", cried out Manoj "And if you rat out of this, then I would have to fight that palewaan or that crazy Gopala Swamy himself."

"Shhhh, the room has no door now thanks to you, the voices will carry to the entire house, not just the study room now", Raj tried to calm Manoj down.

"Excuse me", came a lady's voice.

Both Raj and Manoj jumped back expecting to see Sharada Devi at the entrance, instead it was a much younger woman, the woman Manoj recognized at once as he saw her on a banner and leaving her mother's study just that evening. It was Suguna, her voice, her demeanor were so like Sharada Devi herself.

"Yes, what do you want Miss soon to be Mrs?" started Manoj.

"Firstly I want you to leave the room please", she asked Manoj.

"What the…." Manoj began.

"Or even better, would you come with me to the terrace?" she now asked Raj.

"No, we are in this together, it is either the two of us or none", Manoj replied.

"Me and her makes two mama. So I think it will be fine", Raj smiled as he left the room leaving behind a shaken Manoj.

"Mom has a message for you", started Suguna as Raj accompanied her to the terrace.

"She couldn't give it to me herself?" enquired Raj.

"Not with Gayathri and dad having dozens of questions for her. She guessed they might not allow her to come near you or you to her. So she asked me to give you a message", answered Suguna.

"Oh alright, go ahead", Raj folded his hands as he considered her. His earlier conversations with Gayathri made him wonder if she really was Sharada's daughter indeed. However a discussion with Gopala Swamy made him realize she was his reflection whereas the elder daughter got everything from her mother. Her calm demeanor, her wits, her voice, her authority over the situation, everything.

"Ahem, you mean leave Manoj here and flee?" Raj sounded off "I thought it was a message you had for me, not a threat."

"I am not sure, she just said she would allow you alone to leave the house just for the one day and then you must come back the next day or else…. you need not come back for your friend any other day", Suguna said it as though she was asking Raj to explain the meaning of this rather than she explaining to him.

"If I leave, I really need not return cause I know what Gopala Swamy and his confederates are going to do to my cousin. And today made it clear that even your mother cannot stop your father in some matters after an extent", Raj replied. "Anyway I think what your mother said makes sense. I am much more valuable than my cousin to her and myself. I will consider her offer" he finished.

Suguna was about to leave when she stopped and turned back to him.

"Can I pay you a compliment?" she asked.

"About my looks?" Raj sounded exasperated.

"No, your wits. I understood why you introduced that upasarpanch thing in the challenge today. You made sure dad cannot send one of his muscle men to fight in the challenge cause the winner would have to contest for upasarpanch, eliminating all his henchmen. He would then have to either ask his panchayat gang or their kids to step in who you might find easier to handle. That was quick thinking. Your type are rare in this village. It is usually mom and maybe…me…sometimes who can do that" and then she left.

Raj waited by, his mind in deep thought. Suguna saw right through him, a feat which her mother was not yet able to achieve. She might be much more of a threat to Raj than her mother. Maybe leaving the village for a day wasn't such a bad idea, he would have one less thing to worry about. He would get some more time to think too.

Chapter - 20

THE UNLIKELY PAIR

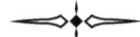

Sharada Devi woke up early in the morning (if one could call getting out of a feigned sleep so). She passed the entire night wondering what would happen the next day though the duel was one more day away. She went as quickly and silently as possible towards the store room. She needed to check if Suguna was able to drive some sense into the millionaire.

Luckily the store room had no door now and Sharada was avoided the trouble of knocking and waking up the fellow foreigner and half the house with him. As she peeped in, her heartbeat started to ease out, there was only Manoj there who clearly was drunk to near death. But she was not reassured altogether, she had to check the entire house once to make sure (atleast the washrooms and other public places within the house).

She scanned through all the washrooms in the house, her study, main hall, lawn, foyer, folly and finally went for the terrace. As she ran up the terrace, her heart only beat fast due to the physical exhaustion, her brain was completely relaxed. Raj was clever indeed unlike his father. Of course, there is a chance he might not return but the fellow foreigner was still here and she could make him spit out Raj's or Ravikant's address as easily as her husband spits out his gutka. She laughed at the thought and settled herself on the cradle to catch her breath.

As she was catching her breath, a strange sight caught her eye too. On the road that runs beside the house below leading to the beach, a villager was laughing the shit out of himself as someone beside him was standing by on a cycle having something. She stood up to see the cyclist's face which was earlier blocked by the villager and now by the coconut through which the cyclist was having a drink. As he lowered the coconut, Sharada's heart skipped a beat. It was Raj on the cycle.

She wanted to shout out to him but was afraid she might wake someone up. She had to run down the stairs in a hurry now, and almost fell off twice. As she was running past the hall, she accidentally kicked a copper vessel with water which went straight to the sleeping Murugayya's head. He fell down the cradle he was sleeping on (in the main hall) onto Tommy the dog who was sleeping beneath it. The dog shouted, shitted and then bit Murugayya on his buttock in protest. As Murugayya got up and began to run with Tommy at his back (with his lungi in its mouth which it pulled out as

Murugayya winced in pain), Sharada ran faster before the voices of Murugayya and the dog (though it was hard to distinguish which was which) woke up the entire house.

As she came out, Raj started cycling off. She shouted at her milkman who was still laughing.

"Oh ammagaru, good morning. You consider us dumb witted right, get a load of this. I was about to throw the packets at your gate when this strange "*cityodu*" who you think is smarter gave me 500 rupees for an hour on my cycle and coconut milk. I think the coconut milk has not worked. I think he has drunk some of his city brand kallu which is not affected by our coconut milk", laughed out the milkman Mattayya.

"Go run behind that guy and stop him", Sharada Devi ordered and no one in Sivasamudram dare defy it.

Mattaya's smile drained out instantly as he ran behind Raj. There was some discussion between the men and Raj turned back with a smile to look at Sharada. Raj rode the cycle back while Mattayya started running back shouting at Raj again asking to let him come on cycle too. Raj skid right in front of Sharada as she closed her eyes in fear.

"Morning athayya! What a coincidence, I was just wondering who could help me out and here you were trying to reach out to me", started Raj.

"Just stop all this nonsense, I gave you all the help I could. I sent word for you to flee for the two days and come back after the duel. Huh, I even agreed for you to leave the village if you left your joker?" shouted Sharada.

"Amma….gaaarrruuu…..haa…..please don't…..tell……me…..I have to give him back……the 500", panted Mattayya.

"Get out", Sharada just let the word out when the already panting Mattayya again ran for it leaving behind his cycle and milk cans.

"You think I am like that guy who would just run away when you ask him to", smiled Raj.

"I say this for your own good my dear boy. I thought you were cleverer than your loser of a father. And you prove yourself dumber than him. Even Varma would not dare challenge my husband and have the audacity to think he would survive it", Sharada held her head which started to turn as a result of her early morning exhaustion.

"Why don't you sit down athayya? I will take you back home on the cycle", suggested Raj.

"Yeah right, I think I need a breather", panted Sharada and she mounted the rim of the cycle and sat in front of Raj, "But make it quick and make sure no one sees us like this" she finished.

As soon as Sharada mounted the cycle, Raj turned it around and started to cycle towards the sea, away from the house.

"Hey, hey, HEYYYYY!!! What are you….? Oh my god", Sharada was blabbing as she saw where Raj was headed.

"Relax athayya, I just wanted to have a tour around the village, especially the places that concern me. You know, the sea, that Ovulayya's farm etc. I needed a guide and since I only know you, mavayya and dad who could show me around, and because dad is not here and I can't go to mavayya, I thought I will take your help", Raj spoke back lovingly.

"What nonsense! What would you do once you look at those places?" Sharada tried to look away as people around them started noticing this unlikely pair.

"Hey isn't that Sharadamma?" "Who is that with her?" "Are they eloping" "Is this the city guy whom she fell in love with when she was studying there, that guy doesn't look so old though?" "Does Gopala Swamy know about this?" "Hey I need to take a picture of this, FLASH!!!"

"Oh god! Their tantrums kill me. Listen to their bloody imaginations. They use up their brains for such stupid tales. First they call me mad, then they call me a gold digger, now they call me ….I don't know….a woman cheating on her husband for a younger lad. This is sooo embarassing", Sharada tried knocking some sense to Raj but the latter was least interested. He looked so pleased with the pleasant weather and seemed to enjoy the fresh breeze coming from the sea towards which they were headed.

As they reached the seashore, (with many more tantrums and weird faces the farmers were giving them en route.

Not to mention the spitting out of tea, choking on coffee, dropping of the water vessels used instead of tissue paper by farmers as they went to their early morning farm visits) Sharada immediately got down.

"Athayya, I have given that milk guy 500 bucks for an hour which gives us....45 more minutes. Now you drove him away and I can't take back my money. So why not we just go around these places and talk. You try convincing me to leave the village in that time, and in case I find your argument logical, I promise I will leave right then and there. Is that a deal?" Raj held out his hand.

"But....do use your sense....I mean I ask you to leave for your sakes?" blurted out Sharada.

"Is that a deal athayya?" Raj extended his hand further.

"Oh forget it, alright, it's a deal" she shook his hand as a passerby corn seller dropped his stove on his foot, and ran into the ocean as Sharada gave him a stern look.

"Wow, look at that. Dad was here when he wanted to strike a deal with you and now I make a deal with you here. What an irony" Raj smiled. He brought some coffee for the pair as they started walking along the coastline. Just when Sharada was about to start her argument, a sheepish looking Paidi thatha (the boatsman who was supposed to take Gayathri to Dubai as per the Queen's plan) came in front of them.

"Ammagaru, this is not good at all. I can see this guy is slightly handsome, though not so much as me, but better looking than ayyagaru, but that doesn't mean you....ori bhagavanthuda (my god)....start seeing him. And you clown!!! Don't think this place is a corrupted shitpool like your big cities. People here still have an honor and code to live by. And if you mess with one of us, you mess with all of us. Look at me, LOOOK AT ME!!!" shouted Paidi thatha.

Sharada offered the oldman her coffee to improve his looks. Just as he was running away into the sea to cool down his coffee drenched face, she shouted back at him, "I guess this man looks better than you now Paidi. So please mind your own business, and by your business I mean your lousy boat business alright."

Before anyone else could interrupt her, she started, "Look Raj, I know you think you are smart and you think you can handle my husband. But logic only works if you are dealing with someone logical. I spent a lifetime dealing with these people and believe me, they believe in the only logic they understand, fight. Hell, if an Isaac Newton comes and tries explaining them about gravity by dropping the apple, they would steal that apple from him and eat it. That's who you are dealing with, so please don't make the mistake of thinking you can convince them with your charm or your wits. Why do you think I made that deal all those years ago? Why do you think I neither advise my husband nor take any advice from him. It's useless even talking to them. I tried a lot in my initial days of marriage to deal with reason. You know what I have been called? A witch, a mad woman, an educated fool and many more. And they are the ones I heard of. God knows how many more names I have been bestowed without my knowledge. So please leave, prove to me you are logical. I beg you. Do not listen to your father inside you." Sharada was surprised at her own feelings now. She was never this open with anybody else. Was she so desperate?

"Athayya", Raj sounded serious now. He held her hand and faced her as he spoke, "Since we are near the ocean, I will try this example. You know how a kingfisher hunts? Just the way an eagle does but cleverer. An eagle spots its prey from up above and dives right down. Just when people think it is about to crash, it swerves parallel to the ground, picks its prey and soars right up again. But a kingfisher hunt is one step ahead. It has to time its dive anticipating the dive from below. It has to think like the fish it is about to hunt and dive down when the fish decides to dive up. Right when the fish bounces up the water, the kingfisher catches it and rest is the same as the eagle. Do you get it? In the eagle's example, the eagle chooses its time as the prey is hardly moving or aware of the hunt. But in the latter example, the kingfisher has to follow the fish, observe it and right when the fish is too confident and bouncy in its arena and decides to rise, it strikes. Your husband thinks he is at the top, as this is his arena, which is what I want my fish to think when I strike."

Sharada was silent for the rest of the walk in the sea while Raj was enjoying the waves hitting his feet. He kicked the water back, felt the salty water on his face and enjoyed the sunrise. She was trying to make sense of what Raj meant by his example. Was he the hunted or the hunter in her hunt? Was she his fish too?

They then cycled to the fabled Ovulayya farm where the deal took place. She introduced Ovulayya to Raj and Raj to Ovulayya (of course she mentioned Raj was just a guest at her oncoming daughter's wedding). She showed Raj the spot (more or less) where the deal was done as Ovulayya stayed back near the fence trying to make some sense of what the other two must be talking about.

As they started walking back towards the cycle, Sharada stopped Raj, "Listen, your life is much more important to me than it is to you. You are part of the deal, you are mine now. I intend to give my daughter's hand in marriage to you if everything works out well. So please do not risk your life. Go away just for tonight, come back tomorrow night, everything would be sorted out by then. I understand you only deal with honesty, and this is honestly why I don't want you here tomorrow. Now deal with it."

"And for God's sakes, don't take me back on that cycle", she continued as they reached Ovulayya and Raj climbed the cycle. Ovulayya was standing near the fence pretending to feed his cattle again.

"Athayya, half the village has already seen us on the cycle. And they will make sure the other half finds out. So what's the point? Besides, it was a dream of mine to take a beautiful village girl with me on a cycle", Raj winked at her and Ovulayya together (Ovulayya as usual had grass stuck in his hand from where the cow was now directly consuming).

And they rode back the road just like a happy couple riding towards the rising sun. As they reached the house, they could already see a lot of faces popping out of windows, balconies, and the barred window of the store room. But for the pair, only one face which was at the terrace mattered. Gopala Swamy stood there fuming (his cigar added to the fume too), and Sharada noticed that the fish was at the top now.

Chapter - 21

THE FIGHT AHEAD

Manoj was eating his favourite Sushi at the Ixi restaurant. It was half finished when the other half was taken by someone else. He turned to see his ex-Stacy smiling at him and staring romantically. He was pleasantly surprised to see her there.

"Hey? What the…when did you come here Stace?"

"What happened ayyagaaru…are you ok?" replied Stacy.

"Huh…my God! Look at your language! How did you get it? Yuck", replied Manoj not understanding whether to feel amazed or disgusted at Stacy's learning power.

"Did you have the ooru special kallu? Then, why are you asking like this? I usually speak like this only right?", replied Stacy speaking so fluently in village dialect in a completely contrasting western outfit. "You know, I always wondered how you get this broken English-Telugu which you speak. Could you teach me too, so that I can impress our neighbour Surayya in Times street?"

"Surayya? Who is that...that...village side brook? Did they come to the States as well now?" asked Manoj in panic, looking around the hotel, as if he will be able to recognize that beedi-taking, lungi-wearing, turban-bearing oldies looking at him from Ixi restaurant and sitting on the road, doing their private work in the public place and laughing at him.

"What are you speaking ayyagaru? Are you dreaming? Wake up...the sun and the hen have risen. Your friend has fled. How come you're left here? Didn't you keep an...what is that you foreign kurrollu (youth) keep...yeah alarm?" asked Stacy in a worried tone and shaking him.

Slowly, the waiters in the restaurant became the old rustic village lungi batch. The clean posh shelves of Ixi became the damp old smelling shelves with rusty brass items. To his biggest horror, the beautiful skin and face of Stacy transformed into a rough scaled, brownish wrinkled one of a middle aged village girl whom Manoj wished to call Pentamma looking at her appearance.

"F***k, f***k,f……."

"Ayyagaaru! Stop! Stop! I can't listen to that. There are children living in this house. No, I've come to wake you up and inform regarding your friend's escape, as you remind me of my brother-in-law Malligaadu. You need not thank me now. Later, you can send me a rose and a letter, along with one Paris perfume and a flight ticket and…."

"Hey, get lost! You half cooked dung! Leave me alone", pushed Manoj and he continued his song of swear words.

"That's what I'm saying. You're alone now and your friend has left you. Do you remember what the rule in duel was, if your friend isn't there or if he loses?" asked the lady (preferrably Pentamma for Manoj).

Her words had miraculously put a full stop to the melodious song of Manoj, who realized the bigger picture or to say the bigger danger.

Without noticing or even understanding what he was doing, he pushed the lady aside and took out his half opened bag, threw random stuff he caught hold of in the room, closed the zip, crying and imagining Raj who would now be laughing in a 5-star hotel…or maybe a roadside dhaba considering he was bankrupt…and thinking how Manoj's face would be looking once he finds out or once he steps into the duel ring.

"No…no…I won't. I won't…I should run. Come on Manoj. Just…just…just recollect the running scene from Forrest Gump. You need to run like hell. The only difference is, now you would be running from hell. All Fathers, give me strength! May the judgement day arrive soon to this idiotic village and punish all of them for troubling a pure soul like me, and not to forget, burn alive the Varma's family for making fun, fool and everything out of me. RUN!!!"

Saying so, Manoj ran out of the room leaving behind shouting and horror struck Pentamma. He took to the stairs beside his room, jumped 2-3 at a time, and landed on the foot of an old man, who shouted throwing his beedi from his mouth. Ignoring him, Manoj pushed aside the kids, the general giggling girls…who for some reason were not giggling now…instead were looking outside of the corridor. But, he didn't let it stop him. Now, no more village girls or their beauties can stop him. He continued his run, passing the dangerous rooms of Sharada Devi's, the Panchayat oldies' and he was finally onto the ground floor where to his shock was a big long queue.

Was it the crowd which had gathered to witness the duel? The duel was for tomorrow. Then, maybe these are the farther stupid generation of that Gopala Swamy or maybe his to-be brother-in-law side. But, how can he get past them? He slowly kept going through them, gently pushing them. He kept hearing tantrums like "Hey, he is the one, the friend of that Foreign Bullodu (foreign kid)", "Why do you foreign people behave like this?", "Don't you know the difference between ages? Dating an old lady?", "Is this why you guys come to India? Find innocent married women and trap them?", "Don't you have any shame, coming from Mother Teresa's homeland and visiting her holyland for things like this?", "Gopalam! Why did you leave them like this?" He kept looking grudgingly at each of them and then saw to his right, where everyone else was looking. To his surprise, he saw the very same person whom he had cursed; Raj. Then to his shock, he saw the person along with Raj, who was the one granting his curse, Sharada Devi.

Both of them were on a bicycle coming towards them, as if they had been enjoying the situation and discussing how much share each of them should get from the collections of the duel match. Even Manoj for a second couldn't believe or understand the view. "Oh my God! Oh my…oh God. Now, what is this asshole upto? Was he thinking of mesmerizing Sharada Devi and eloping? In order to escape from the deal? Did he forget…now it's the duel, not the deal which mattered."

"What are you all looking at? Grab this monkey. He's the one who's giving ideas to his friend. They both are eyeing to loot Gopal uncle's wealth and fame", came the voice of Sravani and she was standing alongside pacifying Gayathri (sorry again Queen Gayathri) who was exactly mimicking crocodile tears.

"Aaayyyyyeeeee" came a roar from the ground floor herd who were zeroing in on the little pigeon Manoj, who immediately sat down covering himself tightly.

"STOP!" came a calm voice from outside, and everyone turned unknowingly in the form of a Mexican wave.

It was as if everyone had been trained to stop at hearing that voice from ages. Sharada Devi entered and suddenly all the herd spread out giving her way. At the circle, was Manoj who was still crouched not daring to come out of his self made shell. Sharada Devi came towards him, looked at him in a when-would-this-guy-change manner, patted and signaled him to get up and go up. Weeping, he slowly got up but quickly went up all the way looking at Raj in an angry (no tearful.... whatever) manner. From the storeroom, he could see Raj waving and smiling at the group who were cursing him, pushing him and stumbling him.

Ring….. Ring…..Ring

And suddenly, everyone turned towards Manoj whose phone just rang. He ran much faster as the crowd was again drawn to him. He swore under his breath and picked up the phone as he reached the store room. WHAM!!!

A kid who was waiting for someone to enter the storeroom just catapulted Manoj's soft muzzle under the ribs with an iron pellet (the one used for popping soda bottles).

"Hello my dear monkey. Ready to speak?" came the voice on the phone.

Manoj playing frisbee with the catapult and holding the kid by his hair answered, "My God! Is this you again, doesn't your daughter have a phone?" and he released the kid with his leg and his hand.

"I don't have time for this nonsense. Just tell me when do you have time for me", asked Rajagopal.

"You think I have time for your nonsense? What is this? Did your counsellor ask you to call your favourites and tell them how you are feeling, to help cure your boiling brain?", Manoj asked, he seriously saw neither purpose nor meaning in these calls.

"I want to show you the presentation my team has been working on for the past few weeks. Also, by the way, shouldn't it be the other way round? You guys calling us and eating our brains to show the status of the presentation, which you've invested for", Rajagopal's patience was reaching its limits.

"Seriously? Is that why you're calling? What presentation is it that you guys are so squeezing out to show? Is it about you all dancing wearing bikinis? And at last showing our restaurant and saying to come if you want a live free show? The caption would be: The show is free, the food is not" cried out Manoj.

"Oh yeah, will I get my 10 lakh rupees for that? Is that your limit?" laughed Rajagopal.

Manoj laughed harder, "10 lakhs for what? Your bikini dance? I don't think your physique would fetch more than a thousand".

"Give the phone to Mr. Raj. And tell him that he's gonna realize why no one dare challenge Rajagopal", boiled Rajagopal.

Just then, Raj entered the room.

Manoj shouted, "Hey Raj, it's Raja on the line? I think we need to take his phone away from him. And he wants to talk to you."

Raj took over the phone and spoke in a twisted lady voice, "Raj who? Oh, you mean that handsome friend of yours who went for the donation drive? Should I imitate him? And who is this Raja? Is he as good as you?" Saying so, Raj gave sounds of kisses he could make as naughtily as possible.

And Rajagopal reached his boiling point, "Oh I see, is this why your interest in me is waning monkey Maharaj? You are with the monkey queen I see. Why don't you tell me on my face that you don't care how many innocent children, middle aged people, adults, oldies, dogs, cats, squirrels and owls your friend's company is killing by the day. You only care about your "masculine macho power" and girlfriend dates while hungry Indians eat the poison your company sells in packaged *******s. My presentation is going to be an eye opener or rather a mouth opener or maybe a mouth closer too. Your mouths will be wide open in realization and then shut when offered to eat your own shit. You corporate monkeys will get a taste of your medicine or rather a taste of your own poison. I will make sure I will chase you down the........." Raj hung up the phone with a girly, "Bye bye goldie oldie".

Just as he hung up, Manoj caught up. Firstly, he caught up some breath, then he caught up with Raj's stupidity he just saw, and finally caught Raj's collar pinning him to the wall and instantly, a large foam of dust left it. "Hey you forever acting American Psycho millionaire! Don't think you can bluff me like you're doing with almost every person in this village, city, country and planet. Maybe you can flatter girls or provoke the men with your acting skills, but you know one thing? You can't fool me with it."

"Woah, you are rather good at dueling buddy. Should we swap our places for tomorrow? It can be you vs Gopala Swamy then. And if what you say is true and my acting skills neither flatter you nor provoke you, then which gender would you fall under?" Raj said as he pried open Manoj's hands from his collars.

"What's all this going on? You go on a cycling ride with an old woman, that too Sharada Devi, kiss an old man on phone pretending to be a girl, my girl rather. And you have a bone crushing duel tomorrow and….and…. you are bankrupt….. and wait a second, can you whistle for God's sake?", Manoj shouted/asked/questioned/weeped/all in one.

"Now, I can say you're better than me in acting man", replied Raj. "Showed me all the Navarasas (9 emotions) a human being is capable of exhibiting. All that in a single sentence. You remember that dialogue? Any state, any centre, single hand…Ganesh (film of a yesteryear South Indian actor Venkatesh)? And yes, I can whistle. Don't know why you have asked that for. Did you want a cheering applause for your performance?" Raj started changing and then realized Manoj broke the door of the store room and fell on the bed in his baniyan and pant.

"No, not an applause, a warning you damned damsel in distress. I thought you abandoned me today morning, just like you abandoned your father and ran away to India. And that sick lady said it so plainly as though I should have anticipated this yesterday itself. Wait, you didn't flee, does that mean you are going to fight tomorrow?" Manoj asked.

"Or run away tonight", Raj yawned as Manoj pulled him aside to face him.

"Then I run away right now", he said.

"Good luck with that, now that I've seen you have become a villagewide celebrity. Everyone wants you. Might I give you an idea? Just go and show your charm to those girls party of that Geeta... Gandhari... Gari... whoever she is. Ask one of them to come with you, and run away so that the village goes into believing that this is what we came for. Your native love story. And, even you will find it easy and enjoyable to run away as that village girl would know the ways of running, and your dream of having an Indian girlfriend would also be fulfilled", saying which Raj took out his mobile phone intending to check for any messages. He found his father had called him some 58 times over the last few hours. Just as he was scrolling down....

Ring.....Ring.....Ring

"Huh...not again. Well, speak of the devil and...", Raj kept his phone aside waiting for it to go off. But, whether to get the doubts clarified, or just to annoy Raj, Manoj grabbed the phone and both of them started fighting for it. Kids were looking at the fight from outside the storeroom and started cheering for the pair (some for Raj but mostly for Manoj, they were calling him Khandala Kothi or Muscular Monkey).

Finally, Manoj got a grip on the phone and answered, "Uncle! Uncle! Mission abort! S.O.S! S.O.S! Please help. We're gone. We're finished. Your son is going to get all of us killed, atleast you and me to start with. He is playing with everyone here. My God! Where did you raise him uncle? Is it your acting skills when you were in this God forsaken village that he imbibed?"

"Hey! Hey! Get my son on the line! Get him!!!" shouted Varma. And Manoj thrusted the phone towards Raj with the speaker activated, but not handing it over to him.

"He's on", Manoj panted.

"See Raj……..Wh…….WHAT HAVE YOU DONE WITH MY MONEY!!!!" shouted the villager in New York. "Couldn't you have left me with one thousand dollars atleast? I would have gone to Switzerland and started a bee farming business in your name by now, I would have had a picture of you with a garland on it too. Now day by day, I sit in this office waiting for that foreign monkey lawyer of yours to come laughing at me, nodding his hand, shaking his finger along with a dozen S.W.A.T officers with their bulletproof vests. And then they would drag me down in front of all these bureaucrats and media channels to the Statue of Liberty, shoot me down on a ferry and dump my body in the lake", cried Varma or the villager (there was little distinction left).

"Pops! Please stop thinking and please stop drinking. With the level of words you're bringing out, I doubt if there is any wine bottle left in our house. And your imagination skills are just comic book level, you could start writing one for a living, instead of bee farming. Why don't you start with your own biography for instance? You can call it How to sell your son for a business. And by the way, I am doing good, thanks for asking." Raj started.

"Doing good? Good in what? Acting? Cheating? Abandoning? Provoking? My son, you turned out to be a bigger scamster than…" gulped Varma. "Than who? My father, you mean?" goaded Raj.

"Raj please stop trying to anger me, I don't have any more secrets to share. So please start sharing yours for a change. What have you done with all my money? Our money? Are you going to be married to that village girl soon?" started Varma. "Better still, he is going to fight her father's henchman in a duel tomorrow" cried out Manoj.

"What? Oh man! Was this the idea you young fox? The age old village intelligence of challenging that Gopala Swamy for your release? My stupid son, this wouldn't work. You're thinking it is going to be like a professional kickboxing match but that's not how a village fight is. God, I miss those fights when we all used to gather around, they were then followed by a Kacheri from Chintamani…stop…stop. What I am trying to say is Sharada made me sign a goddamn CONTRACT, and won't be nullified by a game like in that movie "Sye"." Varma facepalmed himself.

"It has got nothing to do with the contract pops. This is what my beloved cousin got me into", Raj looked at Manoj scathingly.

"No issues. No issues. Let's use some posh management theories. 3 things - Firstly book 3 different flight tickets - 1 from India to U.S, next from U.S to Switzerland and last from India to Switzerland. Secondly, you and Manoj plan out and loot the treasure inside that scum of a house and bring how much ever you can get your hands on. Thirdly, inform the local police that a person named Gopala Swamy is trying to kill you, and you will be needing protection. So that when he realizes the money is gone and goes to the police station, the cops would get him first. ADHI LEKKA, I mean, BINGO!" shouted out Varma (to which the entire floor at his office came running to check if their boss had any good news to share with them).

"Pops, 3 things as you said. First stop having any more booze. Secondly, stop trying to reach out to me or worry about me. Thirdly, your money is now my money as you gave it to me yourself, so do not try running away or anything. You are left with nothing to take or nothing to worry about now, and you're welcome for that. Now sit tight and just wish me good luck for the fight ahead", and Raj disconnected as he could hear nothing but a sob from his father and a worried voice of Mr.Savaroy (Asking if Varma was actually crying).

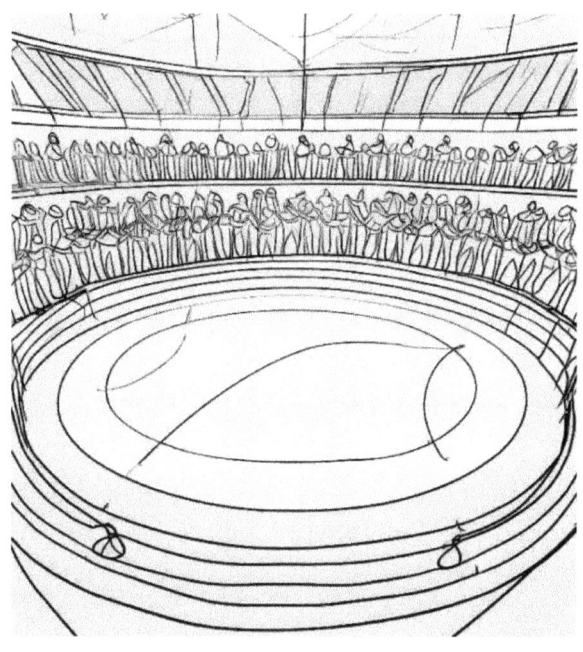

Chapter - 22
THE DUEL

It was as though a Megastar movie had released that day. The crowd that showed up at the village centre was an ocean in itself (besides the actual ocean just behind the centre). The panchayat members who showed up there neither had a clue as to why there was such a gathering of numbers today (was it for Gopala Swamy's campaign announcement or was it for the duel?) nor as to why there was even going to be a duel that day.

A Mexican wave of applause and whistles rose from the crowd silencing the sounds of the adjacent Indian waves, as Gopala Swamy arrived on his jeep, along with Subbu's son Phalguna at the rear, Kireeti in the driver seat.

"Just look at how Gopala Swamy controls his future servant-in-laws, one is driving on behalf of him and the other is fighting on behalf of him", sniggered the panchayat members. Gopala Swamy ascended on to the stage and tapped on the mike to silence the crowd. The only sounds that were audible now were that of waves crashing onto the rocks.

"Welcome one and all!!!" shouted Gopala Swamy (temporarily ignoring the fact that he need not shout out loud as there was a mike for that very purpose). The sound was deafening (not Gopala Swamy's but that of the crowd in response to Gopala Swamy's welcome address). "I am glad that my entire family has done the honor of visiting me atlast. You see, all of you standing here, you are my family. And now, my family has come to bless me and my daughter or rather their daughter on this auspicious day", Gopala Swamy just went on with his speech ignoring all the shouts, tumults of applause and of course taunts as to "Is there going to be a duel today or not? Where is the kallu compound? Is it true your wife is in love with a young foreign musician?

"I now have two announcements for my family here. Firstly, our beloved Suguna as you all know is engaged to Abhigaadu here. And now I am ecstatic to announce her wedding date, and of course I also need to inform you all the date of the elections too. So it is 25th of this month i.e., in about 10 more days", shouted Gopala Swamy.

There was some visible confusion in the crowd. There were murmurs here and there. Finally an old man rose his hand and addressed Gopala Swamy, "Arey Gopi, which date did you announce? Is it Suguna's wedding date or the date of the elections?"

Gopala Swamy smiled even wider and wilder, as he was just waiting for that very question, "It is the same day for both" (This information was not shouted out but just whispered into the mike). For a moment there was silence and then the crowd there just went berserk as everyone's vocal cords and ear drums were tested. "And let me add that the entry to my daughter's wedding will not require you to show an invitation card, it will only require you and the majors in your family to show your inked thumbs and declare that you voted for our family", Gopala Swamy added. And there was a roaring applause to say the least.

Then there was a commotion in the crowd again. Was this it? But they were told there was going to be some fight happening? Some Indian vs American thing and they would all get to witness how Olympics happen and how the crowd there cheers for their country.

Now, it was a young good for nothing college bunking village youngster who addressed the speaker without raising his hand, "Is there going to be a fighting contest today or not? If you say no, I assure you there is going to be a 100:1 fight now."

Gopala Swamy expected the question too, but didn't like the youngster's way of putting it. Nevertheless this was the cue, "You silly street fighter, why do you think I brought Phalguna here. And why do you think none of my inner family is here? They are already waiting for you all at the seashore where all the arrangements for the duel have been made. And before you all shout again, let me just say that Phalguna is not just representing me or you or this village. He is representing India today, and he is going to fight for his country. Today he is going to seek revenge upon that Americans who invaded us, stole our wealth, our freedom, and killed all our freedom fighters and….and now they are stealing away our kids too. Every graduate these days has just one dream, to go visit those foreign lands and work for those white foxes who once visited our lands just the same. This foreigner in particular, has come here to defile our village values. He flirted with our daughters (at this point, the youngster shouted "and your wife too" and there was a wave of laughter from the crowd)…ahem…ahem…and he is trying to settle down here. And about that wife thing, you may laugh now but what has happened with my wife yesterday can happen with your wives tomorrow, remember that."

To this last statement, the laughter drowned in the ocean of people instantly and there came a tsunami of anger. Everyone was bloodthirsty now, all of them were surged with uncontrollable patriotism and devotion towards their country. It was their duty to make sure that India wins this battle and the Indian flag and anthem should stand high today. All of them marched towards the shore singing "Jana Gana Mana" followed by "Vandemataram" and then their own versions of yesteryear telugu patriotic songs like "Punyabhoomi na desam", "Janani Janmabhoomischa" etc., in a random mixture of groups and songs.

At the shore, near the duelling ring Gopala Swamy's actual family along with Subbu, Raj, Manoj and Phalguna cum Kireeti's friends were looking at the oncoming procession led by Gopala Swamy's jeep driven by his servant-in-law and seating all the panchayat members and the other servant-in-law.

"Why are they singing patriotic songs mama?" asked Manoj. "Is today some day of national importance?"

To this, Sharada replied. "More importantly, it is a sporting event. The last time I remember this happened was when there was this India vs Pakistan match last year. And on the actual independence day this year, there were just these Panchayat folks and a few children who came for the sweets that will be distributed only after they stayed for the flag hoisting and sang Jana Gana Mana (as none of the Panchayat members knew the song in full)."

Raj just had eyes for Gopala Swamy who inturn was glaring at Raj behind his cooling glasses. He jumped from the jeep and came beside his wife. "Firstly it was the British who invaded us Gopal, not the Americans and secondly you need not shout into a mike, the mike is meant to magnify your voice", greeted Sharada.

"Oh, were those the only parts of my speech you could hear, or they could hear", he asked pointing at Raj and

Manoj. He asked this because Raj who was now going to face the brunt of the crowd had not even flinched.

"Oh we heard it all right. But I guess we didn't care", she replied.

As Phalguna descended the jeep, village women came and gave him a harathi (a tradition of having burning small camphor balls and moving it around one's face to ward off evil), gave him a "veera tilakam" and a teary eyed "Jai Hind". Children threw flowers at his feet as his friends came and lifted him on their shoulders while some over enthusiastic village youngsters covered him up with a sticky Indian Flag (sticky as it was pretty old and taken from a discard pile of a fancy shop).

Phalguna threw back the flag in disgust but quickly covered it up as though he gave it away to his girl fans on whose heads the flag now fell. The crowd quickly circled the existing circle which had the ring and Gopala Swamy clan + participants of the duel and their correspondents now.

"Go show this foreigner what Indians are made of", "Get out from our mother land", "Inquilab Zindabad", "Jai Balayya" were being shouted all around. Both Raj and Manoj stood there bewildered watching the crowd. Did they enter a wrong event? This was just a friendly personal contest, why were these villagers behaving as though it was Gandhi vs Churchill.

As Phalguna got to the other end of the ring, his friends gathered around and started giving him abstract instructions like "You are an Italian Tanker", "Mhaari choriyan choro se kam hai ke" (Dialogue from a Hindi film saying "Are our girls lesser than our guys?"), "Yudham chetha kani vaade dharmam gurinchi matladathadu" (Dialogue from a Telugu film saying "Only those who cannot fight speak of justice"). And they tore off his shirt and removed his pant leaving behind just his boxer shorts (which too some of his drunk friends tried to tear off but he kicked them in their private parts).

At the other end, Raj (who was wearing a cut baniyan and a sports track suit bottom) started warming up. As he was about to enter the ring, Sharada came by his side (much to the shock of the villagers, some shouted "Told you so" to their fellow villagers. Gopala Swamy broke the headlight of his jeep).

"You just heard and now you just saw my husband's politics. That is pretty much how he has become a successful politician. There is nothing fair in this fight, nor is there a purpose served by it other than my husband demeaning you and getting some much required publicity for his campaign. This is pretty much the only work his brain does and thanks to the brainless folk around him, his half functioning ideas do work. So, step aside and push your cousin or friend or whoever that is into this fight", whispered Sharada. All around villagers thought she was giving him secret strategy or some weakness she observed in Phalguna. Phalguna's friends started warning him too "Bro, careful out there, I think she just told him where that college girl hit you with the burning wooden log when you tried proposing her". The villagers started shouting at Sharada, "Hey Sharada, you traitor, betraying your husband, betraying your country, shame on you". But they were immediately silenced just by her glance towards them. Even Gopala Swamy quickly changed his expression to mild curiosity as she looked around.

And then, he cleared his throat and spoke onto the microphone he was given, "Enough talk, let's have the fight. Fighters, step into the ring". Both Raj and a boxer clad Phalguna stepped in as people behind them were still giving him strategies like "Get him in the ribs, make a pivoting leap and kick his face, just hit him in the head, all his body parts would fail, shall I get a flag with Hanuman on it?"

Gopala Swamy continued, "The rules go this way, this is just a friendly contest. So, no usage of weapons, just fight with bare hands. Also, this is not a professional kusti match or a boxing match, so there are no rounds or count downs or points to win. Let us say fight until the other person is out of the ring, oh no that would be too easy, then let's just say your opponent must either accept defeat or fall flat on his back for hmmm 1,2,3,4,6,5,10…10 times. Oh, and yeah, try not to hit each other in your touch me not areas or face (as you need both of them for your marriages). Lastly, fight for the country not for the crowd."

Almost none of the crowd really understood what the rules were, neither the participants nor their correspondents understood much either. But Raj and Phalguna didn't seem to care. They took their positions as Gopala Swamy walked towards Phalguna drawing him close so that his mouth was inches from Phalguna's ear. "Your dad must have told you this. If you win, you get Gayathri. And just look around what I have done for you. The entire village looks up to you as their leader now, win this fight and say you pretty much lock your seat as the Upasarpanch. I have done all of that for you now. All you need to do is get that white chick ling over there".

And then, he went back to his jeep and sat on the bonnet with his microphone and shouted "Begin"

Just as the sound had come, as though the bull had been shown the red cloth, Phalguna pounced onto Raj who didn't even take a stance. He started giving continuous punches onto the chest, the ribs, the stomach and every inch of the mid portion of Raj. While hitting, he kept shouting different agonised statements like, "This one's for my Maths teacher who unnecessarily kept hitting my hand with a stick, but unknowingly made it stronger, "This is for my Kallu partner Seenugaadu who never misses to drink a single day and never cares to pay for the same", "This is for my Kota Rani (Palace Queen) Gayathri", "This is for my…my…my Sarpanch mama, then…my village…my state…my countryyyyy". While hitting, he kept staring at encouraging crowd smiling and kept winking at the blushing village girls.

With every shot of his, the crowd cheering and ranting like "Adhi Sivasamudramodi dhebba! (That's how the punch of Shivasamudram guy is)", "Kummeyi mama (Hit him mama)", "How are the local punches white rabbit?" "Mera Bharat Mahaan (My India is great)" grew louder and louder. Phlaguna's friends tore open Saara packets and started pouring onto the stadium and onto Phalguna's and Gopala Swamy's photos (brought for campaign). The village girls started whistling and pouring flowers alongside the path which Phalguna would take to come towards Gopala Swamy. Gopala Swamy and Subbu looked at each other proudly and took out beedi to light it together with a common lighter.

Gayathri's friends were enjoying the fight and commenting on how good Phalguna's face was, his muscles were, his shots were. While Gayathri just yawned and was a little dejected with the boring fight and the foreign guy not able to entertain her.

Meanwhile Sharada Devi facepalmed herself on why she didn't take a forceful action on abducting Raj with some local goons and keeping him in a safe place until the day of duel was over. Manoj on the other hand was shouting and sweating equally saying, "Mama! Use the double ninja technique on that Srihari from the Hello Brother movie", "He's not even equal to the least paid bouncer of yours or the gym cleaner whom we used to play friendly matches with and have fun hitting him", "Mama!!! That's too much, maybe you're deliberately losing so that next I would have to play. I would have to? No, no, what should I…?"

"BANG!!!", "NOOOO!!!"

The crowd went mum on seeing if the match had finished and if the shout was from Raj or Manoj, as it was a male voice. Gopala Swamy and Subbu stopped at the spot of lighting their beedis and saw in a finally-done sort of a way at the stadium. Sharada Devi did not dare see what had happened and was just trying to lift her head slowly.

A sudden single drum beat stroke unexpectedly came from behind the crowd. Everyone looked back and Kireeti recognized that old saint who blew the shell as a foundation for his engagement ceremony or more like cremation ceremony. The saint gave an eye-to-eye contact with Kireeti who lowered his head instantly not to give away.

The saint was laughing and waving his head and said to Kireeti, "I warned you. Should have done that with him as well. But, how could I? I didn't know he's gonna be the next scape goat."

Saying so, he then looked at the crowd and directed with his eyebrows to look back front. Every person's head turned exactly like a mexican wave and saw to their...*don't know shock or surprise*...Phalguna's friends stepping into the stadium and slowly lifting him and pouring Sara onto him. Phalguna was conscious enough but was finding it a little difficult to stand and was gesturing his friends to stop and let him think what had happened.

In a split second, Gopala Swamy's eyes turned red and smile went dead. All village girls stood with their mouths open as if their whistles stopped in between. Gayathri looked at her friends who were not speaking and were surprisingly looking at her already.

With this sudden silence, which Sharada Devi generally liked, but wasn't friendly with this time, she looked up instantly. Within her eyeballs was the image of Raj, balancing on one leg with his hands clenched into fists, and the other leg pointed towards the spot where

Phalguna was now getting up, spitting out a few drops of blood, while Phalguna was literally vomiting blood.

"Mama, get up mama, you're alright mama. Think of Gayathri, or Rathaalu. It was only one shot mama. You've hit almost 100 shots. Now, drink one shot and get back."

Phalguna's friends were massaging Phalguna at the hit spot which was at his throat. He drank some Saara and roared back, knocked aside his friends and raced towards Raj, lifted him up and threw at the crowd, who threw Raj back onto Phalguna.

But Raj using the momentum of the throw, had punched at Phalguna's throat again (which again resonated with another single drum beat from the beggar cum saint). He stumbled and fell down, choking his throat as though stopping it from crying, he again did some Rakthaabhishekam (blood pouring ceremony) to his motherland.

Raj stood back on the ground and gave a thumbs up to the crowd, who were all murmuring now instead of shouting or cheering. He looked curiously at the saint who was laughing as if neither Raj nor the crowd would understand his thoughts.

"JAI HIND!", shouted Manoj who was wiping his tears and looking at the angry crowd like a child who had opposed his parents' command of not to eat chocolate. "You forever smoking and gossiping village crows! My Mama might be brought up in the States, but was born on Indian soil and with Indian fire. Jeez! I sounded like a side comedian who turned out to be the hero's boot licker in that...*what was that movie*...haa INDRA."

Raj looked at Manoj with a mix of *seriously?* and *you-put-me-through-this* manner as a response. Sharada Devi murmured something like "Gosh! These men don't know how to solve matters peacefully. Always end up in fights"

Gopala Swamy spitted his beedi and stood up shouting through the microphone despite resistance from Subbu beside, "Rey Phalu! Is this the only magathanam (manhood and bravery) you have got to become my son-in-law and Upasarpanch? Even a Seema pandi (village pig) will fight better. Get up! Get UP!!!"

Slowly, the men in crowd started chanting "Phalu! Phalu!" and his friends looked with teary eyes at the crowd and joined them, though the women in crowd lost attraction and started looking at the latter, who was now looking at the chanting crowd with interest and then at the rising Phalguna who was slightly shivering.

He took the sand below and wiped at his neck but suddenly gave a small scream, looked at the sand having small rocks and threw it away. Then, he charged towards Raj and started hitting with force but in random like a child who was sad with his father not taking him to the exhibition. He stopped shouting now, either due to pain in his throat or losing his cool to impress the crowd.

He tried mimicking Raj by aiming at his throat which Raj was consciously ducking, though receiving other blows. The entire men were now singing Phalguna's name and dancing removing their turbans and waving them. Manoj again became a small innocent cat and kept looking at Raj as though trying to understand his next move.

With every blow, Raj kept getting up back and again fell with a blow but was again getting up. With all his hitting exhausting him, Phalguna took a small break and again looked confident with himself glaring at the crowd and at the gir... *BANG... DRUMBEAT... BANG... DRUMBEAT... BANG BANG....*

It was now Raj getting up and hitting Phalguna who immediately blocked his throat understanding Raj's move. But, after 2-3 blocks, due to his exhaustion of delivering the earlier energetic punches he gave, he gave a pause. Raj used it to his advantage and gave a kick at his legs making Phalguna lose balance and remove the block.

Before he could fall down, Raj gave a kick to Phalguna's throat again and he fell back rolling thrice, leaving trails of blood in his path. "PASSION OF THE PHALGUNA! HAHA" laughed Manoj and kept shouting at Phalguna to give up now and showed various signs which villagers couldn't make head or tail of.

As Raj kept limping forward, the village girls started moving to keep watch on him, and were asking Gayathri's friends about his details and confirming if Gayathri was to marry him or his joker friend if he wins. Gopala Swamy kept shouting louder, "Get up you dumb ass! What happened to your trainings at Kusti, Karrasaamu, lifting weights before Lord Hanuman statue and village fights. Can't defeat this icecream stick of a guy. Let's call this the end of round 1. Listen. Hello?" he watched at his mike and then followed it's wire to see Manoj removing the wire from behind and then running away looking at Gopala Swamy.

With Raj approaching, Phalguna caught his throat, tried getting up and fell back. To his luck, while Raj was coming, he suddenly stopped and caught his limping leg and knelt in pain. Taking this as a chance, and with Gopala Swamy and Subbu shouting together *"FINISH HIM AND TAKE OFF THE SHANI (GOD WHO CONTROLS AND DECIDES ON MISFORTUNES) FROM THIS VILLAGE"*, Phalguna kept running and accumulating all his strength into his legs and right hand.

The old saint kept hitting the drum continuously and the crowd also started chanting mixed names (Men except Manoj shouting Phaluuuuu, Women except Sharada Devi and Gayathri shouting Babuuu).

Phalguna charged making a move to punch with all his friends pointing Raj for him, and the audience watching the upcoming result keenly.

And then, for a second of silence, the birds from trees flew away, and the sea waves were audible and drum beats of the saint ended in a high. Without looking back, he kept walking away saying "Gopalam! I will come back on the election cum marriage date. Make sure you prepare a delicious meal for me. You were looking for a nice son-in-law for your daughters but got yourself a nice mogudu (husband)."

REWIND... Phalguna is performing reverse somersaults thrice and lands in front of Raj attempting to punch him, while Raj's hand is at the intersection of jaw and throat of Phalguna, and Phalguna goes back running reversely.

PRESENT... Phalguna was lying unconscious on the ground, tired of performing three somersaults after taking a blow to his jaw. His friends kept shouting, "Hey you cheater! How dare you act like that and then hit! Mama, you're acting right. Just waiting for him to come near you not knowing that the tiger is just lying there watching. Get up Mama! Girls are seeing you. We all are waiting for your sudden magical move!"

"AYYO!",shouted Subbu and he came running into the stadium at his son and hoisted him onto his feet and kept hitting to wake him up.

The crowd just kept watching at Raj, Gopala Swamy, crying Subbu and Sharada Devi.

Then, one of the other members in Panchayat shouted, "NO! We won't accept it Gopalam. We won't let a foreign bullodu (young boy) sit beside us. We need to send another person to fight as per the rules. Send Kireeti, come on go...go". Saying so, he started pushing Kireeti who was suddenly aware of the situation and kept saying "WAIT! WAIT!"

"Why send Kireeti? Why don't you bring in your pothus (bulls)?" asked Raj looking bleeding but blazing, to which all village girls and Manoj whistled.

"And by the way, as per the rules, if one of the representatives gets knocked down, the main person should come in", replied Raj.

With these words, the entire village gasped. Manoj hiccupped remembering the rules. Immediately, Sharada Devi ran in front of Raj, "Enough! Enough of games both of you! This was supposed to be a friendly match and it's definitely becoming more and more deadly and foolish."

"Step aside Sharada. It's the matter of my dignity which that foreign monkey has challenged. I don't care if it is friendly or not. But I will end it up once and for all", retorted Gopala Swamy who unwound his turban and threw it aside.

The audience became bound to their positions again with silence, when Gopala Swamy started walking towards the stadium crushing the flowers thrown before. He stepped into the stadium and kissed the sand with his hand.

"Perfect!" replied Raj to confusion and murmurs of crowd.

"This is what I wanted. My mavay...I mean to-be Sarpanch stepping into the stadium to face me. That itself makes me feel equal to him, as a contender. I'm now happy to have impressed Gopala Swamy garu as well as his utmost caring Sharadamma", he replied looking at the crowd and at the Panchayat.

"But, also as I am an Indian by birth and values, I will never lay hand on my Guru and will only lay hand on his legs for blessings. Bless me for now", saying so, Raj joined both Gopala Swamy and Sharada Devi together and touched their feet, to which both went back.

"I give up!" said Raj to "What!" from Manoj and then from village girls and then by the men.

"Yes, it's enough for me to be treated equal to Sarpanch. Let him only decide his Upasarpanch. I will return when he calls me. Let's meet at the election date and marriage as well. God! It's my first ever live Indian marriage and elections. Vote for Gopala Swamy!",shouted Raj which the crowd in confusion didn't return.

Even Gopala Swamy kept looking at shock mixed with anger towards Raj and then at the crowd. Raj again looked at the crowd in surprise and said, "Arey? What happened? Won't you vote for Gopala Swamy unless you get a Saara bottle in hand? Come on guys, show some energy".

Entire crowd just shouted following the culture, "Jai Gopala Swamy!" and then kept discussing "Bhale Kurrodu ra (What a guy!)", "Showed who was more worthy and then left it as a paddhati (good tradition)", "What paddhati? He donated it! Whoever will sit in that position now from that namesake Panchayat sons will be a fool"

As the villagers began to disperse towards the kallu compound (mostly men and a few women too), they heard a high frequency sound from the speakers. As they turned back, they saw Raj holding the microphone that Gopala Swamy dropped. And Gopala Swamy slapped Kireeti which was a signal to stop the jeep, he didn't turn back but just sat there listening.

"As we all are about to leave and discuss this duel today, I just want to give a vote of thanks for my sponsors and people behind this exhibition match. Firstly I would like to thank our leader and the running candidate for sarpanch Mr.Gopala Swamy, his dear wife and all of his family members for arranging such a grand event on such a short notice. I also would like to thank Mr.Phalguna and his supporters for being a great sport, I hope he recovers soon and takes a well deserved kiss from his fan girls. I also would like to thank the members of the panchayat for handling all the hiccups and making this event such a grand success and also for kickstarting the campaign. Also, I thank the police department of Sivasamudram for handling the crowd and finally all the people of Sivasamudram, I love you all (with a namaskaram)."

As everyone cheered (with a much deafening roar than the previous ones), Gopala Swamy felt as though he joined legions with that begging saadhu he saw today. He was given alms by that foreign monkey and he had no choice but to accept. SLAAAAAAP.

"What is keeping you waiting you moron!!! Do you want people to lift the jeep up and move it with their hands above their heads", shouted Gopala Swamy at Abhigaadu (Kireeti).

"Oh, and last but not least I would like to thank my buddy Manoj who was the brain behind this fight today (though it was my body behind the fight today). It was he who suggested this duel to Gopala Swamy garu who instantly liked the idea and took it ahead. And while we were discussing our strategy today, he opted out of the fight due to his immense respect towards Gopala Swamy and also asked me to give up in case Gopalam garu steps in. He said, "Mama! You might win the fight but it should be the head of this family (village family) that must decide who would help him lead the clan. Only Gopala Swamy can decide who the next upasarpanch must be, not a silly fight". So three cheers to Manoj", Raj added.

The villagers behind Manoj lifted him up as though he was a rockstar who jumped onto his fans and shouted, "Manju babu ki jai (All hail Manju babu), Mohan babu ki jai". And carried him and deposited him at the rear seat of Gopala Swamy's jeep beside the angry Subbu (Phalguna was rushed to a nearby village tantric in a temple for primary medication).

"Welcome Manju babu", smiled Subbu. "Gopalam, can you drop me and my new friend Manju babu at my house. I want to thank him for his absolutely phenomenal idea of this duel".

As the jeep drove ahead pushing aside the people as though some Moses or Vasudev was splitting the ocean into two halves, village girls started gossipping about that spiky foreigner Manju babu. The Queen and her friends looked flabbergasted (as though wondering if their plan had succeeded at all) but their looks were nothing compared to Sharada Devi's. She was not sure of Raj's intentions anymore. What was the point of all this? Why did he agree to fight? Why did he add the condition of Upasarpanch in the duel? And if he got it midway, why did he throw it away? Did he want to impress her husband? Nonsense! Her husband was agitated to say the least and Raj looked happy with it. What is your play youngman? Where are you leading to?

"Athayya, I think I can't walk back to the house. Can you arrange for a vehicle back or even better could you cycle me back home?" smiled Raj.

Chapter - 23
MANOJ'S FATE

"Now where were we?" Subbu asked Manju babu as he passed on a glass of wine to him and poured himself one too.

"We were at the seashore and now we are in our house", replied one of Subbu's henchmen (or Phalguna's friend).

"Now do you get why I don't offer any of you a drink? It is because you guys are always drunk you useless pack of pigeons", scoffed Subbu, "Now now Manju babu or Mohan babu whoever you are, you answer me rightly. Where were we?"

"You are under an illusion that I am somehow responsible for the fate of your son the falcon or falgun or whoever he is", quivered Manju babu as he took a sip from his glass (only after ensuring Subbu drank his) "and my name is Manoj not Manju", he added.

"No no Manoj babu, I don't believe you are responsible for my son's fate. I believe one is responsible for his own fate. For example, you are going to be responsible for what fate has in store for you now", Subbu gave a laugh which sounded exactly like Gopala Swamy's.

"I haven't done anything mister", Manoj added with a sob.

"You think your ideas are so good huh. The duel, and then the one where you ask your cousin to give up if Gopalam enters the fray, that was just out of the world. You just became a hero without even fighting for it", Subbu pointed his finger at Manoj as he spoke.

"None of the above were my ideas you village weirdo. I don't know why everyone is intent on giving me credit for anything that happens. The duel was some stupid girl's idea and the last one was Raj's idea. I didn't even know he would do it until he did it", Manoj gulped down the entire drink.

"There are two choices my friend. One, tell us the truth about who you clowns actually are, and what your intentions are, and be responsible for a grand feast written in your fate. Choice two, act smart or act dumb like you are doing quite brilliantly now and be responsible for the grand feast written in the fate of the entire village on the occasion of your demise", Subbu smiled and hiccupped.

"I no longer know why I am here to be absolutely honest with you old monk, the brand you drink has turned you into one too", Manoj tried pleading.

"Oh I see, you decided to be dumb originally or atleast act dumb. That is completely fine by me. It is just that my son's friends here don't like it when someone is dumber than them. And I don't like someone being the hero without fighting for it. So why don't we have a duel here (your masterplan)? It will be the dumb vs the dumber, and by that I mean all of the dumb drunkards who call themselves friends of my son and you", Subbu turned towards the drunkards and announced, "Who so ever wins this duel gets all the wine I have in my possession till date. And I shall judge the winner as the one who has the most number of Manoj babu's teeth in their hand. Consider it the money you pay for the drink and the highest bidder wins."

All the drunkards started circling around Manoj's chair ready to pounce.

"Now wait, wait, wait a second, I will match it. Aren't you guys interested in some foreign stuff, whiskey, rum, gin, vodka?" Manoj offered.

The boys stopped circling Manoj and stared blankly at Subbu.

"Did you pigeons decide to become vultures? What are you looking at? Do I look like a swapna sundari? (dream girl)" Subbu blabbered.

Slowly, the boys started moving towards him.

"Alright I get it, I am dumber than you all to trust you. Ok, I will get you the fabled Paani gadi biryani (Paani's biryani) along with the drinks, now stop coming towards me and bring his teeth", Subbu cried out.

Now they looked back at Manoj.

"I can get you all some crispy hot chicken wings from the nearest KFC wherever it is", Manoj sweated.

They stared back at Subbu now.

"What do you want me to say? Should I offer you a kacheri from Rukmini?" Subbu shouted back.

"I will offer that, I mean I can pay for it", offered Manoj.

"Hey, I was going to offer that", Subbu stood up.

"And I already offered it", Manoj shrugged.

"You don't even know who she is, how will you organize it?" laughed Subbu.

"But you know right, guys lets not leave him till he organizes it", and saying so he grabbed Subbu's collar.

Instinctively all the others grabbed Subbu and started chanting "Kacheri, Kacheri".

"You idiots, th.... a.... ts what.... I...... said....... grab....... him........not me you stupid sparrows", choked Subbu. Manoj closed his mouth and said, "Don't say another word, just nod your head in agreement and we will understand".

After struggling a lot (trying to kick the beholders made Subbu receive a few knocks to his stomach, then buttock, then people started tickling his feet), he finally nodded.

"Yay!!! We did iiiittt. Now let us go and get ready", Manoj released Subbu and just ran for it while all others shouted in jubilation and started congratulating each other.

Subbu got up and spat at the floor.

As Manoj reached the store room in Gopala Swamy's house at top speed panting, he found Raj dressing up as though for working in the fields. He wore a white shirt with a white dhoti and a kanduva (a side garment like a towel worn on the shoulder). On the sofa, there was a lavish black kurta and a matching red pajama with a red kerchief to the kurta pocket.

"Hey man, had fun with your village buddies. Told you, you have become a celebrity of sorts here", Raj winked.

Manoj launched himself on Raj, "Did you think I wanted to become an Indra or a Narasimha Naidu in this village? What the hell were you thinking elevating me and making sure people literally elevate me? I almost had to buy a fake set of jaws because of you, you bliiiinnnnndd farmer. And I say blind because of your dressing sense, you have the dress of a prince at your side and you dress up like a peasant? You are not Mahatma Gandhi my dear man, you just fought a duel remember?"

Raj pried Manoj's hands open and pushed him aside, "You better remember that before you attack me next time and spoil my dress (to which Manoj let out a sound which meant *can someone even spoil this shit dress*). And by the way, the dress of a prince should be worn by the prince not by his arrival announcer", he said adjusting the folds of his shirt where Manoj's fingers left their mark.

"What do you mean?" Manoj blinked. "The dress is for you mama", Raj smiled.

Manoj let out a whistle as he looked upon the dress. "Not so fast my prince charming, you don't miss this watch", said Raj as he put a golden watch to Manoj's wrist.

"And don't take much time, the party is about to start soon", Raj said.

"What party?" Manoj asked.

"Don't you know, it is a custom for Gopala Swamy to throw a party when he wants people to believe he did something for them. But this party is for me I guess", Raj said.

"You? You humiliated him in front of the entire village today, why would he throw a party to you?" Manoj laughed.

"To turn that statement around. He is going to pretend I am a…what shall I say, a coward for not willing to fight him, oh or he would say if I had fought that duel with that foreign chicken, I could have served chicken biryani to you all tonight, something of that sorts. He wants people and most importantly himself to believe that he won the duel today" Raj smiled "Now get your ass ready, I will be waiting and she will be waiting".

"She? Who is 'she'?" Manoj blinked. But Raj merely gave a naughty smile and left.

As Manoj began to undress thinking of what Raj might have meant when he said "She will be waiting?" Did he mean Sharada Devi? Didn't sound like it though, it sounded like someone was waiting for Manoj and not Raj. Could it be Stacy? Has she come all the way from Spain unable to forget him (after their rather embarrassing breakup in front of the entire RV family during the opening of RV Spanish chain which Manoj neither expected nor understood. She scolded him for not letting her know that his cousin was the heir to the RV empire, why would she want to know that anyway?) She was rather friendly with Raj after that opening somehow, maybe she wanted to keep an eye on Manoj without him knowing it, he smiled to himself.

And CLICK, CLICK, CLICK, FLASH, FLASH, FLASH.

Manoj came back from his thoughts as light hit him. As he looked towards the source, he realized the store room door was broken (by him) and he was undressing absentmindedly. It seems a kid just noticed this and ….. "WHAT THE SHIT!!! Hey you dirty little racoon. Give me that phone" Manoj shouted and started walking towards the kid.

"Oh Archimedes, don't come out like that or else my photos would lose their value" the kid smiled showing yellow teeth.

"Yuck!!! Have you never brushed your teeth since your birth", Manoj closed his eyes.

"Hey, I know who is going to say Yuck, ask you some private questions and close their eyes too. Let me show them these photos, hero" taunted the kid. "And if you start dressing up, I will run around asking everyone to see what's in store in the store room", he added.

"What the ***** do you want from me you gay monkey? Why shouldn't I dress up" Manoj thundered.

"Hey, I missed these poses, you look better when you are angry", the kid laughed. "Okay okay I will bargain and you close it soon otherwise someone else might come and see your ground reality" he added.

"Okay, I need an iPhone (photos come a lot better in them) and your watch", the kid spoke looking at his phone.

"This is not my watch", Manoj started.

"Precisely, that is mine now", the kid batted his eye "And what about the iPhone?"

"I am giving you nothing", Manoj threw a cushion at the kid.

"Oh then just give me another pose" the kid opened his phone and CLICK, FLASH.

"Ok, here you go, the watch is yours", Manoj threw Raj's watch to the kid.

"What shall we do about the iPhone then?" the kid demanded.

"Let us do this, you give me your phone with your left hand and take my iPhone with your right hand all right" Manoj bargained.

"Done deal" and the kid ran forward and reached out both his hands, one empty and one with the phone. But Manoj grabbed the kids legs instead, lifted him upside down and thrashed his buttocks and took pictures of the kid crying and started pulling off the kid's pants laughing at him, "Who's the boss now huh?" CLICK, CLICK, FLASH.

"What the heck do you think you are doing!" shouted Sravani (one of the Queen's chamber maids).

Manoj immediately let go of the kid and he ran out of the room without his pants crying out "The mad guy tried to take my private pictures."

"Let me just explain what happened…" started Manoj and Sravani ran off from there as he started approaching her. "I think she was the girl I called pregnant", Manoj spoke to himself. He sheepishly dressed as fast as he could before anyone else arrived.

As he went downstairs, he saw Gopala Swamy and Sharada Devi were in some sort of a puja (worship) as a priest was chanting the mantras. He looked around for Raj and finally found him talking to Suguna.

"And you can then add up all the expenses, calculate the cash flows expected to net present value and net them off to see how much profit you make. Then you make sure your restaurant is viable and zero in the location. So yeah it is not just making good dishes", Raj was explaining Suguna.

"Woah, I had no idea there was so much behind it. Okay, I have to go now, let's catch up some other time. And by the way, congratulations on your duel once again", and Suguna ran off.

"Are you out of your mind mama? You are talking to the would be bride, if that mad head of her father gets to know this, there will no longer be a duel, there will be a bounty on your head", shouted Manoj.

"Oh, then thanks for shouting this out loud", Raj rolled his eyes and continued, "Anyway, never mind that, it was just a casual discussion, it seems she once wanted to setup her own business, so she wanted some insights on it. What took you so long? I told you she was waiting for you."

"Oh damn, I completely forgot why I was excited because of that little imp. Anyway you never mind that. Tell me who she is, is she Stacy?" Manoj asked looking around expecting a saree clad Stacy to appear. "I knew my dream had some meaning to it" he added with a teary eye.

"No its not Stacy you idiot, I asked you to stop thinking of her. It is someone else who lost their heart to your machismo and quick thinking in today's duel" Raj raised his eyebrows naughtily as he said it.

"Bullshit, you fought the duel", Manoj reasoned. "But she fell for you mama, love is blind. Maybe she didn't see it was me who fought the duel" Raj reasoned back.

"Alright who is this Pullamma or Ellamma or whoever she is, I will just go and tell her...", Manoj stuttered.

"Oh, there she is", Raj pointed out towards a girl descending the stairs with a plate full of diyas.

"I have seen her somewhere", Manoj said.

"Yeah, you died for her in your last life", Raj pranked him.

"No, I am serious, I.... oh, shit this is that girl I called pregnant and she saw me pulling the pants off a kid and taking pictures of him", Manoj hid behind Raj.

"You did....what?" Raj whispered back to Manoj.

"Should I repeat it, isn't it bad enough once", Manoj whispered back.

"You crazy karate kid, what is it with you? Why do you get into all these things which children themselves would find childish?", Raj was irritated.

Manoj was shocked, in this entire trip, Raj was never this angry on Manoj except when he waited for the luggage in the airport or when Manoj entered Gopala Swamy's house alone for the first time or ....oh never mind he was angry. But Manoj was confused as this seemed a small matter, and Raj was not angry with him when he told him about the duel too.

"What happened mama? Why are you angry?" Manoj asked Raj getting back in front of him again as Sravani left for the main hall.

"No, not angry, I am exhausted with your tantrums. Now go and apologize to that girl", Raj pointed in the direction Sravani just went.

"Are you crazy?" Manoj exasperated.

"This is what she will ask you when you go to her, just try convincing her that you indeed belong to the homo sapiens species. This is my order", Raj sounded stiff.

"Oh, your order! I have told you remember, you can give orders but they are useless unless I obey them", Manoj scoffed.

"If you don't do this, I…." Raj began.

"No. if I do this, then you are going to tell me exactly what you are upto. And by that I mean you will tell why we are here, what you were doing here, what you are doing here and what you intend to do, is that a deal?" Manoj asked.

"Agree to the first two, I will tell you why we are here and what I did, I will not tell you what I am doing now or what I intend to do. If you don't agree, then I would go give that girl a letter I would have written on your behalf", Raj dealt with it as though he dealt with a supplier for lowering his price.

"Fine then, I will go tell her it was no mistake of mine if she is fat or the kid is cranky", Manoj said.

"You will apologize to her and ask her out, because as I said she is in love with you, and she showed me so", Raj said.

"She 'showed' you so?" Manoj questioned.

"Yeah, I could see the elation in her face when villagers lifted you up today, I saw concern in her face when you were infected with dog sickness, I saw a smile on her face when you do all your stupid things, is that enough cause I had enough. Now you go", Raj ordered again.

"I will just go apologize", and Manoj ran towards the hall.

As he gave a sudden blind turn, he bumped into the priest who fell back on the lighted diyas and his dhoti caught fire. The priest had to then run (and as he ran, the fire spread wilder), undress himself and to his horror, the inner wear was on fire too and he finally jumped into the water used for washing the cattle in Gopala Swamy's shed. He was cursing Manoj and his ancestors and his descendants as people around watched Manoj in disgust.

He ran rather carefully this time and asked around for 'the girl who...uh...was a friend of sister of the bride'. After a while, he sounded stupid to himself. He knew only one way this could work. He started asking for 'the bride's sister' and was instantly directed towards the queen chamber. As he ran up and entered the room, which was filled with the queen and her chamber maids (who got him to fight a duel...well almost), he felt a sudden rush of fury.

"Well, well, who do we have here?" smiled the queen with an oddly satisfied smile.

"If it isn't the unofficial upasarpanch himself", laughed a chamber maid he was not looking for.

"Look here, I neither have business nor interest in dealing with all your shit. Now, I am looking for uh…..what was her name? The one who I said looked preg….I mean….where is that girl who is in love with me?" he asked awkwardly.

"In love with you? Are you dreaming?" laughed out the queen.

"Oh I know you wouldn't be able to understand seeing no one would ever love you apart from your loser of a daddy", Manoj gave a greater laugh.

All the women let out a great gasp as the queen stood angrily and came ahead to slap him.

"What? You want to duel me huh? After your village palewaan failed?" said Manoj as he held the queen's hand that came towards him. He twisted her arm and pushed her back roughly onto her maids or friends or gang.

They caught her, ran ahead together and started kicking, punching, biting, slapping and finally crying on every bit of Manoj they could reach out to.

"What the hell is going on here?" came a voice from the entrance to the room.

Chapter - 24

SHARADA CALLS THE BLUFF

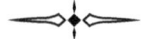

The occupants of the room turned on the spot as if doing a ballet and found Sharada Devi in a traditional and vibrant saree with gold necklaces, bangles on her (resembling Goddess Durga by appearance but Goddess Kali by her eyes and tone) and right behind her, a shivering Sravani.

"This…this guy here tried to…tried to", Gayathri started crying.

"Don't you dare test my intelligence Gayathri. You think the tricks your doting dad falls for would work on me?"

shouted Sharada, as if reminding who the actual queen there was.

This shut everyone up and all the girls huddled together sheepishly as Manoj (with his brand new dress or rather Raj's dress all tattered and torn, ridden with dust from the floor) got up nursing his back which endured all the apes at once.

"You tell me what's going on here Manoj", Sharada asked (or commanded) and she immediately raised a hand to Gayathri who undoubtedly would have asked, *You trust this clown over your daughter?*

"You damned damsels in distress, with your two cent drama of being a queen!" cried out Manoj as one or two girls sniggered, stifling a laugh. "I have actually come to see her", Manoj said pointing out to Sravani behind Sharada, "And tell her I was sorry, but I would wish to date her for a while before accepting her love".

All the girls gasped and looked at Sharada Devi.

"See mom, that is why we gave him a thrashing", Queen Gayathri defended herself.

"Shut up!" shouted Sharada and Gayathri withdrew to the fag end of her group.

"And you", she spoke to Sravani, "You just had some time with some foreign funky guy and you start having feelings for him don't you?"

"As if you didn't", murmured one of Gayathri's cousins as Sharada gave them a glare asking the person who murmured, to dare come forward.

"If I hear one more reference to me or to my actions, you will see for yourself what my actions actually are and you would be used as a reference by others whenever they try to explain my actions", Sharada added in a low tone, which somehow always has a greater impact than her shouting voice.

"But pedhamma (maternal aunt), I neither love this crazy guy nor have asked him to love me", sobbed a teary eyed Sravani.

Sharada looked at Manoj to explain himself.

"No she hasn't told me, she actually showed it and by 'showed it', I mean showed it to Raj. And he told me", Manoj blabbered.

"Are you trying to test my intelligence now Manoj?" Sharada folded her hands.

"No I am serious, Raj told me everything. I mean…how she stares at me daily, how she was impressed with my dueling skills, I mean arranging for that duel and people lifting me up, and how she cried when I was ill or how she laughed when I, you know, show off. And because Raj has a lot of experience with girls, and especially with girls trying to get his attention, I knew what he said had meat. I am a rather shy person and fail to notice this stuff", Manoj went on a monologue marathon.

"Or such stuff never happens to you", added Parvati to which all the girls there (except Sharada and Sravani) giggled.

"Now quit all this tomfoolery all of you and get downstairs for the Pooja", ordered Sharada Devi and one by one all the girls dispersed out of the room without so much as an eye contact towards Sharada.

As Manoj tried to leave too, Sharada held his arm and Manoj's heart skipped a beat.

"Not you smart boy, I will just have a few words with you. By then the Pooja would have gotten over and we shall start serving the dinner and you can hop your way to the lawn for that", smiled Sharada and she shut the door. Manoj whimpered, he hated being alone with Sharada Devi or her husband.

"Your mother did take a fancy to the foreigners", Paravti looked sympathetically at Gayathri as they saw the doors close.

"Now tell me straight what were you planning on doing here? Another duel? You are always upto something, trying to manipulate these giggling gang of girls", Sharada sat down on the bed as she questioned Manoj.

Manoj drew back to the wall as though a child ready to be punished by his class teacher.

"I told you the truth, and besides, the duel was arranged by those giggling apes themselves, not me. They manipulated your husband. Today, I was here because Raj asked me to apologize to that girl....what was her name....I keep forgetting, the girl who loves me", Manoj cried out.

"You don't know her name but you know she loves you?" mocked Sharada.

"Raj knows she loves me and he is never wrong about girls. And I know of the two (me and Raj), I am the better looking guy, so that girl had to be showing her love to me and Raj observed this", Manoj gave a blushing smile towards the end.

"Ok apart from all your lousy deductions, the only fact in the monologue remains that RAJ told you the girl has feelings for you", Sharada bit one of her nails as though assessing the result of an experiment.

"And he is never wrong about girls. Even that is a fact", Manoj added.

"And he asked you to go apologize to her and ask her out for a..ahem ahem..date?" Sharada asked.

"As in, he didn't specifically ask for the latter, I just felt I owe that girl a chance at least. Otherwise, when we go back to the states, and don't return (and mind you we shall not return), she would become a depressed girl turned into a psycho woman and she would show it all on her poor would be husband. So out of my humanity and respect, I thought she deserved a chance", Manoj answered proudly.

"And now when the girl said she had none such feelings towards you, didn't you get back to your senses?" tired Sharada.

"No. I mean not "no" to me getting back to my senses part, as in I am always true to my senses. I mean no to what you said earlier. The girl, as most of the Indian girls (barring you) are too shy. She couldn't express herself in front of everyone else, especially those apes and you", Manoj defended.

Sharada laughed out aloud.

"You remind me of my husband a lot", she continued.

"Excuse me, you want to date me too?" Manoj was shocked.

Sharada gave him a *You better hope I don't* look to which Manoj was relieved but was afraid at the same time.

"I meant you don't understand when you are being manipulated and when someone tries to point this out to you, you think they are trying to manipulate you", she laughed again.

"I don't get it", Manoj said.

"My point exactly", she nodded her head in laughter. "Now let me ask you something else…"

Ring….Ring….Ring…..

Manoj dug out his phone from the pockets of his pajama and saw it was from Rajagopal. For the first time in this trip, Manoj felt so happy Raja called him and prayed his thanks to the heavens.

"Sorry ma'am, my dearest friend, my buddy, my soulmate has just called me. Need to take this, if I miss his call, he would miss me so much that he would make a painting of my face with his blood and talk to it", Manoj ran to unlock the door.

But Sharada was cleverer, instead of trying to race him to the door, she held his kurta and pulled him back and spoke in his ear.

"How are you related to Raj?" she asked.

"I am his best friend. I mean cousin first, as in first cousin", he blabbered.

"How are you his cousin?" she asked irritably.

"By birth", he breathed back, hoping Rajagopal doesn't cut the call soon.

"Should I call my husband now? I asked how are you two related? And if you say by blood, I will take your blood and his blood and see how they are related?", she spoke as though she was talking to a child or a primate ape which could understand Telugu.

"Oh I got it, my father is a sort of first cousin to his mother, so technically I am his brother-in-law", he spanked himself for being so slow, as Rajagopal cut the call.

"I see. I see it. I see it all now", Sharada gave out a laugh that reminded Manoj not just of Chandramukhi the ghost but every other female ghost he had the misfortune of seeing, be it Indian, American, British, Korean, Japanese, all at once.

As he prayed to the heavens, his phone rang again and it was Rajagopal again, Manoj turned back and pleaded.

"Please let me go, for my friend's sake. His life hangs on me lifting this phone now", and Manoj even touched Sharada's feet who was still laughing her heart out.

"Get lost you funky fellow and listen, ask Raj to meet me in my study after dinner. And tell him if he doesn't I will call his foodie father", she added on a serious note and kicked Manoj's hand off her leg.

He ran out of the door and answered the phone.

"I love you dude. Thanks for the call, you are the true savior of masses", cried out Manoj.

"Hello? Is this my friend Monkey Maharaj?" Rajagopal sounded confused but elated nonetheless.

"Oh yeah it is me", Manoj spoke as he went to the lawn and for the first time in his life, he watered the bushes. "Oh god, such a relief", he added.

"Why thank you my monkey. By the way, are you free tonight? Our presentation is done with and we would like to show it to you, take your inputs and then go for Mr.Raj Varma" Rajagopal spoke in as soft a tone as he could possibly make.

"Oh, what, no. I am not interested in this marketing campaign shit. But thanks for calling me, an elderly woman had locked me in her room refusing to let me go and thankfully your call helped me get away from there", Manoj spoke enthusiastically as though explaining Raja about a miracle he had performed without his knowledge.

"You millionare morrrooooonnnnssss. You insolent, insensitive, careless, soulless, cranky, lousy monkeys. You are worse than the Indian board of directors or that Vijju here. They don't cross paths with me unless their stars turn their asses on them. But you monkeys play with me, you ask for my wrath. You dare challenge me and when I am about to win it, you just, YOU JUST, MAAAKKEEE A FOOOOLL OUT OF ME!!!!" shouted Raja to which Manoj could hear a lot of people around him and around Raja on the other end came around concerned.

"Hey listen oldie, I don't know what you are talking about", Manoj started angrily.

"You know nothing you combinational monkey and a donkey. You are only fit to build your body to raise your boss's load and entertain him with your circus tricks from time to time. You know nothing about what your boss does for his living and what it does to others' living. Millions of people lose their appetite for the healthy, traditional native foods, millions of animals suffer to either get into these dishes or later eat these dishes thrown away by partying passionate pigs around the world. You don't know anything about how your boss fools people with his advertisements or celebrity campaigns or whatever the hell he decides to do. You only care about your money, you mongrel. And when I try teaching you all a lesson, you are busy with a monkey maharani or a monkey princess and you are happy I helped you get rid of them so that you get around to a monkey priestess…" Rajagopal had this knack of building a never ending conversation wherein he would be the only person talking or rather swearing and the person at the other hand helps the conversation by neither listening nor reacting to it.

Manoj waited for a while and then hung up the phone. Why is he getting these swear calls from that retirement officer? God knows why. Oh shit, he thought to himself and he ran back, now asking people for the whereabouts of Raj or the fellow foreigner.

When no one could tell him, he started asking them if they saw an odd farmer (remembering what Raj wore that day) and was instantly pointed out to the lawn where he saw Raj serving food to people.

As Raj went on serving, he reached Gopala Swamy's plate. And Gopala Swamy stood up immediately holding Raj's hand up as though declaring him the winner of the duel now. Raj looked at him confused.

"I see you are in the mood for another announcement mama", Raj smiled at Gopala Swamy.

"I remember you mentioning you became a fan", Gopala Swamy smiled back.

"For heaven's sake, not now Gopal. Let us eat peacefully atleast", Sharada asked from his side.

"Everybody here, hello, everyone pay attention here", Gopala Swamy shouted out to all the village that was in his house tonight. All of them, which included Kireeti, his friends, Subbu and other Panchayat members, most of Gopala Swamy's family (Suguna, Gayathri and her friends included) and a few policemen who came for the food on pretext of protecting the panchayat members looked up.

"Let me introduce you all to the winner of today's duel, I don't mean introducing him as the winner. I meant let me introduce him to you. You guys didn't seem to recognize him, some of you even thought he was a foreign wrestler or something, well he is not. He was born right here on this very village soil. But you fail to recognize him because of his rather misleading attire. Now that he is in a much more, what should I say, fitting attire, you can attempt a guess. Let me give you all a clue, he is serving us food", laughed out Gopala Swamy as Sharada tried pulling him down.

"Gopal, please listen to me, you promised me you would not tell them. Gopal please, are you drunk?" Sharada tried in vain.

"Do you all remember Mr.Ravikant Varma garu?" Gopala Swamy smiled.

People looked at each other and everyone nodded back in confusion.

"Who are you referring to?" asked Subbu.

"Oh sorry, let me give him a more recognizable name. I will address him by the title the village had bestowed him with 'Vantala Varma'", Gopala Swamy's eyes looked so menacing and happy that Sharada stopped trying to stop him.

Many of the elders there (as younger generation had no idea) said "Ahhh", many of them laughed as though reminding each other of that queer animal they encountered, few of them whistled, few knocked each other on the ribs to stop them from laughing and choking on the food. Gopala Swamy deliberately held back and looked at Raj as though asking him to look at his father's achievements.

"Yeah, what about him?" Subbu asked as the unrest had finally subsided.

"What that clown dreamt of achieving, his son has achieved. He is feeding us all right now", Gopala Swamy raised Raj's hand that held the bobbattu (a sweet delicacy) he was about to put on Gopala Swamy's plate.

Everyone there (except for Manoj, Sharada and Suguna) laughed out loud. Some of them started giving Raj names like "Vantalodi Varasudu" (sarcastic name for cook's heir), some started giving out merciless comments like "Nuvvu kuda ammaye na?" (Are you a girl too?), someone else correcting it with a "Ammayi kadhu atu itu kaani vaadu" (Not a girl, a girl soul trapped in the body of a boy), "Saadhinchesavu babu mothaniki" (You did it finally), "Nanna unnara leka non-veg item ayipoyada rabandhulaki?" (Is your father still alive or has he served himself to the vultures?)

Raj stared at each of them silently but his eyes radiated an intensity which Manoj had never seen in him before. He looked as though he was holding back a bomb load of energy inside him, but not letting it come out. As though Sharada saw it in him too, she let go of her seat and held Raj's hand (instead of her husband's this time) and asked him to follow her. Everyone started laughing at Gopala Swamy now who was surprisingly happy still (as though he no longer cared about what people said about him).

Sharada took Raj straight to her study room. She had planned to have this after the dinner, but the cat was out of the bag now and she had to act. Once they reached the study, she bolted the door, pushed Raj onto a chair and stood in front of him. As Raj looked up at her, he saw firecrackers being burst in the night sky behind her, glittering through the window.

"I am sorry Raj, I didn't expect this from my husband tonight. I thought he would try pestering you into a re-match or humiliate you for not facing him (just as Raj had anticipated too) but this, this I didn't expect. You drove a different personality into my husband which I admit I failed to do till now. You made him think. For the first time, he tried defeating his enemy mentally rather than physically or politically. But enough is enough, the game is getting out of hand now", Sharada spoke, handing out a glass of water to Raj.

"I am not done with your family yet athayya", Raj simply held the glass and looked down. "What about my marriage with Gayathri?" he asked.

And Sharada Devi smiled back. Raj looked up and saw her smile. He was confused, wasn't she supposed to be angry at her husband and sorry for Raj. Why did she smile?

"I can have you married tomorrow. Or better, I can call your beloved father right now, give him a day to reach his hometown and have you married the day after", Sharada smiled victoriously.

"I…what…what did you say?" Raj muttered.

"No more tricks boy. Your game is kaput. I call your bluff, liar", Sharada looked into Raj's eyes as he looked back at hers, trying to make out if *she* was ….. Bluffing.

Chapter - 25
CARDS ON THE TABLE

"Frankly athayya, I don't see where you are going with this", Raj attempted to leave.

Sharada stopped him and pushed him back, "Don't you take me for a fool Raj. I hate it when people test my intelligence. And you my foreign friend have insulted it. You just saw what my husband is capable of when he uses his brain. You haven't seen what I am capable of when I use mine, you just heard of it from your precious petty daddy."

"If this is what I get for leaving my family and wealth for you and your daughter, then I better leave now athayya. I don't know how you think I insulted your intelligence, but you sure are insulting my honor over here", Raj defended.

Sharada gave a roaring laughter to this. Raj did not flinch, she must be bluffing.

"Oh my dear boy, I for a second heard your father in you there", continued Sharada.

"I am proud of my father and all his achievements, whatever he has done" Raj said.

"His biggest achievement sits right in front of me boy. And you know what you have achieved till now, a win and a loss. A win against my husband in the duel but against me you lose. I have seen through your play. I surely don't know what cards you hold, but I know now what final sets of cards you play for. I have seen your show and I will make sure you don't get anymore lifelines from any of the players in this invisible game of cards." Sharada looked at Raj intently.

"I hear your husband in you now", Raj looked back at her just as intently.

"Is that so? Do you want to hear me out? That's great, do you think you can manipulate me as easily as you manipulated your half brainer of a cousin into believing that stupid Sravani fell for him? Do you think I am so blind I would miss the most important piece you dropped even though that card was not meant for me? You see boy, you don't just play to defeat one player in cards, you have to beat them all, this is a bigger chess. You have to observe every card that is being drawn, dropped and picked up. It is not the cards in your hands, rather the cards on the table that give you a picture of the game. And I saw right through that Sravani card you dropped for your stupid cousin to pick up. Though he didn't get the intent behind it. Your cousin thinks you did it for him to win, or maybe for me to lose. But you did that for your own selfish reason, your win", smiled Sharada.

"That's all very good athayya, but I still don't get where you are getting it all from", Raj defended.

"Sravani is Gayathri's cousin. I don't know who told you this but you found out exactly how they are related. Her mother is my husband's first cousin or to be exact, she is the daughter of his paternal aunt, which makes Sravani Gayathri's sister. And your silly cousin is actually your brother-in-law, or in his own words 'technically so' because your father and his mother are in a way brother-sister. So if you ensure he ends up with Sravani, that would make you and Gayathri siblings or brother-sister to each other. It was a carefully woven trap you set and tried with no success, to mask it up as a casual drop. That way, I could not have you married to my daughter, very ingeniously thought of. Your mother must have been a smart woman", and Sharada gave a fake applause to Raj.

"Nonsense, I hadn't thought of it. I didn't know how Sravani and Gayathri were related. I just saw she must have been infatuated to my cousin and informed him. It is a completely harmless and natural thing that goes on between boys", Raj was on his feet mentally, though physically he was still sitting. Sharada Devi was getting close, he thought and he tried hard not to give away (the fact that Sravani actually told him right in his first meeting with the queen exactly how she was related to Gayathri).

"That won't work Raj. I never wondered why you had come all the way to this village. But I did wonder what the point of bringing your stupid accomplice along was. It all makes sense now. You brought him here for a very selfish reason. Manoj could not help you in your scheming due to his lack of brains but he can surely help you by being a gullible part of your grand scheme. You realized there was a chance to play with the human relationships if you brought him with you. And that poor soul thinks he was brought here to be entertained", laughed Sharada.

"Again athayya, does this mean you want me to leave right now?" Raj raised a brow.

"Huh, no. This means precisely the opposite, you can't leave here. I caught your plan to escape. Oh, and by the way, how could I forget the duel? Though the deal was set by my husband, you agreed to it instantly. Because you were waiting for one such opportunity to arise. And you would have been laughing at me inside all the time I was showing concern to you. Because just like it was for my husband, the duel was a publicity stunt for you too. But just not for you, it was a chance to bring Manoj to the limelight and make him a sort of a celebrity or a dream boy in the village. This would help you in softening up Sravani or her father and getting her hitched to your cousin. That was exactly what you did. After you won the duel, you simply stepped aside from the fight with my husband forgoing your fame. But you made sure Manoj got the credit for your scheme", Sharada was running away with her thoughts.

"You seem to be letting your imagination get the better of your senses athayya", Raj cautioned her (though he flinched a bit now).

"You say so, then how do you explain your sudden loss of money. I admit I was completely baffled by this game of yours boy, again must be your mother's genetics. Right in your first meet, you gave me two conflicting pieces of information. One, that you intended to marry my daughter, and two, that you are bankrupt. At an initial glance, it could have been seen as a gesture of good faith that you confided your bankruptcy to me. And I tried really hard to believe this notion. But it made no sense, if you really knew who I was or how I think, you would not have given away your penniless if you wanted to marry Gayathri. You should have masqueraded yourself as a multi millionaire and I would have gotten you hitched to my daughter within a week. And then you drop your charade to reveal your worth. But no, you told me you were done with but you still wanted me to give my daughter's hand to you", Sharada rested her arms on Raj's chair and glared at him.

"I was being honest with you. I thought you had a heart bigger than your head. It seems to me I was mistaken", Raj moved her aside and actually stood up now, she would see it in his eyes if he sat still any longer. He moved away from her and faced the firecrackers in the sky.

"You are mistaken Raj. I am all about my brains and don't try to play out my heart now. Heart only gives me anxiousness and fear, my head steadies me. I know for a fact now that you never intended to marry my daughter. Your play (with Sravani and Manoj) showed me the hand you are playing for. I admit I do not know for sure if you are truly bankrupt or if it was all a complete farce. I am inclined to believe the latter. You somehow managed to move your money elsewhere, some 'binami' (sort of a rat who hides someone else's money as his own) must be holding it or you must have shifted it to another bank account or…or…some such scheme. And you thought if you made me believe your pretense of bankruptcy and still ask for my daughter's hand, I would be double bluffed into believing you. And if it had worked, you thought I would have kicked you out of my house because I made that contract only for your worth. As I said, completely ingenious except for one discrepancy, you never underestimate Sharada Devi's wits. But you did, you are from this village after all. You are all born with it I guess. All of you think I am just a mad woman who thinks too highly of herself, and time and again I have to prove myself", Raj heard Sharada's voice quiver at the last sentence.

He looked back to find Sharada with a tiny tear in her eye now. "There is no one as thick as the one who thinks he/she is cleverer, stronger or braver than he/she truly is", Raj replied. "Accept who you are and move on with it", he continued.

"I am not thick you fool. I know exactly what I am capable of, and it is time you, your father, my husband, my family and this entire godforsaken village sees it", she sounded touchier than Raj ever heard her before.

With this, she went to her study table beside Raj and picked up her phone. Raj waited for a sign as to whom she was calling.

"Hello panthulu garu (priest), I asked you for a date on Gayathri's wedding remember, when is it? Oh wonderful, I need one more date from you, a date for the wedding of one of my nieces, Sravani. You just tell me what I asked for, or I will tell you things about you which you neither asked for nor dreamt of", and she hung up the phone and dialed again.

"Hello bava garu (brother-in-law), it is me Sharada. No, I haven't called for my husband, I want to speak to you. I am in my study room, but its okay, we can talk over this great technology invented by Mr.Grahambell. Right, so you just heard about Vantala Varma's son right, stop laughing or you will start crying my dear sir. Because that son brought an assistant with him. Yes, that crazy guy. The assistant is trying to woo your daughter Sravani and get her to date him, you know the phenomenon so famous abroad where a boy and a girl start a live in relation to see if they are compatible. No, no, no marriage is far fetched here, they just want to know how things would work out in case they decide to marry. After getting Sravani pregnant, that guy might just decide that things aren't working the way they are supposed to and leave your child and his child with you.

No, my dumb baava, it is not that assistant that you should be taking care of now, it is your daughter. I had a word with our family priest and he is looking for a good date, you now look for a good groom to get her married and make sure this happens within a week right in front of that crazy assistant and his boss", and she hung up the phone without listening to a further word from the other end. The calls which she made were always on her call.

And she picked up the phone again.

"Hello Varma", Sharada spoke with a loving prowess in her voice.

Raj turned to her as she smiled at him, and gave a teary wink. He attempted to take the phone from her, but she stopped him.

"I don't think my voice needs any introduction", she continued and she put the phone on speaker now so that Raj could hear his 'petty daddy' tremble. Raj rolled his eyes and tried signaling Sharada to stop this but she wouldn't budge, Raj had taken it too far.

"First things first, your son is a charming and dashing young man. I am glad he got neither your looks nor your wits. But unfortunately he hasn't got my brains and it would take my brain to outwit me. Your son unfortunately tried doing it and failed", she laughed.

"Please spare me Sharada", cried out Varma at the other end.

"Wow, look at your doting dad, he didn't ask me to spare you, rather he wants me to spare him and his wealth. That's how he was, he is and will always be", she turned to Raj.

"Now look Varma, I have neither the time nor the interest to play a bargaining game with you. I played enough of them with your entire family now. I just called to tell you (not ask you) to get your well fed ass down to Sivasamudram by next week. Because it is my daughters' wedding (in plural) and your son's wedding too. And if you find yourself too busy and unable to come, nothing to worry, cause the marriage will happen anyhow", and she hung up the phone again without listening to a single word from Varma.

"And I meant every single word I said Raj", she glared at him. "I have had enough games with you and your dad. And if you think you want to play me again, I am not going to play with you, I will play with your dad, and I don't think he needs more of them at this stage of his life. So for God's sake and for your dad's sake, you will do nothing more than come sit at my elder daughter's wedding followed by your wedding the very next day (as my priest told me just now that it happens to be an auspicious date too)", she finished.

As she reached the door, she stopped and half turned back to see Raj still standing near the phone.

"As for your wealth that you have hidden from me, I don't expect you to live out your life here in this village. You know why? Not because your father did the same and you are his son, but because you too are educated and clever like me. Hence you too must feel the same why I do about this village. It is just not for people like us. Deny it if you may, but you are more like me, than you are like your dad" and she closed the door as she left, as she knew Raj will be incapable of words or actions for a while now.

She incapacitated him finally, just like she did his father. But she destroyed Varma with just a phone call, his son proved to be much more formidable. She smiled to herself as she walked down to the people beneath her (physically and otherwise too), also leaving above a man who was finally beneath her now.

Chapter - 26

THE SECRET SIVASAMUDRAM

Raj was just loitering around in maada veedhi that midnight. He had been thinking hard, very hard actually. He didn't listen to whatever Manoj was saying or asking. He could vaguely make out things like "Whyyy.... fun.... your father?", "You.... show them.... what.... capable of". He could only think of Sharada Devi, her words echoing in his head.

As he was mindlessly wandering, he bumped into an old monk whom Raj recognized as the person who was playing the drum to Raj's beats (literally).

"My youthful son!!!", the monk spoke dramatically, "I heard you are living in Gopala Swamy and Sharada Devi household. And also that Sharada loves you and Gopalam hates you", he gave a huge laugh that must have echoed all around the village.

Raj neither had the interest nor the intention to respond to this beggar. He attempted to move aside and leave when the monk stopped him by the shoulder and continued, "Believe me my dear boy, both the things are equally dangerous. I usually see it as an omen when people are under the attention of either of them, but you....oh dear....I certainly don't envy you. You are under the attention of both of them."

Raj pushed aside the monk's hand roughly, "If you are done, I would want to leave. I am pretty sure I am trespassing in your house", Raj mocked the beggar by showing the footpath.

"Listen up, do you want to know where I used to find your father a lot?" the monk smiled as Raj was leaving. On these words, Raj stopped on the spot and half turned back.

"I think you are mistaken, my father doesn't live here", Raj tried out testily.

"Of course, your father left the village, but has the village left him?" the monk raised one of his eyebrows.

"And who do you think my father is?" Raj was even more cautious now.

"As you yourself said, he is your father", saying so, the monk clutched his stomach as he couldn't control his laughter upon his own joke.

Raj mouthed a few swear words within himself and just started leaving.

"Malligadi kallu compound", voiced the monk, now lying down on his living hall (the main road). Raj stopped again, he heard of this place before, when his father was describing the deal. He didn't turn now but the monk knew he had Raj's attention.

"Did you ever try kallu?" goaded the monk.

"No, and by the looks of it, you drank enough to keep you high for the rest of your lifetime", Raj was pissed at this suggestion. He expected the monk to give him a secret piece of information he needed, maybe the place where Sharada Devi hid the contract or maybe something related to Gopala Swamy.

The monk gave another dramatic laugh, and Raj was sorry he entered into this conversation in the first place. The monk was either trying to make Raj laugh or laugh himself loud enough to wake up the entire village.

"I do go there once in a while, you know why?" the monk came closer to Raj now and spoke in whispers directly into his ears.

"I can only see two possible reasons, either because you are sad you haven't married your entire life or happy you haven't married your entire life", Raj scoffed and attempted to leave but the monk gripped Raj tight.

"No, you would find people's secrets in there. You see, it is not here (he held up Raj's palm), it is here (he said, placing an empty kallu bottle in the palm). Once anyone has this, you need not tell them anything about their destiny like a priest or a fotune teller, they tell you that themselves. Just like your father", the monk now relaxed his grip as he was sure Raj wouldn't leave now.

"What are you talking about", Raj spoke to the black darkness ahead of him and the white monk behind him.

"No, you should ask 'what was he talking about?' " the monk whispered back.

"He told me about the money he got from Sharada and what he wanted to do with it, he bought me my drinks too that day", the monk sniggered.

"Wow, very nice. Good to know. Oh sorry that was nothing I wanted to know anyways", Raj spoke but didn't leave.

"Then go", the monk replied, as Raj closed his eyes trying to make a decision, but just like his father felt on the day of his deal, he was not able to think of anything except what he heard from Sharada Devi that night.

"Go to that kallu compound. You will hear many more secrets there", the monk whispered, "Just like I heard today, that you are Varma's son."

As if he was given a decision he was trying to make, Raj opened his eyes. "And oh, now that everyone knows, if you tell Malligadu you are Varma's son, you might get a discount on that kallu order, and many nice anecdotes about his discussions with your father" the monk added as he walked back towards his palatial bedroom.

It wasn't very difficult to find the compound. Raj just had to ask around and walk towards the shore for a while. Once he was there, there was no mistaking the only open and happening place in that village that late an hour. It was just a short two storeyed structure with thatched roof at the very top. There were a lot of clay pots either placed one above the other or hanging from the concrete ceiling separating the ground and the first floors. As Raj stepped in, he saw a few pictures which reflected the humble beginnings of the place and its owner. The place sure grew along with its owner.

Malli gadu was earlier a short skinny man with a thick moustache and a beard, from the photos Raj could see. But as he asked a waiter for the owner, he was pointed towards a fairly stout, still short man with a white moustache, without a beard. The man was entertaining a crowd of people who weren't so drunk yet. The hefty drunkards already started dancing to their own tunes, while others sang it. A few of them were shouting and scolding random villains of their life such as a village landlord, sarpanch of the nearby village, their brother in law, chief minister of the state, prime minister of America, the British Queen and Mahatma Gandhi.

Raj pushed himself through the crowd towards Malli gaadu and faced him.

"Hey! I know you, you are the guy who won the duel right?" Malli questioned Raj.

"Then you actually don't know him", came a voice from the seat facing the seas (a premium seat no doubt).

The crowd turned towards the source to find Kireeti along with his gang of friends/followers/people who couldn't afford their own drink.

"Oh, he looks so much like that guy who smoked Phalguna then", Malli wondered. "And I thought you would be asked to go next Kireeti", he added mischievously.

"Look, I am here to talk to you in private", Raj tried to break the chain.

"I wouldn't fight a woman Malli", Kireeti stood up "Or a trans for that matter", he added.

"Thanks for that, I am relieved", Raj mocked and turned back to Malli.

"What did you drink Kireeti? Or rather how much did you drink?" Malli asked. "I surely didn't think you would lose your mind over a few pots, you are the reigning champion when it comes to the drinking capacity of a tummy".

The crowd cheered and taunted Kireeti, who for some reason was not happy with the praises he was getting.

"I surely can't fight him (sorry I meant 'her') or her woman of a father though Malli", Kireeti smiled.

"Brother, you have come here to drink, I have come here to talk. Looks like both of us are wasting our time now. Why don't you get back to feeding those poor souls?" Raj answered this time pointing at Kireeti's gang.

"Ashamed of your father, are you?" Kireeti shouted. "Ashamed of the legacy he left behind in this village, and in this compound", and Kireeti spat on the floor.

Raj turned back to face Kireeti now, "Brother, all your father did for you is feed you and sell you to a man with money, just like one would do with his pig. My father gave me a life none of you could ever dream of, and he gave a lot others that life too. Now if you ran out of money to pay the bill and are staging a diversion so that your friends could skedaddle out of here, then don't worry. All your rounds are on me. In fact, with the money my father had given me, I could buy out this compound. So cheers", and he turned back to face Malli, who along with the crowd was looking baffled as to who Raj was.

The crowd started muttering and shouting. Confused, Raj turned back to see some of Kireeti's gang (who were not yet fully drunk) strenuously holding back Kireeti from charging towards Raj.

"Then why don't you tell them all who your beloved father is, you foreign brand of cheap liquor?" shouted Kireeti as he struggled to set himself free. "His father was a premium customer of your compound my dear Malli. And as Raj rightly pointed out, if he had some money in his earlier beggarly days, he would have bought your compound out and drank it all himself. He was your reigning champion then, and an all time record holder too. This is the son of the legendary 'Vantala Varma'." Kireeti added.

The entire compound roared in laughter. Kireeti's gang finally let go of him as he too stopped struggling and stood victorious, proud of the effect he had on the compound.

There were a lot of taunts now, "Oh my god, with the build up this foreign dude gave, I thought he was the son of some Italian Mafia", "I thought he was the son of Superstar Rajnikanth", "And I thought his father was the King of America", "Has your father managed cooking, or is he still begging?", "Do you have the same drinking capacity as your father had? Want to challenge me on that? Your father defeated me on a bet of hundred rupees those days?" "All of us here speak of him so often, he used to drink with us and entertain us so that we pay for his drinks", "We all miss his contributions to this compound", "I will offer you two free pots of kallu just for old times sake, but you need to pay for all your father's previous drinks. He never paid any of them, and I have them all noted down in this book here", Malli added at the end with a tear in his eye but a mischievous cackle in his mouth.

Unfortunately, no one was holding Raj back as Kireeti's gang held their boss earlier. Raj just launched himself feet first on to Kireeti and kicked him out through the window that broke into a hundred pieces. All the taunting and humdrum stopped, as the compound fell silent (but for a few hefty drunkards who were still singing).

As Kireeti's gang ran out to lift their boss, Raj dusted his shoe and turned towards Malli.

"Now, can we have a word in private or do you want to have a fight in public", he asked.

Just then, all the near sober gang of Kireeti along with the man himself pulled Raj back dragging his coat towards them and threw him on a nearby table. The pots on the table, along with the table itself gave up to the force as people all around were drenched with the splash of the palm wine.

"Wow, I remember you saying you wouldn't fight, what was that, 'A woman or a trans'. Does that mean I am a man or you are no longer one", Raj said as he got up.

And a fight broke up which broke a lot of things around too. Random members from the compound started supporting random fighters. The support was initially verbal and had soon become physical. People started hitting each other with some old history in heart, or for the money the other person had with him or to avoid paying for their bills by joining the ruckus and making a quick detour or just for the fun of it. Just like his friends abandoned him and danced to their own tune during his engagement rally, most of his gang had abandoned Kireeti in his fight too, as soon as they realized Raj was too much to handle (and they finally saw merit in that duel which Phalguna lost). They just started hitting random passersby which they could use as a cover up when Kireeti would ask them what the hell were they doing (if he was capable of speech by the end of this).

In the thick of the fight, were Raj and Kireeti. Raj was always tactical in his approach while Kireeti just tried to employ brute force and punches he saw had an impact in movies. Raj on the other hand, rarely used his hands now. He was either kicking Kireeti with his thick leather patent shoes that surely had an impact on wherever they landed, or was using his surroundings to his advantage. He was throwing Kireeti onto some pots or throwing the pots onto Kireeti. This was hurting Kireeti and was getting him slightly drunk every time they hit him, thereby incapacitating him.

Malli trembled as the compound started to tremble too. He was cursing his premium customer Varma who still seemed to have a great impact on his customers. Making a mental note to add the bills to Varma's earlier account (which Varma never repaid), Malli ran out of the compound with his phone.

As an hour or so of the ruckus passed, lots of the inhabitants abandoned the store as they knew what was in store for them. However, Raj was still not through with his frustration and continued to beat the heck out of Kireeti who seemed to have mentally abandoned the long lost fight. Kireeti's gang were trying to hold back Raj now and then, just so that Kireeti noticed they tried. They stopped this once Raj punched a guy who tried to stop him punching Kireeti.

And then came the siren. Kireeti's gang tried to flee but they were too late for that. The cops immediately grabbed the left overs from the compound (drinkers and the drinks too). Raj stopped the fight as soon as he saw the cops, but kicked Kireeti again as the cops were taking him away. As the drunkards were being shop lifted into police vehicles, they realized they had hit an off duty officer too, who had come there to have a drink.

The off duty officer happened to be the Sub Inspector of Sivasamudram. He held Raj by his collar and breathed, "Come now Mr.Varma. Let me show you a place in Sivasamudram which your father never visited during his stay. You could describe the place to him as a secret Sivasamudram then."

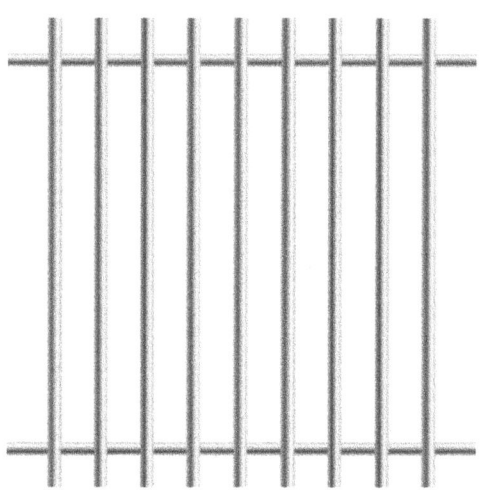

Chapter - 27

THE PHONE CALL

"Can I have my phone call now? I need to talk to my lawyer" asked Raj as the Sub-Inspector was getting back to his senses after the all night party the police station had with all the wine they confiscated from the crime scene. Kireeti and his gang were placed in a separate cell and Raj along with some drunkards who were too drunk to run away were in another.

"I already made your phone call, mister. Gopala Swamy garu has been informed of the situation, he said he will send his lawyer to do the needful", the SI hiccupped and struggled to get up.

"Was he informed about us too?" Kireeti questioned. "Yes he has been. After all, his law needs to save his son-in-law first, right?" laughed the SI. Kireeti sank back into the cell.

Around afternoon that day, the station was graced with the presence of Suguna along with Gopala Swamy's lawyer. She handed some papers (legal and monetary) to the SI as he examined them carefully.

"Excuse me madam, the papers only specify the bail for Kireeti and his friends here. I told Gopalam garu that the foreigner in his house is my guest too", the SI blinked.

"I know, but….it is just them", Suguna shrugged. To this, Kireeti and his friends whistled and started showing off. As they were released, Kireeti winked an eye to Raj and said, "Now do you get why I 'deliberately' lost such an easy fight with you yesterday. I knew that the law (I mean father-in-law) would stand by my side. And as you are an American who enslaved us for so many years, I knew you would not be set free by the Indian Justice Department".

"Hey, get lost before you get arrested or thrashed again", the SI shouted, "Are you sure you want to marry that guy?" he asked Suguna who got up too.

"Thank you sir. And Kireeti, you go along with your friends to your house and get yourself some medical help. I have some small business with Raj here", Suguna replied.

Kireeti and his friends were shocked to hear this, "Hey! What private business do you have with this dumbo? I am your fiance' and I forbid you from talking to that man" he demanded.

"Oh, it was actually a message my mom had asked me to give him. If you forbid me from giving it, then I shall go back silently and inform mom that my husband hasn't allowed me to do the job", Suguna smiled innocently.

"Hey, hey, I am not a backward low lying villager who tells his wife whom to talk to and not to. I give you full freedom to do as you please alright", Kireeti immediately changed his stance and slithered away.

The lawyer stood out too, as he knew better than to question Sharada's judgement. Suguna gave what looked like a lunchbox to Raj.

"I am sorry about this. Dad didn't want you to come out and mom couldn't protest", Suguna said.

"I know your mother could have handled your father quite easily if she desired to. If she didn't, that doesn't mean she couldn't. It only means she didn't want to do it. I know you know it too", Raj replied as he took the lunchbox.

"Yeah. But that was my mom's message and lunchbox that I delivered", Suguna replied sheepishly.

"I need you to talk to Manoj. You know him right? Ask him to reach out to my lawyer and get me out of here", Raj continued.

"I can't, mom locked him up in the study instead of the store room now. The store room no longer has a door right. And she likes to put all her valuables in the study.

The material she has there keeps reminding her of the intelligent woman that she is. Your friend is one of those now. I am also pretty sure she confiscated his phone, and scared him off talking to you. So, all in all, both of you are locked up", Suguna hesitated but opened up nonetheless.

"Right, thanks for the honest info" Raj bit his lips.

"Don't worry, mom said it is only till my wedding you would be here, and I would keep delivering you your meals on a daily basis", Suguna replied.

"Why you?" Raj was confused.

"I am the only person mom trusts", she replied.

"But you are giving me all the info", Raj raised his brows.

"Mom trusts me to use my brain. She never confiscates me from doing stuff like she does to Gayathri. And I tell you things you need to know, not things you would want to know", she answered.

"Sorry about that, but can you please help me with one phone call. I need to make it", Raj replied. "It is for my father. He would be worried about me", he quickly added.

"Sorry I cannot. But in case you need me to deliver any message to mom or your friend Manoj, I can do that", she answered.

"I will think of something and tell you when you come next", Raj gave up. But just as Suguna was leaving the station, he shouted back, "Tell your mom Manoj has a phone in the study room, and he needs to dial just one person. That person is neither my father nor a lawyer. If she is okay with it, then I will give the person's name and number when you come back".

"I can call her right now and confirm, then you can give me the number right away", Suguna said and she went out of the station to talk to her mom.

After five minutes or so, she came back, "Right, give me the number. But mind you, mother will be there along with Manoj as he makes the call".

"The person's name is Rajagopal and Manoj has his number in his phone. He is just an employee from the marketing team in my company. Tell Manoj to ask him about the presentation Rajagopal was to show me this morning. And if the presentation is ready, he is free to show it to Manoj this evening or tomorrow. Your mother can sit through it too if she is suspicious", Raj said.

Suguna appeared confused but nodded nevertheless and bade Raj farewell for the day. As she came back home, she went straight to the study where she was sure she would find both the people to whom the message was intended.

"And Raj said you could sit through the presentation too in case you…ah…want to", Suguna finished Raj's message to both the parties.

"Is Raj crazy? He has been arrested for God's sake. I am under house arrest here, and I have been told Varma mama is coming to India this week. Now, all he wants from me is to talk to that mindless old swear word king and listen to a shitty marketing presentation from him? Unbelievable man!" Manoj was exasperated.

"Does that mean you don't want to do it?" Sharada asked him.

"Yes it means I don't want to do it, not that I won't do it. Raj is the only person here I trust and God knows I am the only person here he trusts. So, yeah I will make that phone call", Manoj cried out.

"But mind you, I will put the call on speaker and if I find out anything fishy like you mentioning your arrest here or Raj's arrest there, or talk in some code language or ask the …well the other Gopal for any help or money etc., I will hand you over to my husband", Sharada warned Manoj.

"My God, you seriously just gave me all those ideas, do you realize that? I had nothing of the sort in mind and even if I had something like that, Rajagopal is not the person I would trust. You will get to know him now when we call him", Manoj gave a wry smile.

Sharada dialed out the number in her landline, put it on speaker and beckoned Manoj to stand beside her. Suguna was asked to leave and make sure no one enters the study.

Ring….Ring….Ring…..

"Who the f**k is this? If you called trying to lure me into an insurance policy, mistaking me for an innocent, God fearing, ready to die old fat dumb sick piece of shit who wants to feed your company their premiums and die soon without getting back so much as a paisa to his distant cold family members who not so much as call him to find out if he is alive, then kindly cut the call", shouted Rajagopal.

Sharada looked at Manoj and smiled in a way that seemed to mean *A perfect Varma's employee.*

"Hey it's me Manoj speaking, you know, Raj's cousin", Manoj proceeded carefully as he had never heard Rajagopal in such a foul mood before.

"Oh, it is you, my monkey maharaj", swore Rajagopal (to which Sharada gave a silent cackle of laughter and patted Manoj).

"Ahem, ahem, yes it is me. This is regarding some presentation you were supposed to give Raj this morning. I know this is evening now, but good for you, you got a chance to deliver the presentation now", Manoj answered slightly indignantly.

"You pretending orangutan. Have you checked your phone at all today? Have you checked how many times I have been calling you every 10 minutes right from 9AM today to 3PM? You now call me at 5:30PM asking me if I am ready, you softening gorilla." Rajagopal was just at his foulest mood today.

Manoj now understood the reason for Raja's mood. As he looked towards Sharada, she raised a finger as though ordering him not to mention anything about his phone being confiscated from him or him getting 'arrested' or Raj getting arrested for real.

"Oh that, I am sorry. I have been….busy….with some official work", Manoj stuttered.

"Oh my God, did you say 'official work'? I am so sorry darling. I just wanted to ask you if I could buy a few extra potatoes for the curry I was planning to prepare today. And if you don't mind me asking, am I allowed to feed the remnants of yesterday's meal to the beggars or the stray dogs? Or would you rather eat it yourself or feed it to me? I would be forever indebted to your affection if you feed it to me" Rajagopal spoke in a fake feminine voice.

Sharada was thrown into fits of uncontrollable laughter.

"Hey, will you please drop it? You are just an employee under Raj. Don't you think he has many more things on his plate?" Manoj protested.

"Don't you dare justify yourself, you good for nothing mongrel. It was he who picked the time today. And if he had some sense of responsibility or an ounce of shame or dignity within himself, he should have informed me of his unavailability yesterday, today morning or atleast by this afternoon. My team worked their asses off making this presentation for almost three weeks now and your ass of a cousin cannot afford a few seconds to inform me that the presentation has been delayed? Now I am done playing around with you, give the phone to your goddamn boss, I have news for him", Rajagopal as good as stood beside Manoj and shouted all those words in his ears.

Manoj gave Sharada a helpless glance as she returned a wry smile and a nod again.

"He has been really busy sir, please understand. And I don't have him with me now", Manoj dropped all pretense and started pleading.

"I get it, I get it all now. He just wanted me to go on a wild goose chase. All this presentation thing was a sham. He played a prank on me, now don't you deny that. I have been a blind fool all this time. I should have realized it the moment Raj gave me your number and not his. He was just having fun at my expense, distracting me from the actual marketing campaign all the while. Wow, what a neat but dirty trick that was. Now, I would not be a hindrance to your costly campaign to fool millions of people and deprive them of their staple diet. And I bet Vijju has already completed the ad campaign, the social media shit and all the donation drives. SPANKKKKK", Rajagopal slapped himself as he said it.

"Hey, hey, don't let your imagination get you", Manoj sounded concerned as Rajagopal was just busy weaving his own theories. Manoj and Sharada could hear a lot of indiscernible swear words and surely the sounds of a lot of fragile things breaking in Rajagopal's office.

After a whole ten minutes, Rajagopal was back on line.

"Now listen to me you joker, I just confirmed from my team that Vijju has actually completed his campaign work, so I caught your ruse. But don't you dare think that I would let this go so easily. I am going to take this far, so far that all you corporate criminals would land in jail trying to chase it", Rajagopal's voice sounded very intense and hurt.

"He is already in jail", shouted back Manoj as Sharada grabbed Manoj by his collar.

"Now shut up and tell your boss this. He wanted to see my presentation but is too busy to actually see it right? Not a problem at all. Tell him he is going to find it in every social media handle he can lay hands on, be it Twitter, Facebook, Whatsapp, Linkedin, Reddit, Quora, Insta, Pamphlets, Posters and anything else I can afford. Ask him to view that and give me my appraisal, you dumb piece of shit you cook", and Rajagopal just cut the line.

"How dare you defy my order!" shouted Sharada.

"You crazy woman! Didn't you hear what that guy was saying? He thinks Raj is some posh corporate guy who doesn't care about the people who work for him or people who buy from him. And this stupid oldie is going to do great damage now. Let me call someone from the company and try controlling that clown", and Manoj started to dial again as Sharada unplugged the cord of the phone.

"You will do nothing more. Your friend wanted you to make this call, and you made it. That's all. Now if you are so interested, I can show you the presentation in social media that has been leaked and then we can decide upon a message we can deliver to Raj, along with some suggestions for damage control. Nothing else", shouted back Sharada.

Manoj could do nothing, he was in her house, in her control now and God knows for how much longer. He just took a deep breath and sat back on the chair.

"That's better. Now Suguna is going to deliver you some food. Have fun and oh, you are free to read any book you are interested in. Consider yourself a political prisoner", scoffed Sharada as she walked out of the study.

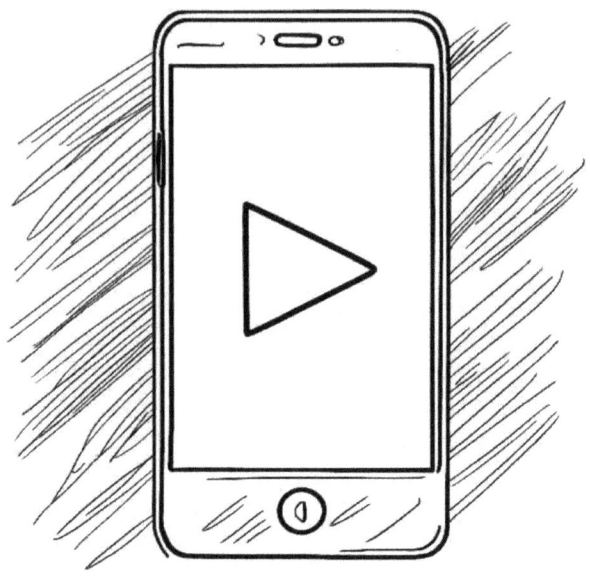

Chapter - 28

DAMAGE AND CONTROL

"It's really bad", Sharada sounded off as she handed Manoj a phone with the presentation video that Rajagopal had released on social media. "I thought it would be some childish marketing campaign that the crazy shouter had made. But it is actually a documentary of sorts, revealing some stuff about the RV chain which I hope is fake".

"Documentary? What sort of stuff could that Old Monk brand have shown?" exclaimed Manoj. *Did he by chance get hands on that video? Where I was flirting with that pop singer cum chief guest of a girl on the 22nd anniversary. GOD I hope he censored the sign she showed me that day .STUPID OVERCONFIDENCE OF THAT CHICK! THINKS SHE CAN OVERPOWER ME JUST BY SINGING FAST!*

Manoj clicked on the play button expecting a pop singer starting to sing in abusive language about RV chain. On the contrary, there was that Old Monk Rajagopal in a vintage news reader attire wearing his reading glasses looking as disinterested as possible.

"Yewww! Right now, I lost interest after seeing this man's face. He didn't even change a bit. The same look of an immature child trapped in a bearded lost man's body. Why doesn't he even shave or apply dye?" remarked Manoj.

"Welcome everyone!" started Rajagopal. "I mean welcome in two ways. Firstly I welcome y'all to the world of RV restaurant chain. BY THAT I MEAN THE ACTUAL WORLD OF RV CHAIN!" he shouted suddenly hitting the table in front of him.

"The world which is so preciously hidden, like the healthy food which gets covered with unhealthy oil, maida, additives just to make it look good, smell good, taste good and what NOT. And then served in the hands of an unbearably clean and unwillingly serving waiter who just knows the big scary cum posh words of the dishes which we innocent recipients can't speak or spell. But, you know what? He knows something more. He knows that by any means, he shouldn't dare to eat that very dish he's serving, if he wishes to stay alive. The...URGH...let's get to that in the later part of this video." controlled Rajagopal.

"Secondly, after seeing this video, I hope it's going to ignite some fire in the rotten useless stove cum brain of yours! Where I hope y'all will cook some meaningful dish to serve yourselves" he scoffed.

"Then, when you thank me before you thank God for sending me onto this planet, I wouldn't be able to check or receive your comments. As I've become way wiser than y'all not to waste time spending hours trapped in the web of the internet, waiting for a spider of a corporate giant to swallow my data and...URGH....will get to that again later. So, you are welcome for that." pointed Rajagopal.

Manoj gave a loud and clear facepalm for starting this video. Just to stand by the word given to his friend, he continued to watch. For the remaining 15-20 mins of the video, he felt he could have watched even the most boring videos he ever watched on the internet twice or thrice.

According to him, he would have given an R Rating for the video, not that any violent or grotesque content was shown (like a chicken or a pork or fish being slaughtered, crushed, or burning oil being poured live on them). The video had Rajagopal showing some dumb stats, which Manoj could never understand why any board member or stakeholder showed so much interest in, and some content details of famous and even his favourite dishes of RV restaurant. And then, he was saying some stupid rumors on each of the board member of RV chain (them collaborating with competitors and doing some...some...pricing he was saying, linkups with mafia people), about his colleagues like Vijju and their daily unofficial activities.

Manoj would have given R for the abusive language being used by Rajagopal, and for his expressions whenever he went into Poonakam (state where women go into a trance during worship of Goddess) his favourite state of mind.

For every dish being shown by Rajagopal, he was concluding either death or forever loss of memory as the end result, which Manoj wished, if true, should be served to Rajagopal atleast 6-7 times a day until he either dies or becomes just a blank old kid who could be used for laboratory testing.

Once the video stopped, Manoj stared blankly at Sharada Devi and said, "I agree that the video is bad, and by bad I mean bad as a video. But I don't see how this is going to affect RV or Raj. There were no proofs shown or videos of RV employees or customers crying about some great scam going on within."

Sharada facepalmed herself just as loud as Manoj had done just a minute ago, "Oh God!!! Why does God make rich people foolish or rather foolish people rich? This has nothing to do with evidence my dear Manoj. This 'other Gopal' is not trying to bring a raid on restaurant chains of RV by the Food Commision of India. This is about your IPO, do you even know what it means? This video is going to have a detrimental impact on the market sentiments in case it goes viral. And it is going to take a very huge positive marketing push to bring the stock out of the abyss. And what's worse is that the video has been made and posted by a whistleblower from within the company itself".

Manoj had his eyes and mouth wide open. After a while, he came back to his senses and muttered, "I need to go and inform Raj about this then. Been telling him not to trust this sandbag brain of a guy! Now look at what he's done! Can't even hold his tongue or urine. Just released whatever he likes, I mean dislikes, about the RV chain! PLEASE LET ME GO!!!" he blabbered at the stopping and glaring Sharada.

"Even you said it will impact the IPO of the RV chain", he revolted.

"Don't pretend as if you understood what I had said about your IPO or how this video will affect or damage it" Sharada replied plainly.

"Ma'am, please! You don't know about this guy Rajagopal. If we do not get him arrested or make him delete this video after beating him up before his daughter, he'll keep posting it on every other platform and he also said he will distribute it offline as well" urged Manoj.

"Your job was to review this and give a message to me, to be shared with Raj. Now, please do that in 5 mins or else it's goodbye for now and I'll lock this cage", decided Sharada.

"No! No! Wait. Let's think about how to control this damage. Urgh…come on…come on. Shall we connect with any famous female celebrity in this state? And release a video of me and her dancing in front of the RV Indian restaurant chain. We can even give you and your husband a bit where you bless us both. NO! NO! Don't go" cried Manoj when Sharada Devi threw a look with a clear message of not to waste her time, and started walking.

"Shut up! Don't even dream of thinking ever again. Let me send Suguna and give information to Raj. Will ask if he has any known contacts from the Indian branch here, so that we can discuss with them on legal actions or negotiations with this…this…good for nothing depressed soul. Gosh! Why do these big giants make such small mistakes, recruiting useless brainers like him and you?" remarked Sharada closing the door with a noise which gave up the actual intensity her calm voice had in it.

Manoj stood there like a child who was house locked by parents, who warned him not to tear the house apart before they came back. His eyes slowly opened the gates for tears.

Once Sharada Devi came out of the study room, she ran into Gopala Swamy who, for some reason, was looking so happy that he hugged her (which he hasn't done for many years now).

"All these days, I was so worried. I wasn't able to understand where you were getting at. Was worried what you were becoming, with these foreign pigs entering our house. But, for the first time, and am sure it will be the last time, you rectified the mistake. And by last time, I meant going forward, there won't be any mistakes or misunderstandings between us. Let us live our life the way we wanted to. Let's first do the best in making Suguna's marriage her best memory and celebrate it to the fullest. Then, we'll sit with Gayathri, know what kind of a guy she wants, and look out for such a guy from a nearby city. In that way, you would also be satisfied that he is a graduate guy and educated equally for your status" Gopala Swamy almost smiled and cried together.

"Come, the guests are arriving and there are only a few days before Suguna's marriage. My God! We are about to fulfill one of our most important responsibilities, and it's just days away! I am just not able to stop my tears. Will drink an imported brand today", saying so, Gopala Swamy grabbed Sharada's hand and started taking her downstairs.

Downstairs, Sharada could see everyone greeting the recently released heroes Kireeti and his friends, and were discussing things like *Even Gopalam never went to jail...but his son-in-law has gone and come back..he's the face of the future*, *This is unavoidable in politics sir..I say leaders are born in jail.* At the centre of it, Kireeti and his friends were all blushing and waving hands or joining them with those guests who wanted handshakes from the celebrities.

With the arrival of the couple, everyone shouted in celebration and applauded. Gopala Swamy tightened his grip on Sharada and lifted their hands in response to another huge applause. He then started his speech which he was so good at.

"Thank you everyone! Thank you. I am feeling so proud of our village kurrollu (youngsters) who never disappoint our village, and are taking us to a bright future through their path. Also, it's been proven again that my... I mean our selection of son-in-law never fails our expectations. Good job Kireeti! I am so happy for you and Suguna. I also wish that Gayathri will be as lucky as her sister in getting another jewel of a husband."

YAYYYYY...shouted the crowd and suddenly Kireeti's friends blushed even harder imagining their chances. Even their parents started pulling them close and hugging them. Sharada Devi, realizing the damage her action had done unexpectedly, patted Gopala Swamy and whispered, "I'll have a small word with our daughters".

"Sure! But don't be late, as we don't want you and them to miss the celebrations. They would also have been surprised and happy, and would want to share their happiness with their mother privately", said Gopala Swamy, simultaneously gesturing to a plain faced Suguna and slightly puzzled Queen Gayathri to come.

Sharada Devi grabbed both her daughters' arms and took them both to Suguna's bedroom. She indicated them to sit on the bed as she didn't want their tall heights to dominate her and make her feel inferior.

"Firstly, I want both of y'all to relax and get yourselves out of the noisy revel happening downstairs." she said.

Both of them bent down slightly into a relaxed and comfortable position. Gayathri was about to speak when the actual Queen Sharada Devi gestured not to.

"Let me discuss with Suguna first", she replied.

She then turned to Suguna who stared blankly at her.

"What should I say? The one good thing which is happening to you is that you will be here with us. So, anything that gets out of hand can be handled." Sharada gave an honest answer.

"I don't know what you think about or seek from that Kireeti. But, I'm happy that you're happy. The only catch is when he does such foolish village acts and gets arrested, you will have to bear with him and spare him. For this, you will at the very least be here with us and so, you need not worry about what might happen. We'll take care." she answered.

"Also, as an elder sister, you have one small responsibility i.e., your younger sister. Let's give her a better life", Sharada added with a tone of responsibility in her voice.

Both Suguna and Gayathri looked at each other.

"What'd you need to do for that? Well it's simple. I have made very good arrangements for her and even controlled the situation. You just need to keep visiting the police station and delivering the carriage along with some messages to that smartest and the most eligible bachelor", saying so Sharada indirectly brought the topic and Gayathri as well into the discussion.

"As for you, well kid, your stars have aligned now. It was so difficult with your character and behaviour, and also with a completely contrasting intelligence of your would-be", Sharada Devi remarked.

"What? I don't understand" asked Gayathri, not understanding what her mother was saying or where she was taking this topic to.

Sharada continued "Yes. The one whom you've been thinking with your foolish brain to be my crush is…" "Not just me, the entire village is of the same opinion," intruded Gayathri.

"Enough! He's your would-be husband. I had to use all the brains I had and use it to an extent that I have never done in the past 25yrs. But now I have done it all, ensured that he arrives in India, and comes to our house and is now waiting to be released to get tied to you", she concluded.

"Yuck! That guy who has been flirting with old Queens and is now in the dungeons? You wish me to marry him and stay proudly in this house. What an awful taste you've got mom", rebuked Queen Gayathri, this time not paying heed to the gestures of both Sharada and Suguna.

Sharada waved her hand as if to slap Gayathri and stopped mid way.

"You fool! You fell for his tantrums and misleads, have you? I wished you fell for him in the right way. But, one more thing just struck me with your reply. You're also lucky enough to be leaving this village and being the first ever woman from our village to be setting foot on foreign land. Seriously, you've been gifted with a golden spoon which was molded so hard by me", Sharada was annoyed with not getting recognition for her efforts in mending her daughter's future.

"No! I will decide as to where I wish to go, not where you or this foreign poet takes me. I'll speak to dad on this", Gayathri was about to get up and leave, but stopped seeing her mother wasn't stopping her, rather she had an evil smile on her face that Gayathri had never seen before.

"Well, please go by all means! Why did you stop? Oh, were you waiting for me to stop you? No, I won't. Why should I always be the one who worries and thinks? Try thinking for yourself for the first time, Gayathri."

Gayathri just stopped there, not able to understand what to say.

"Well, shall I say what's running in your brain now?" started Sharada.

"When you inform this to your father, and mind you he already knows about this proposal, he will immediately get a third class villager buffalo who hasn't even cleared his first class and would have gone to 'dungeons' more than school", Sharada smiled with no response from her daughter and continued, "Then you'll be trapped within this house and just be dreaming of how it would have been if you'd have listened to your mother."

"Let me also brief you about my proposition now. If you get married to this foreign poet, you'll be living in a bungalow which is the size of this village, along with servants who would have studied 10 times harder than you've, just to get to that job of being in 1 floor of that bungalow", Sharada Devi stood just beside Gayathri now.

"But, knowing the importance of the status you're about to get should also make you equally responsible now. Know that there won't be any aunty of your silly friends or maids there who keep praising whatever you say or do. There'll be graduates from IIMs and MITs who keep questioning you on what to do in order to keep the business and kingdom running. You'll be needing to give them decisions. So, grow up and learn from there when you reach. Don't worry, I'll also be visiting your home and office from time to time in order to check on you and guide you." Sharada Devi concluded as usual in her terms.

Upon hearing this, Gayathri just stood there and fell down abruptly, while Sharada gestured Suguna to come with her and leave Gayathri alone for a while, to think.

"As I was saying, in order to fulfill your duty as an elder sister, go to the police station now as it's almost lunch time and give this message to him. Just listen to whatever he has to say, and inform that you'll discuss with me and then pass it on", saying so, Sharada left Suguna's hand and gave her the lunch carriage from the dining table.

She was now feeling happy and relieved to have controlled the damage about to be inflicted. She went down to the ground floor and joined her husband and the other guests in celebrations and arrangements for the function. Once in a while, she was just looking for either Suguna or Gayathri to turn up but she was sure the latter wouldn't turn up for a while now.

Almost after an hour, Suguna had come back and was asked by Kireeti first, followed by Gopala Swamy on where she had been. She was saved by Sharada Devi intruding and informing that she had sent her to a nearby temple to give some offerings and also serve food to the Brahmins there, as she had prayed to do so.

"What happened? Why did it take so long?" questioned Sharada.

"It was just as usual, the cops taunting him about his father. I had given him the message and he was enquiring about the video contents. So, he asked me to be there and give him information silently while he was eating, so that the cops wouldn't get any doubt", she replied.

"Smart kid, that one. Always on caution to not let any cop give information to my husband about him. Well, did he give any message as to what to do?" Sharada questioned.

"He didn't say much about the action, but was content that his marketing team would take necessary action against the video and just wanted Manoj to speak with Rajagopal and check what the video had. But, upon listening to the information in the video, he wasn't much worried and also requested to send a message to his friend in the study," Suguna replied.

"Come with me. Will give that joker lunch along with this message." Sharada said.

When both the women went and opened the study, they found Manoj lying in the middle of the study floor weeping and sleeping, reminding them of prisoners of some war. Upon seeing them, he immediately got up, wiped his tears and looked serious and manly.

"Take the lunch and have it soon. We have just given your message to your friend", replied Sharada.

In an instant, Manoj again became that enthusiastic kid and kept shooting questions. What *did he say...when do we start...how do we get out...who is going to come.*

"Hey, get back to senses! He said his marketing team will take care of this", Sharada replied.

"And did he send me any message?" Manoj asked.

"Yes," Suguna replied.

"Which is?" asked both Manoj and Sharada Devi.

"TAKE CARE AND GROW YOUR MIND. PLEASE READ THE 1ST CHAPTER OF EVERY BOOK AVAILABLE IN THE STUDY"

Chapter - 29

JOB DONE BILLION DOLLARS TRANSFERRED

"What have you done!" shouted Vijju as he entered Raja's office.

"I have resigned, thanks for your concern, Vijju. I must say I am touched by you trying to talk me out of it. But it is already done", smiled Rajagopal (sarcastically of course).

"Yeah, it is already done you snaky snack", Vijju pushed the books Raja was just packing and threw them onto the cabin door.

Rajagopal just smiled, "Now you get some part of my frustration Vijju. Good to see you using your human antics once in a while. Anyhow, I have submitted my resignation as soon as I posted the video so that you don't get the satisfaction of firing me."

And as Rajagopal was packing his nameplate, Vijju snatched it from him, "This neither belongs to you nor is deserved by you, you beacon of bullshit. While the entire company feeds people tasty food, you fed them utter bullshit."

"That's the exact point I tried to make Vijju babu. Just because junk tastes good doesn't mean you devour it, and just because medicine tastes bad, you don't avoid it. All the while we, I am so sorry, you fed people tasty poison, everyone was happy. But now, I have given them a bitter medicine, and you all, a taste of your own medicines. Now, they might not be happy but they will be healthy eventually. Just as a matter of interest, not that it interests me anymore, could I know how much have you guys spent on the worthless campaign you presented Vijju? As a matter of FACT, I have merely spent a month's subscription of the MS Powerpoint and 3yrs of self-research on my presentation, and look at its impact", chuckled Rajagopal.

Vijju grabbed Rajagopal by the collar, "You think we will let you get away with this Raja? Do you think the company is going to give you a single penny post your retirement?"

Rajagopal straightened his glasses," Woah woah! What Vijju? Do you want me to make a sequel to the video?

Regarding the culture of the RV chain, starting with the majestic grabbing of a whistleblower's collar by the shameless marketing management? You will become an item of meme for everyone Vijju. And then, about the retirement money you were mentioning, I am not the moneysucker as you guys are. I worked for, and always work for my passion and satisfaction, and haven't even touched your basic level, where I have to sell my soul for a salary, at the cost of the ignorant customers. If you don't believe me, then for your kind information I have just forgone 10 lakh rupees for the truth to come out to the public. I do not expect your corporate cobra to give me alms or leftovers of the junk he sells. I have already asked the HR to complete all my settlements as on date. A call from them is the only thing separating me from slapping you in front of all the marketing team here. I am sure I will get a tumultuous applause from them all, they would slap their own hands as they can't slap you, but consider each and every clap a slap."

Ring…. Ring…. Ring…..

"Well, so long Vijju. Couldn't have imagined that we would be together so long. On a side note, if you do not wish to get slapped, then please run away from here or slap yourself in front of the team. Hello", Raja answered the phone from the HR.

"Mr.Chary, we have prepared your sheets and settlements, we would need you to come down and sign it", said the HR.

Raj signed the report placed on the table as he was handed back his wallet (empty now) and his watch.

"Make sure you do not cross my path Varma gaari kodaka (Varma's son)", the SI remarked.

"Well, to those who have emptied my purse, hope they are educated enough to realize they even took my credit cards. The EMI is long due, I reached my spend limit and they will have to pay for the bill when they swipe it. So, please don't try using it and especially for any expensive ones, as the police, I mean you will have to arrest yourselves for it. So, avoid giving it to your spouses or mistresses altogether...*beep*...*beep*", signed off Raj ending his sentence in English intentionally.

"What is it? What did he say? What were those last words", SI got up yelling.

"Am sorry. For that, you'll need to study and learn basic English sir. Merely watching *beep* films won't help you there", chuckled Raj.

Murugayya, Gopala Swamy's lawyer and Raj left the station (as the constables strainfully held the SI back saying words like *Sharada Devi won't like it, Gopala Swamy is the next Sarpanch sir*).

Murugayya addressed Raj as they started back in Raj's BMW, "Abbayi garu, today is Suguna papa's wedding. So Sharadamma garu wanted you to attend it too. We have got you out on a bail, but please don't do anything stupid again."

"Oh! Shit, I forgot about that, Murugayya. Shouldn't you have told it a couple of days earlier? I wouldn't have hit Kireeti straight on his face. How is he looking now? Is he wearing a flowery paaga (turban) to cover it up?

And what about his assistant bridegrooms? That guy…the one whose jaws are no longer straight…who caught me in the back, not realizing the back hook I had given him with minimal force. And more importantly, has our beloved Phalu been discharged? Will he grace us with his presence at the wedding?" mocked Raj.

"Hey, stop the car if you know how to", shouted Raj and he took the wheel from Murugayya who simply couldn't drive the car.

As they reached the….it was no longer looking like a house. It looked like a flowery castle, decorated with multi coloured, mutli fragrant variants of flowers, mango leaves, banana branches and huge cut outs of Gopala Swamy, Kireeti (clearly back dated as he was not covered in bruises there and was showing all teeth), Phalguna (same goes true for him), Subbu, other panchayat members, random villagers (who were in cooling glasses, riding bikes, holding sickles, named as Gopala Swamy vaari fans association). There wasn't any picture of Sharada Devi or Suguna and only their names were visible at the bottom of the cut outs, and Suguna's on the wedding board.

Raj got down, and then climbed up towards the store room. The reaction of the relatives was completely in contrast to the reception that Kireeti and his friends had got when they arrived home from prison. Now, there were angry retorts from the elders, comic jeers and taunts from the middle aged and much angrier retorts from the youth (most of whom looked like members of the Fight Club). As Raj reached the store room, he saw there was neither his nor Manoj's luggage there.

Realizing what must have happened, he changed course and went towards the study (as Suguna told him Manoj was imprisoned there).

As he started his journey, he went across the usually smirking lady gang of Gayathri, who were now completely silent and just murmuring. As they shifted their gaze towards him, they had clear shock on their faces. He stopped, looked confused at their reactions and then tried bringing voice out of any of them. With no response from them, he smiled, winked at them and left them with a bigger shock on their faces. He knocked on the study door.

"Welcome alludu garu (son-in-law). Ready for the weddings?" smiled Sharada. She herself was adorned in a rich orange saree, lavish ornaments and not to mention a big victorious smile on her face. "Today is her's (she indicated Suguna downstairs) and tomorrow is yours. Do not worry, I have already informed your father, and also told him not to worry about the catering. He need not cook, we will have his dishes for the rituals after the marriage. I hope you are mentally ready for the wedding, now just get ready physically. I have bought nice suits for you and your cousin. And between us, I think your cousin needs some consoling. Whatever suggestion you gave him on reading something, doesn't look like it has worked in cooling his senses. He has been crying a lot. I can only imagine it is for Sravani, as she is getting married this weekend too. Must be a heartbreak for him. Now, I am really busy acting happy and hiding my actual happiness, so please get ready soon." and she unlocked the study.

Raj expected to find Manoj, but he found a mountain of books lying one above the other on the floor. And the mountain trembled with the sound of the door as though the movement caused an earthquake within it. As the pile fell to the floor, there was Manoj. It looked as if Manoj had set the mountain up for himself to hide inside whenever anyone came to the study. His eyes were pitch red, whether from reading or crying, Raj didn't know.

Sharada smiled at Manoj and showed him Raj and yelled, "Surprise kiddo, I got you your lollipop. Now be a good boy and get ready for the function" and she shut the door with a bang.

Manoj just kept surveying Raj for a whole 5 mins as if researching him. They were both exactly like two prisoners who were released on the same day from two different prisons. As Raj started walking towards Manoj, about to speak, Manoj pounced onto Raj throwing him onto the fallen mountain, and trying to scream at every body part of Raj available.

"Ok, ok. I get it. You missed me", Raj tried assuring, to which Manoj was taken aback for a while, but then started to soak Raj into the ocean of books again.

"You freaking UBL, why haven't they hanged you in prison!!! You should have got a lifetime imprisonment for your two face plots, you murderer. You are an Afghanistan terrorist, you deserve to be oiled to death or boiled to death. You better have a great plan to escape this hell which you brought upon us yourself. Now, start narrating the plot Holmey, I haven't been able to figure it out from these shitty books", and he kicked the pile of books and Raj within.

"What plot, which books?" Raj slowly got up.

"These volumes you asked me to read, I finished the first chapter of every freaking book here! Well, almost. Some of them were in Telugu and this Sharada didn't even give me a phone to use Google Translate or give me an oxford Telugu to English dictionary. But I have tried everything with the ones I could read. Never have I read so many books in my entire life, I mean…life until now, if ever I have any more of it left, and that too with so much attention. I didn't even read this much for my final year graduation. God, I would have become a CEO myself had I studied this hard.

I tried joining the first letter from the first chapter of every book, stitched them in about 5,628 combinations…. wait I have it all written in this piece of paper I found in the dustbin. And then….it made no sense! I then remembered Interstellar was your favourite movie, and you must be trying to send me a message through the five dimensional tesseract of a bookshelf. I tried talking to each and every book shelf, check the seconds hand of my watch, converted the first chapter of these 45 books into morse, binary, enigma, pictures of the words and then…then…. NOTHING MADE SENSE!!!!" Manoj shouted his lungs out. Thankfully there were the marriage drums and trumpets going on downstairs, otherwise the whole of Sivasamudram would have heard his shout.

"Alright. Great work pal! Hope you would have attained the ultimate wisdom under this…this…roof maybe. I need nothing but a fraction of that wisdom from you. So, tell me this, you have gone through all the bookshelves, cupboards, ruffled all the papers in this room right (and yeah, as you mentioned, the dustbin too)", Raj asked.

"I thought I was some strange colonel S.S.Landa looking for the Jews, but yeah I did. I didn't rip open the floor boards and the false ceiling though", Manoj spoke in great passion as though a mad man had finally found a partner who could see the world like he does.

"Ok, were there any ones you couldn't open? As in locked?" Raj continued.

"Yes, the black one there, the brown one under the phone, this….this cabinet here and the study room door itself were locked. I used to see the trees from this window over the telephone like Anne Franke did. I also tried to chisel off this wall, like I remember from Shawshank Redemption but as soon as I tried, Suguna came in. She said she could hear the chisel, my cry, my fart from the room just below and beside and terrace above too", cried out Manoj.

"Great, that's all I wanted to know", shrugged Raj "Thanks buddy, you were of great help".

"Wha…. aa….aattt? You just wanted to know which ones were locked?", Manoj opened his mouth and as Raj started walking towards the indicated locked cupboards, Manoj pulled him back, sang a swear word rhyme, and asked him (all the while slapping Raj slightly as though trying to make Raj look at him), "Hey, you didn't mean that, take it back, take it back, swallow it and flush it out. Tell me you wanted more, tell me you had studied these books the very first day we came, and imbibed a secret message for me to do something. Tell me you and I are about to be transported to the states by a helicopter right….. now, now, NOW!"

"Hey, get it together", Raj pried open Manoj's hands. "How could I have asked you to check for secret places inside the study through Suguna or Sharada. The message was a code in itself you moron" he said and went to the cabinets again.

"Oh, and I want you to stand outside the study fully dressed for the wedding and let me know when anyone comes in from the commotion", Raj added.

"The….what?" Manoj asked.

"Yes sir, this is your salary account statement for the past 12 months. You need to sign this too just as a formality", Deepika the HR sounded off.

"Hahaha, you mean to say the bank needs me to sign one more bloody form when I have signed like 200 documents already. Are they trying to forge my signature …hey…hey…be honest. Are you trying to screw me huh? Are you trying to rob me?" Raja goaded the HR.

"Excuse me, you never even accepted cheques or direct transfers, we have always paid you your salary in cash just out of respect", she spat back.

"Yeah, that's what. You guys would have been misusing my account for showing it as your company's profits in the to-be-made public report right? Just so that you can escape the taxes you need to pay as a responsible entity to the government, to the public and to this country. You blood traitors!" shouted Raja, snatching the papers from HR and squeezing them.

"Raja!!! Please don't give me an opportunity to call the security and have you necked out of this office. I am trying to restrain myself so hard for the past few hours", Vijju said vehemently.

"It's not me who will be kicked out of this office Vijju. But the entire office which will be knocked out from the IPO and from the country", replied Raja bringing a patriotic voice and expression.

"Sir, please sign these papers, if you want to get rid of this company from your life or vice versa," Deepika pleaded showing the squeezed papers in Raja's hands.

"Well, let me check and withdraw the leftover hard-earned money from the account which I will keep as a token of memory of my self achievement", demanded Raja putting the papers onto HR's desk.

"No issues man, we'll give you the cash now itself. Deepika, please check the balance he has. We'll open the locker and check for some change if available, and give it to this cynic for his treatment. Why get our hands dirty", remarked Vijju.

"Ok. Wait a minute. As per the account, you're having around 10,05,010 rupees in the account sir", mentioned Deepika which was again snatched suddenly by Rajagopal.

"Transfer the entire thing", he said.

"No sir, it isn't possible. You need to have at least 5000 rupees in your bank account which otherwise will get closed", clarified Deepika only realizing later that she shouldn't have mentioned it in the first place.

"Oh wow! What a cool policy! Now, this is what I call an advanced hi-tech robbery which is so well scripted. With your local Indian RV chain having around 10,000 staff working and each person asked to have 5000 rupees left in the bank for y'all and the bank, that itself is giving y'all 5 crore rupees in your pocket. Had I known this, I would have posted this as well in my video. How do I look like to you guys? Huh?", pointed out Rajagopal.

"Looking as handsome as ever mama!" commented Raj, looking at the dressed up Manoj in his gifted suit. "Quick, now that you got ready, get ready for the task." said Raj while the music and noises grew louder from below.

Both Raj and Manoj looked down the study room from the spot where Sharada Devi used to look out. The bridegroom Kireeti and his friends, family, fans all have come to the entrance of the house while the ladies from Gopala Swamy's tent came with plates in their hands to greet the procession.

"It's almost time. All the people will be going downstairs. You too follow the drill mama, and just stand near the stairs. If anyone comes up, send me a message", Raj gave a quick word of command.

"But why should I do? How should I send a message mama? And where will this lead us to? And what was that commotion you said?" Manoj kept asking all the questions made up by his newly trained and wiser mind.

"Mama! Believe me, this is the last time you'll be needing to remain silent and not ask any questions on our trip. It'll get decided now" spoke Raj.

It brought goosebumps into Rajagopal, who got unusually silent which surprised Vijju and Deepika.

"Phew! Finally we brought some sense into you Raja. Cheers for that! Let's get it signed and Deepika, just as I said, withdraw some from the locker and deposit it into his hands. Will get this over with", said Vijju wiping his face with a handkerchief and slowly falling onto the chair.

"Oh my dumbest brains! What is this statement showing and saying?" Raja raged at the HR. "You never look at the dishes you cook, pictures you paint, atleast look at the papers you print. Now what new dish or story will you cook up for this?"

"For God's sake, will you stop looking at the papers we print and just sign it!!! We assure to plant 100 trees for the 10 pages it took to print this" shouted Vijju, "Do it Raja or I swear I will personally neck you out, without calling the security."

"You mindless circus clown, this paper says my account had 1 billion DOLLARS change i.e., 8000 crore rupees change in my account and I have transferred all but this 10 lakhs change", shouted back Raja.

And then Manoj noticed crowds of people running downstairs. Maybe they wanted to greet the procession too, he thought to himself. He was just revising what Raj told to do, within himself. *Wait at the stairs, don't let anyone pass me or pass a message if someone passes. I shall guard the sanctum with all my strength. None shall pass.*

But then, he saw the commotion getting bigger and louder below. *What did you do mama and how is this going to help our cause?* The noises were growing louder.

"Just quit all this nonsense Gopal and get the hell out of here!!!" shouted Vijju.

"I will not unless this woman tells me what this bloody transaction means", Raja stood his ground.

"Well it surely doesn't mean you are a billionaire", Vijju scoffed.

"But it means I was, and who the heck sent it back!!!" Raja argued.

"Well, don't you wonder who gave you the billions in the first place?" laughed out Vijju. "Come on it must be some technical error at the bank, can you pleeaaaasssssseeee sign it? Deepika, just remove the '1' from the amount, must have been a misprint."

"And what about all the zeroes, you zeroes pretending to be heroes. Are they all misprints too, you misfit shoes God threw back to earth" scoffed Raja.

"Sir, it is a personal transaction, and this firm has nothing to do with it. I can strike it off if you wish me to, but just for an info, you are not allowed to use salary accounts for such humongous transactions alright", said Deepika.

"It won't matter, Deepika, he is not part of the RV firm anymore, and hence it is no longer a salary account, it is a beggar's treasury from now on", exhausted Vijju.

"But I do recognize the account you made the transaction with", Deepika added slightly confused.

"Well, well, if it isn't my dear Manoj. What are you doing here abbayi, come down to the celebrations and be a part of it. Your bestie is about to be hitched soon, you can't just stand here. Go get yourself drunk and dance all your worries off", said Sharada as she spanked Manoj's back.

"No, not interested. I am fine, thank you. This place has….a…..yeah….a good view of what is happening below", Manoj spluttered and again started looking straight and focussed.

"What is there to see from here? It's to go experience it. It is time we all unite and plan out what to do after the marriage. You need to show me around New York. Are you waiting for your bestie to come? Where is he?" enquired Sharada with enthusiasm all around.

A sudden horde of people descended the stairs again muttering under their breath, and Sharada started getting calls from Gopala Swamy.

"Oh God, this man cannot either survive alone or let me survive alone", and she tried to pull Manoj with her as she answered the call. But Manoj resisted.

"Sharada, come down urgently. Hello? You there?...." Gopala Swamy said among a million other voices from the phone.

But Sharada looked at the man not talking. She pulled his face towards her to see him more clearly, he was sweating.

"What is it Manoj? Where is Raj? What are you two upto?" she asked with a calm voice which clearly meant a serious warning.

Manoj tried to pull up a blank face as he said, "He is just getting ready. I am waiting for him to come. And he said he needs to use the washroom in the study."

Sharada started climbing the stairs back. Manoj stopped her immediately.

"He is dressing up pinni (aunt). Please respect his privacy", he stammered.

She broke herself free from his arm and started running up the stairs now. Manoj started to run up with a brief *SHIITTTT*. Manoj had to give the message to Raj immediately, so he shouted the words.

"The account seems to belong to the....C&MD....of this company", Deepika muttered.

Sharada won the race to the study and she hit the door with all her force as her cell phone began to ring again.

Ring....Ring....Ring.....

"Yes, who's this?" asked Raj.

"Hey!!! Who are you talking to?" shouted Sharada as the window of the study flew open.

"Hey!!! Who did you think you could cheat?" shouted Rajagopal on the phone, and Sharada at the window.

She immediately answered the phone, not to listen to her husband but to ask him to listen to her and get his ass up to the study room and break the door. But it was Murugayya who spoke from Gopala Swamy's phone.

"Ammagaru, where are you? Everyone's been trying to reach out to you", he quivered.

"Just shut your mouth and give Gopal the phone", Sharada shouted at him.

"Ammagaru, you need to come down right now, there is a huge issue downstairs", he shouted back.

"You just gave me 8000 Cr and took it back you moronious mongrel", shouted Rajagopal.

"Hear me out first you idiot, ask Gopal to come up, not me to come down", Sharada shouted.

"Ammagaru, the wedding….", Murugayya continued.

"To hell with the wedding, it will not stop if Gopal comes up for 5 minutes", Sharada replied.

"What is the meaning of this all? What did you do to me? Or rather what have you done with me?" asked Rajagopal.

"Exactly, the wedding is about to stop. Suguna papa says she doesn't want this marriage, and she said it right from the kalyana mandapam (the wedding stage)", Murugayya cried.

Chapter - 30
ALL HANDS ON THE DECK

"Consider it an appreciation of your efforts Raja" Raj replied calmly, as he unlocked the study room door. "And, to correct your earlier statement, I haven't taken back the 8000 cr I gave you".

Sharada entered the study completely lost for words.

"Bullshit! The statement says here the amount has gone back to your account your corporate conman. I thought your father was a scamster, but he is just a hamster in front of you. You are a cheat right from the core of your heart you pig. You deserve to be killed, cooked and fed to all your rotten employees", shouted Raja.

"Woah, woah, woah, calm down Mr. Crocodile. Just check the amount I have left, not the amount that I took back or rather you gave back, and things will start making sense to you", said Raj as he beckoned Sharada Devi to sit down.

"It is……." blanked out Raja.

"Exactly", said Raj. "It is 10 lakhs short of a billion", he smiled. "Now, does that amount ring a bell? It happens to be the cash prize I promised you in case you submitted the presentation within the timeline as per the contract we signed. And if you read that contract right, which I am sure you have not, in case you submit your presentation, I would have to transfer you your 10 lakh rupees from my account as you transfer whatever amount your account holds at that time, and we had given the bank full powers to exercise this option independently and without the requirement of a further consent or notification from or to either parties involved."

"Oh, and be thankful I had left you the additional 5,010 rupees your account held initially. As per the contract, I would have to take that away too. But consider it my gift on the occasion of your retirement", Raj replied winking at Sharada who sat confused.

Manoj arrived there breathless, and gazed at Raj and at Sharada. Raj looked at him and signaled him to go back to his guard duty. Manoj looked confused but left the study nonetheless.

"Hello? Chary garu, are you there?" Raj asked. This had to be the first time that Rajagopal had remained silent for that long on a phone call.

"But I didn't present it to you, you cheat?" Rajagopal spoke in a low undertone now, indicating how shook he was.

"You did Mr.Chary. I have asked Manoj to have a presentation from you, but you refused. And then, you posted it everywhere, didn't you? And that's when and how you submitted your work to everyone, including me. Thus you have executed the contract, and the bank did so too. I intervened and asked them not to give me everything you had, just the billion dollars I gave you, and of course the 10 lakh rupees you deserved", said Raj, and there was silence at the other end.

"You see sir, if you are what you claim to be, then you wouldn't care about the billions you lost, because you never earned it. You earned the 10 lakh rupees and you have it. So just like you asked me the first time we met, prove yourself worthy", Raj continued.

"But……why? Why did you do this? Why did you give me your money, why did you take it back? Why have you asked me for the presentation? Why did you play the game?" Rajagopal requested his boss.

Raj looked at Sharada, who now understood where all the money had gone when she checked his account. "I have my reasons to do what I did. And I did it *with you*, not *to you*. I did it with you so that you would realize you are also like the ones you point fingers at" and Raj cut the line.

As the study room phone got cut, Sharada's phone started buzzing again as random people tried reaching out to her from downstairs. As she looked at Raj, slightly angry but heavily confused, he smiled back at her, closed the answering chord of the phone and said, "You might have to go down for a while. The elder's wedding comes before the younger one's right. Don't worry, I am going nowhere till you come back to me. And that is because you need to know that your younger's wedding would suffer the same fate as your elder's. When you come back up, we will put all our cards on the deck as I call for a show…. down."

Downstairs was a complete contrast to the calm, silent atmosphere that was in the study. Sharada was forcefully reminded of the day they announced Suguna's wedding to the village, when she avoided all this humdrum and sat upstairs in silence. Now she was brought down, and the wedding was in danger of being called off.

"After all this time and effort, you realize now that you don't want this wedding?" barked Gopala Swamy at his elder daughter.

"I have realized it a long while ago, today is for you all to realize this", Suguna fought back.

"Is it because of the bruises on my face? The doctor said it will be cured within a fortnight, shall we postpone our wedding until then?" pleaded Kireeti who was still sitting in his place, refusing to get up.

"And what about the bruises to your brain? Will they ever be cured?" Suguna responded angrily.

Gopala Swamy was rushing onto the stage to give her a slap. People around Sharada pushed her in urgency to stop her husband. Sharada jerked back from her thoughts and looked at what was happening. She too hurried onto the stage and stopped her husband as he raised his hand.

"Gopal!!! What the hell do you think you are doing?" she shouted.

"What the hell do you think she is doing? Today is supposed to be the best day of my life, of our life. My elder's marriage, the elections, the entire village is voting for me and joining the wedding. Am I to be humiliated in front of them all? What is wrong with her?" and he charged forward again, unable to control his emotions.

Raj kept trying to open the locked cabinets. He memorized two possible passwords for each of them. There were 3 locked cabinets and two passwords each making it six possible attempts. This shouldn't have taken this long. But it did, none of the cabinets have opened. Frantically, he kept trying again, he must have made an error while arranging the passwords. First the black cabinet, password 1 (failed to open), password 2 (failed to open). Ok, no issues, the brown cabinet now. He wiped the sweat on his brow and tried again. Brown cabinet, password 1 (failed to open), password 2 (failed to open). *What the heck,* he muttered to himself. Brother, calm yourself down, there is the cabinet under the phone too. Right cabinet under the phone, password 1 (failed to open), his heart started beating fast, as though trying to replace the drums that were beating earlier and have now stopped...password 2 (failed to open). WHAATTTT THE...

Gopala Swamy kicked the contents on the stage in a roar. The panchayat members below (or rather the entire village) were muttering under their breaths. The cocky panchayat member said to the others, "Woah! We thought Gopalam would be fighting to get Gayathri married, like threatening to die, and Sharada would 'accidentally' kill him. But this seems to be happening for Suguna herself."

"Consider yourself lucky Subbu. If Gopalam would have asked you to give your son to Suguna, you would be on that stage too", laughed the drunkard panchayat member.

Subbu and Phalguna (who was still unable to speak aloud due to the blows he received in the duel) were looking at each other, then the surroundings as though wondering whether it was all worth it. The priest was sitting dejected, as he wanted to ask for the due engagement fees along with the wedding fees on this day. Looks like he is not going to get a paisa for either the engagement or the wedding.

Manoj, who was now told as to what was happening by the chambermaids of the queen, was busy pondering as to whether it was a coincidence or has Raj planned it all. And if he did, why?

Come on, think, think, think you idiot. There has to be something you are missing here. The password had to be one of the two, then why wasn't it working? Was there any other possible password? Just remember what has all happened.

"Suguna, look at me. We talked about this twice. Once, in my study and once in your bedroom. I told you we will be there for you, come what may. What has happened now? If you weren't convinced, then why didn't you discuss it with me again?" Sharada tried reasoning it out with the only person from the village whom she knew listened to reason.

Gopala Swamy was sent down to sit in the front row, as Sharada asked for a few minutes to talk sense into her daughter. He was sitting there, taking deep breaths as though he just swam the ocean beside the house, or he was the ocean himself.

"Because I know you will not change your stance, you will only try convincing me", Suguna let out a tear for the first time that day. She cried, "I thought you were the only person in the house who understood me. And I thought I understood you. But none of them seem to be true. You are just like one of them, though you admit not to be. You have become one of them."

"Oh my dear child, now you are talking like one of them. Please listen to reason. Only if you marry Kireeti, can your sister get a better life, as I said. It is for your sister", pleaded Sharada now dropping all pretense, because Suguna touched a nerve when she said her mother had become a headstrong villager like everyone else. "Haven't I told you what my father did to me?"

"Then why are you doing the same to me?" Suguna cried harder.

"ENOUGH OF THIS!!!" shouted Gopala Swamy. "BOTH OF YOU. SHARADA, I told you umpteen times I am not going to give my daughter's hand to that foreign fart. And I thought…you finally corrected yourself."

"Gopal, this is no time to debate about Gayathri, this is time to talk to Suguna", Sharada shut her husband up. "Suguna please, I can only manage a better life for one of you, and unfortunately it has to be your sister. Only if your father has his will first, will he let me have my will. I never wanted this for you. But I will be there with you throughout this. You will be there with me, with us all."

"Is this about that foreign fighter?" Kireeti asked his mother-in-law, shell shocked. And he just voiced the villagers' mind there.

"This has nothing to do with him, and that has got nothing to do with you Kireeti. I am trying to get your marriage done, and you will shut your mouth, and your brain while I keep mine working", shouted Sharada.

"This has everything to do with Raj", Suguna shouted as everyone in the hall stopped their muttering and looked towards the bride for an explanation.

"He told me he will invest in my dream to set up a business amma. I am going to live your dream, my dream too. He explained it all to me. His team is going to help me with the place, the setup, the funding, everything my business will need. We can do it together, I need not marry this joker", Suguna held her mother's hands as she spoke.

Sharada drew her hands back, and stared at her daughter, as though looking at her for the first time, "What did you say?" she calmly asked.

"Yes amma, I told him about my dream the night after he won the duel, when we had that puja in our house, and he said…he said he will help me out. Lend me some money, arrange for some bright minds and everything else. I finally get a chance to do something, to make you proud", Suguna hiccupped.

"So this is all the doing of that cowardly cocky son of a cook. Now, don't you dare stop me, Sharada. The elections will be done in just a while now, and once it is done, nothing can stop me from a man hunt followed by a human sacrifice. I get it now, the holy Mother Durga wants me to perform a human sacrifice for all that she has done for me. And once I do it, there will be no more hurdles, everything will fall in place", jumped up Gopala Swamy.

He ordered all his henchmen, Kireeti's friends, henchmen of his fellow panchayat members to arrange for all and any kind of weaponry they could lay their hands on. He ordered Murugayya to get his jeep ready for him to hunt. He called his representative who is sitting at the voting and counting centre (as the population was low, counting would be done as soon as the voting is done) and asked him to give an update on the elections every hour. And then he brought his beloved shotgun and sat on the swing that directly faces the stairs.

The Most Eligible Bachelor

Sharada Devi realized the situation had completely gotten out of hand now. She could neither stop her husband nor save Raj. He had gone too far, way too far now. She had to hurry. As she went for the stairs, Gopala Swamy's eyes (which were redder than they had ever been before) followed her all the way, but he didn't stop her. He wants this to happen, he wants Sharada to scare the foreigners to run and then he would hunt them down. As she reached the top most stair, she was stopped by Manoj.

"Pinni, please wait. I don't think Raj is done dressing, he hasn't come down, or maybe he has gotten an upset stomach, with all the prison food he ate", Manoj stopped her.

"You idiot! I sent him food everyday. Do you want Raj or yourself to die a painful death here? My husband is waiting downstairs with his army and ammunition to finish you off both. Your cousin has crossed all his limits and the elections are about to get over. Now there is nothing I can do to stop my husband. So, let me go and talk to that dumbass, we have no time", she shouted off her lungs.

Come on, he had to hurry now. He got the possible third password now, but there are three cabinets to test it on. Now is not the time to think, it is the time to act. Right, the black cabinet, password 3 (failed to open). Run now. The brown cabinet, password 3 (failed to open). He could hear shouts from below and some footsteps towards the stairs. He ran for the cabinet under the phone, password 3, he was moving his fingers as quickly as possible, rotating the numbers to the combination he had in mind.

"Open, open, open", shouted Sharada Devi as she banged on the study room door.

And click, the door opened. Raj's hands trembled as he lay hands upon it.

And click, the door opened. Sharada ran in and caught Raj by the collar.

"What the hell did you do, you moron? How dare you...?" Sharada stopped abruptly as her eyes fell on what Raj had just done, making her forget what he had done earlier.

Raj lifted up the piece of paper in his hand, "My final card, the Ace in the hole. I now put it on the deck", he said as he showed her the original contract she had made his father sign (or rather give a thumb impression on).

"Now it's time for the showdown athayya", said Raj.

Chapter - 31

SHOWDOWN

Ring….Ring….Ring…..

Raj answered the phone, "Yes it's me. Oh, it's great to know. Make sure pops, I mean dad comes along with him at the earliest."

"Mama!!!" Manoj came running "Mama, I am so sorry I let her pass but she said, and I just confirmed from the gang of Gayathri's girls too. That crazy Gopala Swamy is all set for hunting us both down to death. He only waits for the election to be done, so that his position is not jeopardized. Come on, we have to run, we haven't got much time."

"I am going nowhere mama. I have unfinished business with Sharada garu here. You are free to leave if you wish to. Take my car, but I will remain right here", answered Raj.

"Are you out of your mind? These people actually are out of their minds and they will not hesitate to kill you", Manoj pleaded as he kept looking back to see if anyone came to capture them, so that they do not run away.

"Mama, go downstairs. I am going to lock the study from the inside. If they try to stop you, tell them I have Mrs.Gopala Swamy here with me, and I will not hesitate to harm her if they try harming you. Tell them once you leave, they are free to do anything to me, provided they let you go", Raj answered as he beckoned Sharada to sit down for the showdown.

Manoj thought for a while, let out a wail of anger, then a cry with a few tears and went away. *I can atleast go call the cops from a nearby town (as cops here fear Gopala Swamy) to save him,* he thought to himself.

"Now for our little card game Sharada", started Raj, "You do remember mentioning you saw where I was heading to with my game. What was that? Yeah, you saw my final set of cards, though you had no idea what cards I currently hold. And as you have seen me drop a card, you guess what I hold and make sure I don't get any useful pieces to take me to my intended final set of cards."

"This is not time for games now Raj. If you die, no one wins. Neither me, nor your father, nor my husband. Please go, we will think of something later. But one thing, you give me that contract and I shall let you go. If you try taking it away with you, I have to get you captured. And I cannot guarantee my husband is going to let you live, after what you have done to... our daughter", Sharada spoke, trying to hide her emotions.

"We will get to that athayya. But first about this game, I do admit that you saw through my play. I intended to get Manoj and Sravani together to avoid marrying Gayathri. And I also admit I faked my pennilessness to bluff you into throwing me out. But you saw my play, and made sure I lost my card with Sravani and my card with you at stake. I lost all hope that night, as I had nothing left but to drop out of the game. But then, in your reckless victory lap, in your intention for the final kill, you inadvertently dropped a rather valuable card. That card changed the course of my entire play. It became a lifeline of sorts and I had changed all my sets to back it up. It was you who gave me my last chance for a win", Raj went on sitting opposite Sharada (the contract still in his hand).

"Suguna", mouthed Sharada as she remembered what happened after that night

---

Suguna gave what looked like a lunchbox to Raj.

"I am sorry about this. Dad didn't want you to come out and mom couldn't protest", Suguna said.

"I know your mother could have handled your father quite easily if she desired to. If she didn't, that doesn't mean she couldn't. It only means she didn't want to do

it. I know you know it too", Raj replied as he took the lunchbox.

"Yeah. But that was my mom's message and lunchbox that I delivered", Suguna replied sheepishly.

"What'd you need to do for that? Well it's simple. I have made very good arrangements for her and even controlled the situation. You just need to keep visiting the police station and delivering the carriage along with some messages to that smartest and the most eligible bachelor", saying so Sharada indirectly brought the topic.

"As I was saying, in order to fulfill your duty as an elder sister, go to the police station now as it's almost lunch time and give this message to him. Just listen to whatever he has to say, and inform that you'll discuss with me and then pass it on", saying so, Sharada left Suguna's hand and gave her the lunch carriage from the dining table.

"Suguna", Raj confirmed. "You sent her to me. From the first time I saw her (where she guessed the intent behind my move before the duel), I knew she was your heart. She was the only person in the entire village in whom you saw yourself and vice versa. And she mentioned her dream to me, her dream to set up a business. I didn't think much of it then, but once all my other moves were out, I had this only alternative. And you gave it to me on a silver platter along with my lunch. I spoke to her, or rather she spoke to me. She admired my brains before the duel, she thought my type were rare in the village.

Hence, she thought well of me and I could use it. I asked her if she really wanted to marry Kireeti or if she still held the desire to have her own firm. And in her reply, I hear you Sharada. I saw you speaking through her, and just like your father had done, you were making her stay back in the village.

And she cried out her anguish. She felt herself cheated by you, whom she trusted, whom she thought was a projection of herself. And you refused to offer her any help. (Now Sharada understood what delayed Suguna's return from the station the previous day. Suguna lied to her). And so, I offered her help. I told her not to discuss the topic of her dislike towards the marriage with you, as you would only convince her back. I asked her to rather bring this topic on the day of the marriage, at the mandapam (stage) so that the entire village gets to know she was being forcefully married."

"But you didn't suggest that to help her", Sharada spoke looking straight into Raj's eyes. "You did that for your own selfish reason. You used her" she continued.

"As a distraction", Raj completed the sentence.

"Just like you used your cousin as your guard, your shield, your best man and what not", scoffed Sharada. "You made her stop the wedding so that you could search for this contract in my study. Who told you it was here?"

"Suguna did", Raj said to which Sharada looked utterly dumbfounded.

"Nonsense, she neither knew about the deal nor about the contract", exclaimed Sharada.

"But she knew about you athayya. She told me in her very first prison visit that you locked Manoj in your study just like you keep things that remind you of who you are. And the contract is the crown jewel of them all. Where else would you keep it?" laughed Raj.

Manoj shouted out as Raj had instructed, warning the village folk that Raj had Sharada with him and Manoj must be allowed to leave unharmed. He quickly hustled past all the angry, hungry, bloodshot looks he was getting and ran towards the BMW.

"Let's go get him", said Gopala Swamy. "But his confederate has Sharada", reasoned Subbu.

"And we will have his assistant with us. Then we can talk about a trade off", Gopala Swamy breathed out, along with the cigar fumes.

"What if he calls his cousin and tells him we are following him?" asked another panchayat member.

"Then, we kill him", Gopala Swamy threw the cigar into the holy fire on the stage and got down the swing.

"And Manoj showed me the locked cabinets as I anticipated. I thought of the only thing that mattered as I dwelled my time in prison. What could the password be, in case you locked the contract in a safe (which I was sure you would)? Now here, I thought of what Suguna said about you, and I started to think like you. It had to be something that proves your intelligence too, as Suguna put it, "Something that reminded you who you were". Almost every safe has its password in the form of numbers, if it was a name, I thought it would be mine or pops. But what if it was numbers, a date perhaps or maybe the amount you lended my father. But the amount you gave my father doesn't prove your intelligence, the amount that you get back will prove it. It has to be a date then.

And you are not a woman who would choose a birthday or a wedding anniversary. The dates that prove your intelligence would be the date you entered into the contract...", Raj went on.

"I would be surprised if your father remembered that date. Cause if he had remembered the date, you would never have needed to come this far", wondered Sharada.

"Well, he doesn't remember, but that doesn't mean I couldn't find it out. I cannot ask your husband, you or Ovulayya from the prison. And certainly, you or your husband wouldn't tell and there is no telling if Ovulayya remembers the exact date. Then it struck me. As fate would have it, there is a rather old monk or a beggar in this village who helped me (you wouldn't even know him I think). He told me (unwittingly of course) that my father bought him drinks at that kallu compound the day you gave him money. And he also told me my father paid for his drinks too.

When I visited the compound, without actually planning to do or seeing any purpose for the visit, I got a very crucial piece of information. Pops never paid for his drinks, and the owner maintained an account. Undoubtedly, he would have reduced the debt by a negative entry for the money my dad gave him on his last visit to the compound i.e., the day of the contract. As police confiscated the contents of the shop, they took that book too. As I offered the contents of my wallet (willingly) to one of the constables there, I was allowed a look. Does the date 06th December sound correct?" smiled Raj.

Sharada gave a wry smile, "But I changed the password", she mumbled, still unable to grasp how Raj could have gotten the contract.

"Which brings me to password 2, the other date that would prove your wit. The day the contract would be executed i.e., the day you called my dad. You would have seen that day as the biggest day of your life, the day your tantrums would be considered wit. And you called him on the eve of our 25th Anniversary, 16th December. With this info, I assigned Manoj the task to look for the locker and he gave me 3 options. 3 options, 2 trials each, 6 in total was by no means a lengthy task. I just needed a few minutes, and there came Suguna", Raj answered.

"But you are wrong, the password is…" Sharada again failed to grasp.

"Exactly, I made a mistake. I lost a lot of valuable time over a small overlook. I nearly gave up when I realized it. This brings me to password 3. You didn't call my dad on the 16th. It was 16th for us in the US, but for you here in India, it was the 17th of December", and Raj got up as he opened up the contract and started reading it.

As Manoj drove past the centre where the elections were being held, he heard shouts of anger from behind him. He saw in his rear view mirror that he had company. Not only were Gopala Swamy and his panchayat following him, but they had also brought in a lot of voting villagers to run after Manoj, throw stones at the BMW and try puncturing the tyres. He quickly picked up his phone to ask Raj for help. But then he realized if he called Raj, Raj would not have any option but to call the entire party back upon himself by hurting Sharada. And if he did hurt her, there would be nothing left for him to bargain, and Gopala Swamy would tear him to pieces.

Instead, if he drove around to the nearby towns and killed some time, maybe he could give Raj enough time to finish his business with Sharada and escape. And what was better, if Manoj could somehow reach a police station in the nearby town, he could get Gopala Swamy arrested and save Raj. He pushed his feet hard on the accelerator as the car jumped a speed breaker. Gopala Swamy gave a wild smile, his deer was running for life. He raised his gun, took aim for the tyre, and BAAANNNGGGG. He missed and hit the road instead. The BMW was just too fast, touching 150 kmph at ease leaving his jeep behind. He shouted at his driver to take a shortcut turn, but ordered the public to go after Manoj so as not to lose him.

And Raj closed the contract just after going through it for 15 odd minutes. Sharada looked at him and smiled for the first time in a while, "What did you think Raj? You thought I would leave a loophole for you to wriggle out? Or did you think I would not have any other copy or scanned versions of the contract by now? Did you think I was just another villager...like your father?"

Raj looked at her, "My father was a villager, is a villager and shall always be one. But he was not just another villager. He is the most successful entrepreneur this village has ever produced, and you should be proud of him, like I am."

Sharada got up, "Then you should be proud of me too. If it weren't for me, your father would have died unable to feed, unable to eat and unable to stop drinking. He is what he is because of me."

"You did it to him, but you didn't do it for him. You did it for yourself Sharada, this is why I wanted to look at the contract", Raj smiled now, which faded Sharada's instantly.

"I never doubted your capability or wit, hence I never saw merit in looking for the contract, up until Suguna said something about you. She said you wanted to prove yourself above these villagers, you wanted to prove to yourself and everyone else that you are not 'just another villager' "

"What's to know in that? Everyone here knows that" Sharada shrugged.

"There's the catch. I didn't until she told me. She said it to me while she cried that you weren't going to help her out. She told me you did this to Gayathri not out of your love for her, but out of your hatred towards your village and the people in it", Raj looked at her with that intense gaze he gave when people made fun of his father.

"The contract is air tight you stupid boy. I could take your father's entire wealth or take you as my son-in-law and if none of this happens, your father goes to jail", Sharada turned away, unable to withstand Raj's gaze.

"Of course, you can send my father to prison. Cause neither am I giving you my pop's wealth (or my wealth as it stands now) nor am I going to marry your daughter", Raj told her.

"Then I cannot help it. Your father will be arriving soon, just as I heard you say in the call. He will never leave the village. He will spend the remainder of his life in the only place in Sivasamudram he hasn't visited yet", Sharada turned back to face Raj, who was still calm.

"But is that going to prove your wit or worth to this village?" he asked.

The villagers sprang on top of the BMW or jumped right in front of it, as Manoj tried his best not to hurt anyone too badly as he swerved the car, kicked the villagers and dashed past. They were just springing foolishly from everywhere. Had there been someone else driving, the villagers would have surely died, crumpling down under the weight of the car. Now, Manoj was driving along the tortuous lanes of the village to avoid hordes of people. But this meant he was unable to understand which way he was heading. As he was driving, people were throwing stones, vessels, hot water, chilli powder and a few old luggage onto the car from the windows of their houses. Just as Manoj took a turn, he saw a wider road ahead. He drove quickly through all the debris that was intentionally placed to block his path and dashed ahead onto the road. BAANNGG.

The car missed a bullet by an inch. As Manoj looked to his right, Gopala Swamy was reloading. "I will aim for you if you don't stop", he shouted as Manoj quickly swerved left and drove at maximum speed. He could hear sounds of bullets hitting the road and one of the tail lights of the car. But thankfully, he saw the village board ahead, which meant he reached the outskirts after all. He quickly drove the straight road at maximum speed. He saw some passerby cars coming in the opposite direction. Hence he kept his vehicle as left as possible and continued going straight. But this meant if Gopala Swamy reloads in time, Manoj can't swerve to avoid. Hence he prayed to all the Gods he could think of and floored it. And then a bullet hit the left rear view mirror which blasted to pieces and cut Manoj on his left cheek.

He closed his eyes and swerved blindly as he felt a sharp pain along his cheek. And he felt his car hit something big. BAAANNNNGGG.

"I neither understand nor care what you have to say", Sharada looked away.

"Oh, I think you do athayya. You can very well get my father arrested here. But think about this, what sort of reputation does my father hold here, and will the arrest really do anything worse to him from the villagers' perspective? Of course, you can argue it will damage his reputation in the globe, what with the IPO and CEO getting arrested", Raj said.

"Exactly", shouted Sharada, relieved as Raj saw the danger.

"But the CEO has changed, madam. My father's arrest will make me the next CEO of the firm. And the question is, do you think you can handle me? Will you get a single penny out of it? And most importantly, will you prove yourself ahead of these village folk", Raj said it with a smooth demeanor. "No. You won't. You will again be called a mad woman for putting your money on that 'Vantala Varma', 'that man with a woman's soul' and what not. You would have confirmed the villager's notion of being a mad woman" smiled Raj turning her slightly to face him now.

"I....I really don't care", she trembled.

"I thought so until I spoke to Suguna. I thought you would win even though dad loses, but now I know that for you to win, pops can't lose. If people see the man you made out of my pops, you will be hailed as the brain behind the billions. But if my father gets arrested, you will be called the madness behind the man. And that was why I wanted to read the contract. To find out if you had any clause to protect your interests in case my father gets arrested. Do we have to pay you back still, if you get my father arrested?" Raj whispered. "Do you remember adding any such clause athayya?"

Sharada looked defiantly at Raj and he saw a single tear dropping out of her eyes.

"So that means, if pops is arrested, the contract goes null and void right then and there. And we don't have to pay you back anything, zero return on your investment. Or as the people in Sivasamudram would say 'a weird tantrum costing Gopala Swamy thousands back then'. And as for my father, I am ready to gamble all the money he has given me, employ all the legal resources I hold and get him out of the secret Sivasamudram. I can afford to do it, can you?" Raj asked.'

Sharada was silent, but Raj heard her. "Then I guess it is time for you to quote a sum that will prove your worth and time for us to pay back", he said.

Chapter - 32

PAYBACK

"What a shame!" laughed Gopala Swamy. "We were starting to have some real fun when that squirrel hit the police car."

"Doesn't look like one Gopalam", Subbu raised a brow.

"It has a siren Subbu, it must surely be a convoy car", said another panchayat member.

"But for whom? Though the elections are done, counting is in progress", said another panchayat member.

And as the person in the back seat of the car (into which Manoj had rammed his BMW blindly) got out, all the panchayat members gave a great laugh.

"Oh my god! It is the local MLA. Now the squirrel is dead for sure. Tried to run away from a sarpanch but hit an MLA", Gopala Swamy laughed as he got down his car to greet the oncoming MLA convoy.

"But Gopalam, why do you think he has come? Did he come to greet you on your victory?" asked Subbu.

"I didn't invite him, otherwise I would have asked him to come to the wedding too right?" Gopala Swamy turned back and replied.

"And mighty well you didn't, else Suguna would have made you look like an embarrassed dog in front of the MLA", said the cocky panchayat member.

Gopala Swamy turned to him, gave him a rude finger and walked ahead towards the MLA and his guards. The guards grabbed Manoj, looked at his cheek and took him into their custody.

Gopala Swamy shouted something like "Do not let that squirrel escape sir. The sarpanch (he raised his collar as he said it) and the entire panchayat here finds him guilty" as he lit his cigar.

The other door of the MLA's car had opened and a second person now got down the back seat. Gopala Swamy failed to recognize the person. He definitely looked like a rich guy, stout in size, wearing a brown suit over a lavish silk shirt. He wore a branded watch (Gopala Swamy didn't recognize the brand but knew it was a costly one) to his left hand and his right hand had a kerchief which was busy wiping the man's forehead.

The MLA greeted Gopala Swamy, "Namaste Gopalam garu. I heard you are the new sarpanch here (as there is no other candidate, unless 30% of the village gives a NOTA). I am sure you recognize a fellow villager who I am sure made the entire village proud", he indicated towards the other guy.

"Oh, this man is from Sivasamudram too?" asked Gopala Swamy incredulously.

The man extended his arm sheepishly. He was either afraid or feeling very sultry. Gopala Swamy took the arm as he suddenly felt a deep sense of familiarity. He has definitely seen this guy somewhere.

"He...ahem...ahem...hello Gopala Swamy garu", replied the villager inside Ravikant Varma who was unsure whether he was happy being back here.

In an instant, the cigar and the voice dropped from Gopala Swamy. Simultaneously, the voices behind Gopala Swamy picked up from his panchayat members behind. The air of recognition among them saying "Hey it's that Vantalodu", "No no, he was called Vanta Varma or something like that", "Hey Varma, when will you return my kallu bill? I'll add all the interests and you can't escape this time."

"Ah! Finally some nativity is heard. There is a big difference in hearing these swear words from those English ones you speak wearing that tight and hot suit Varma" sighed the villager inside, but in contrast, Varma from outside was just standing and staring at them sweating.

"Varma mama!!! These people are going to kill me and then Raj!!!" struggled Manoj, "I was trying to save him, now please don't tell me I need to save you too."

"Do you know this guy and also them?" the MLA asked. "Looks like you are famous in the village then", he chuckled.

The village voters who were partly turned hunters and party members gave a huge gasp. The local MLA had just spoke to that Vantala Varma as though Varma was as high as him, or maybe the MLA was as low as him.

"Can you please let that foreign guy go, he is actually my….my….distant nephew, and in case he flirted with….I mean misbehaved with any of you or your girls, then I think he is just my nephew's look alike", shivered Varma wondering what effect each of his word would have on the crowd as he spoke.

Though he was slowly recognizing each one of them present, his eyes kept turning away fearing not to see THAT ONE FACE which he feared and wished would never see (which was slowly going to be overruled soon).

Gopala Swamy was the first to recover from all the ones who were shocked there (Varma and the villagers included). "That foreign pig just tried to ruin my daughter's wedding, his confederate tried wooing my wife, they tried to fight me in a hand to hand duel, and now he tried to run away from me", he smoked out the remnants of his cigar which were held back too long.

"All in good humor", Manoj chuckled nervously, while Varma became dumbstruck listening to his son's and nephew's short achievements. He now looked at Gopala Swamy's gun which he was sure would let out smoke just like it's owner, and would be pointed at him.

But to everyone's surprise there, the MLA signaled his guards to leave Manoj (and 'signal' refers to many native swear words which Varma was known for during his stay).

Manoj straightened his dress, folded back its collar and sleeves in the latest fashion (rampant in Rome these days), and then....immediately ran towards and then behind his uncle. Varma who initially expected his nephew running to hug him was shocked, then frustrated and then shit scared. He tried pushing the rat back in front, but Manoj was holding and folding his hand so tight that Varma felt the villager's scream himself. It took all his effort not to shout and give away his fear in front of these bucolics.

"Listen Gopalam, is the election and the counting done?" MLA asked in a business-like tone (after he raised his brows confused at the mama nephew duo. He shrugged it off taking it to be some childish playful banter in the US when people met each other after a long time).

"Yes", said Gopalam as though trying to remind the MLA who the boss there was.

"Jolly good. Then ask your....um.... servants (he indicated the panchayat members Subbu and gang) to clear out that space. Mr.Varma here has some announcements he would like to make", said the MLA.

"But, what about the 'big' announcement? The result?" said Gopalam ignoring the cries of revolt from his 'servants' behind.

"Result? Oh, the elections…ummm…ok let's make Mr. Varma himself the declarer. He will…maybe…give you a picture holding a shield along with my newly announced plant donation scheme…yep..it's perfect. He can just say out the slogan of the scheme umm… 'Instead of using water to spit out ghutka, why not plant a tree and water it?'...that should attract your villagers. Even you yourself can feel like a celebrity for a day, receiving the honor from such an elite NRI and MLA." MLA concluded and signaled his guards and the 'servants' to start their vehicles.

"What's the need for all this humdrum sir? Gopala Swamy garu must be very busy with his daughter's marriage…. oh shit….(he gave a stern look towards Manoj who blushed) I meant elections….yeah….the great 'Sivasamudram Sarpanch elections'. Zindabad Sivasamudram. Now can I just wait here, while my Manoj quickly gets my…. uh….son's look alike and all of us drive off happily?" Mr.Varma twirled his fingers at the MLA.

"What is this Mr. Varma? You drove so far and wouldn't make it to the announcement of my plant donation scheme? I mean even without your campaign kick start? And...you didn't tell me your son is here too?" asked the MLA, shocked at the sudden decision of Varma to leave.

"Yes he is, he is the confederate squirrel I was talking about. He planned it all, spoiling my elder's wedding, having an affair with my wife, planning to marry my younger, challenging me in a duel, fighting with my son-in-law, I mean would be, no would have been, whatever. Oh man he didn't leave a single member in my family, now that I think of it", snarled Gopalam.

With each and every word from Gopalam, Varma's eyes grew wider and rounder, as his feet started going back (but Manoj didn't budge from behind). After Gopalam's monologue however, the MLA had a completely irrelevant expression of joy.

"That's even better then, Gopalam, looks like all of you have got along so very well. That is just splendid. Now let me just....", and the MLA took Gopalam aside.

MLA whispered, "Now listen here you village celebrity, I know you people are narrow minded and naive to such western etiquettes. These foreign people think it is a way of showing their love and affection..."

"My foot affection!" Gopala Swamy intervened. "How is flirting with a married woman who also happens to be my wife...wife of this village's sarpanch A WAY OF SHOWING LOVEEEE!"

"Now that's where they have surpassed us and grew...well...even more mature. They have no concern towards skin colour, marital status, age and...sometimes gender too. I consider it lucky that he didn't come after you and proposed. And I say here old man, start coloring your hair! Need not show off your experience to the villagers. There needs to be a charm in you so that your wife sticks to you only. And I heard his son is a real charmer. If you think of it, it's your fault that your wife had an affair with him, just like it was my wife's fault in my case" said the MLA unnecessarily correcting the collar of Gopalam.

Now, he corrected his tone to a higher level so that others could hear him too, "Now go get your family and Varma junior to the village panchayat space and ask the wedding planner cum tent house cum free eaters to shift all the chairs and decoration (which has anyway got no use now, and you paid for it too) for the announcement. It's payback time."

The entire village gathered there. Gopala Swamy invited the entire village to his marriage, but only about half showed up till the break. He didn't invite anyone now, but it seemed like folk from nearby villages got there too. Each one of them were dressed up for a wedding wearing silk kurtas, silk sarees and golden turbans (which were gifted by Gopala Swamy for coming to the wedding). They were all in a confused state as to what the announcement would be about. Whether declaring the result of elections or the result of the marriage or maybe announcing the new bridegroom or Gopala Swamy's first death sentence as the sarpanch.

Lots of whispers were going around such as "Excuse me, I missed the wedding feast, will the same be served here too?" "Is it true Gopala Swamy's daughter has eloped with a foreign sarpanch?" "Will there be kallu served as the elections are over now?" "Or even better, because the marriage is over now?" "When is the muhurtham for marriage?" "How much would it have cost for the marriage? Did Gopalam get any refund because the marriage stopped midway?"

For the first time, Gopala Swamy felt really uncomfortable at the panchayat place, in front of a crowd who were just discussing him. He looked anywhere but at the crowd. Mostly his looks were towards Varma and the joker who was hiding beside him, behind him, below him from time to time. Word has reached the MLA that the marriage party had started from home and would reach there anytime. The MLA ordered the marriage convoy to be led by Varma junior on the bride groom's horse.

"Mama, did you by any chance bring some US dollars with you? You know our entire cash has been locked up by that tyrant in a saree. If we can check the Emirates' website for available flights, we might make it with MLA's protection. God, my passport is with that lady gaga who went completely gaga. Mama, mama, are you alive?" Manoj was whispering.

Varma always felt he couldn't handle the bureaucrats, but now he realized the bucolics were way worse than any suit wearing chimpanzee. The villager inside him tried recognizing everyone down there, and also noting down his last wishes to do there, before he would be hunted down or hung down. Any moment, Gopala Swamy would shout "Rey narikeyandra (go get these squirrels)!!!" and the entire crowd would just go berserk, removing sickles, knives, naatu bombs from their lungis, handbags, turbans, bikes and go for it, as the MLA would give a trembling look at Gopala Swamy (who will turn towards the MLA and give a wicked smile, and say the MLA is below him now, and needs to do anything he asks of him).

And then came the sounds of drums. Though he knew it was the marriage convoy, somehow Varma felt it was a funeral procession, either his or his son's. He never felt this amount of hatred towards any human being, let alone his son as he saw Raj riding the horse, getting ready for the sacrifice. And just behind Raj, in the ambassador, Varma saw her, and he never felt this fearful for a long long time now. It was even higher than the fear he had for her husband, which was next to nothing in comparison. The villager inside him had no trouble recognizing the woman too. For the first time in the past few weeks, Varma heard no noise from within.

The MLA stood up welcoming the procession, who according to Varma was like an innocent deer abandoned in the forest that felt happy upon seeing a pride of lions coming towards it. Even Manoj tightened his grip on Varma's fat hand, reducing its width by a few inches.

As the convoy stopped, there came a loud reverberating noise. Varma looked around initially trying to find the source, but later checking if others heard it too? Or if he was getting a heavenly omen. He looked up at the sky expecting to see his in-laws and his wife dressed up as imps, asking him to come up offering a vacant seat beside them.

But, when the MLA himself shouted asking who was that idiotic person blowing a conch during an auspicious event, Varma felt slightly relieved. And the crowd parted to show that Sadhu smiling in the gap.

"Every event in one's life is auspicious, my elderly son. That is why even death has an anniversary and is celebrated every year. And this is indeed an auspicious occasion. The beginning and the ending of a battle must both have the blowing of a conch, one starts death and the other finishes it. Ironically, the situation now is both the ending and the beginning of a war", he laughed hard and winked at the MLA (who looked around him wondering if that beggar was indeed referring to him). He ordered his guards to grab that monkey with a tail on its head.

As they got down the stage, the horse had made a loud kneighing noise and they retreated immediately. Raj comforted the horse's neck and slowly got down, though wondering as to why the horse did that. As the MLA looked confused, Raj asked the guards not to trouble the bearded monkey.

"He is just fed up and wants to be fed", Raj said."Give him something to eat and drink, and he will be as silent as a kid in a movie."

"Leave that aside now, please come on stage Varma junior", the MLA smiled.

Raj smiled back and said, "Just a small addition to the event if I may. I took the liberty of calling a few of my friends too. I would appreciate it very much if you allow them to attend the announcement."

"Oh ok, sure", the MLA looked confused as to how Raj knew about that beggar.

And then Raj beckoned towards some cars at the end of the convoy. And from them alighted the marketing team of RV chain, Varma's lawyer Anand and to the MLA's absolute delight and Gopala Swamy's utmost horror a whole host of TV channels.

"Oh boy, oh boy. Time and again you foreign people, I mean Indian born foreign people prove your patriotism towards your country. Truly the next generation knows how to show off, I didn't dream of bringing the media here" chuckled the MLA. "Now come onto the stage Mr. Varma."

Raj ran atop the stage and as the MLA showed him an empty seat, Raj gently pushed the MLA towards it and seated him on it. The MLA looked utterly befuddled by this, he thought he would deliver a speech and then the corporates would give theirs. But Raj took the center stage now. He knocked the mike a few times to drain down the audience's noise until there was just the rush of the waves.

Just for a minute, his mind took him back to the stage at the States where he addressed the RV family announcing his taking up of the CEO mantle from his father. And now, a few months later, here he was on a 10 foot stage addressing a bunch of villagers where a half of them were waiting to settle scores with him while the other half were just wondering who the heck he was. He smiled back and started speaking in his native lingo.

"Welcome my dear Sivasamudram neighbours! Today has been a special day for many reasons. Firstly, it is the day when we are about to decide who among us will be leading our village to the future i.e., our elections will be concluded. Secondly, it is this day when a woman has for the first time opened up on what she wants to become and what she wants to do for her village. Lastly, it is this day when a villager has come back to his motherland, proudly willing to show his mother what he has become, and to offer her a small payback as a gratitude. Let me start by introducing him to you all"

MLA was about to get up blushing with those words when Raj directed towards them. But, it was Manoj who got up lifting the completely reluctant Varma who on the contrary was like a wimpy kid resisting being taken to perform on stage. "Can you please lend me a hand MLA sir? Mama has been growing old. Needs to have a foreign brand post the event to rejuvenate. Please mama, get up and finish it off. Will be backstage waiting for your signal".

The MLA looked taken aback, but the clicks and flashes on his face brought him back. He quickly covered his emotions, bringing on a smile he gave every time he had to announce the party membership he expected, to an opponent. Varma too was painfully reminded of how he was forced on stage just a few months back when he was completely lost for words. His son looked at him, just like on that day, expecting his pops to manage everything, which he couldn't.

The villagers slowly started clapping and as a few started, the entire crowd picked up on it. "Is that Vantala Varma?" "How come he is wearing the James Bond dress?" "Is he Varma's elder son who looks just like him?" The media on the other hand had a field day. They never expected to get so close to the CEO, right before the grand IPO. The marketing team looked worried though.

As Varma got upto the mike, all of them started raising their hands and throwing the same question at him in twisted words. "Are you aware there has been a video doing rounds in the social media?" "It seems that your dishes make people forget themselves, and not in a good way like that in an alpenliebe ad, but as though the person has been hit on the head by a side villain" "When did you reach India?" "When has the campaign started?" "There have been claims that the video is going to have a detrimental impact on your IPO?" "And the person who posted the video was a whistleblower from the marketing team, was he?"

With no words to speak, Varma was highly hoping to show signs which would give clear meaning to the media to back off, some being indications towards lunacy or mimicking a heart seizure or diverting them towards the sea and wondering when the next Tsunami was to come.

His hand was then held by his son from the back and he saw Raj, stepping beside him and then ahead of him pulling the mike towards himself now. "Hey folks! Thank you for the great response or great questions from your end. As you all are aware of our RV style of announcement, let's take the QnA cum rapid fire round towards the end. Let's quickly get to the main event" to which the media people chuckled. Raj took over the mantle.

He then started,"So, let's all together invite another special guest who also happens to be our fellow villager and the most well spoken chief person of this event"

"Oh...why this much propaganda my boy", the MLA again blushed and got up.

"Please welcome Mrs. Sharada Devi," Raj passed both MLA and Gopala Swamy who looked bewildered. Varma instinctively stepped back as though the dog heard Pavlov's bell. Raj got down, took Sharada Devi's hand and brought her onto the stage.

Click....Click....Click....Whistle....Whistle....Giggle...
Sounds of anger

Sharada Devi looked as calm and composed as ever. It just took a two minute glance of hers to silence the entire crowd, on and off stage. She looked at the party on the stage, stared at Varma senior for a whole minute and then at his son.

"Your silence tells me two things. One, that you know me, and two that you don't know him", she pointed at her partner (business one, not the personal one).

Varma was trying hard to stop his fears, and then tried to cover it as though they were tears of joy, or something just fell in his eyes and then just gave away. He tried calming himself down. It was nothing, just the close physical proximity to the one woman he wished he would never lay his eyes on for the rest of his life, it was nothing.

The crowd took it up instantly to the surprise of the media. "Hey it's that Vanatalodu right?" "Do the cooks also wear spyware in foreign land?" "Ma'am, how much is he indebted to Malligaadu?" and some were just whistles and tantrums.

"See Varma" Sharada looked at him, which he couldn't take at such speed. "Some things never change right? We can never figure you in this appearance or take you to be the businessman. Though they are called first impressions, they last."

The media couldn't take their eyes or ears off her either. And surprisingly, not a single soul questioned her as to who she was or how she knew Mr.Varma so well that she addressed him 'Varma'. Varma glanced helplessly for a while, and then just shrugged.

"Never forget where you started from Varma, no matter how far you go. You will be surprised to know your son taught me this. The race always finishes at the start. And the finishing points are decided based on the beginnings. I….uh….don't….have anything else to say", and she looked at Varma junior with mixed expressions of anger, jealousy, hatred and hidden admiration too. She never dreamt of coming across a soul as intelligent as her, or in this case slightly better than her.

He smiled at her, took the mike from her and said, "People here don't know you too Sharada." The crowd instantly went dumb at the last word. The media just blinked, as they didn't know that not a single person within a radius of 32 kms from here dared address her thus (Gopala Swamy being the only exception. He could, but he wouldn't.)

"I repeat, none of them here, your husband and family included know you for who you are" (there were some naughty and angry retorts here and there) "Does anyone here know that Sharada garu was the first person to trust my father? And those who know this (he looked at Mr.Sharada Devi), do you know she didn't do it because she was out of her mind? She did it because she was out of the box. She saw my father for who he would become, not what he was on that day. And both of them were called many names for that. He was called a woman, and she was called a mad woman for what they did that day. Now, as I said, this day is special on three counts. The last one was already revealed and I am happy that I united my father with his motherland. Coming to the second part where I said 'for the first time, a woman opened up on what she wants to become and what she wants to do for her village'. She is none other than Sharada Devi…junior."

To this, all eyes of media went in random directions while those of villagers and Gopala Swamy's family went in one direction.

"Her name is Ms. Suguna. And today, she decided to cancel her wedding ceremony. I can figure out that it would be taken as a bad omen by the village and would force her to shut herself. But, she proved it otherwise by opening up in front of her entire family. It's time that my village…our village…realizes the potential in our women. Do not repeat the mistake you made with Sharada." Raj spoke to a silent crowd who could either be thinking on his words or were just angry with them.

"To signify this, it is time for me to pay back my very first investor who proved that her seed can become a forest today. I was told by her that she wanted us to be family (this time there were no taunts or jeers), and ma'am you are going to be a part of my family, my 'RV' family now. I assign you a tenth of the shares I hold as the CEO of the RV chain. You need not subscribe to our IPO, as you are now a part of those who release it. I hope you invest in your daughter's dreams similarly", Raj announced.

The media went berserk this time, not to mention the entire RV marketing chain who pounced on the cue they got. They banged their hands together to a tumultuous applause. The crowd, panchayat however failed to understand what was going on and why were people clapping as though the hero of a movie announced his next. The MLA however clapped just for the sake of it. The main person Sharada Devi just stood peering through Raj's eyes wondering what they meant. Did she win or did she not?

"My lawyer here. Mr.Anand Raju will take care of the legalities involved", he closed the mike and spoke to Sharada "The contract first and then the share allotment."

"Lastly, or should I say firstly as I mentioned 'it is the day when we are about to decide who among us will be leading our village to the future i.e., our elections will be concluded'. As to the election results, well, no surprises, it is the hunting gun symbol party of our beloved Gopala Swamy which shot the election ballet", Raj directed to Gopala Swamy and panchayat. This time, the media just clapped for the sake of it while the RV chain marketing team kept staring blankly. But, the entire village rose like a high tide and applauded.

"But, in the last statement there was also that 'we are about to decide who among us will be leading our village'. Well, I seriously hope that it could be our Sarpanch (who just won), who leads us. But before he decides to change your lives by launching many new kallu kottus or bringing new kacheri girls, I would wish to bring a small change in the other direction. I want to bring jobs and literacy to my village to give the future Varma all he/she needs. So, I announce setting up a branch of the RV restaurant chain in Sivasamudram in the exact spot of Malligadi kottu (which was being received by shouts of revolt from villagers) and will also arrange for food donation and education drives. I told you I could buy you off", Raj concluded as he looked at Malligadu last.

And then he was instantly separated from the hunting herd by concentric circles of bouncers, his marketing team and then media. As none of them were strong enough to swim through, they couldn't help but to get drowned in them. Manoj and Varma (the senior) quickly made a detour inside the circle as the MLA kept shouting to the walls of the stage, "Hey! Wait! What about my speech? What about my plant donation scheme announcement? Varma! Both senior and junior! Anyone!"

The only person in the crowd who stood her ground and wasn't being washed away was Sharada Devi. She, with her usual talent of not missing on her prey, was able to keep her gaze on Raj, who was just inches from her before, but was now separated by a group of 20-30 beings from the human species. For a split second, they both made eye contact again but that broke when the bouncers took Raj away from the mob.

All villagers gazed with their mouths wide open, as they just got a taster of who Raj actually was. Gayathri turned towards her mom who just got down from the stage, no longer in thought and asked, "What was all that? Who was he?". Sharada smiled, "You pretend to be a queen, he pretended to be a commoner. Both of you have now come back to yourselves, now that the curtains are drawn. What worries me is not who he is, but what he is going to become. What with all the money and power he hasn't used against us yet, if he gains those resources (which he just did), there will be no stopping him."

"He gave you quite some resources too", Suguna said. "That was what he thinks I deserved. Didn't you notice? He hasn't given you anything even though you helped him. He gave me wealth even though I opposed him", Sharada replied. For the first time in her life, she felt truly calm, truly in place. Raj just showed her what her heartfelt desire was, for the village and her family to realize her worth, realize their worth.

"Excuse me ma'am. Ma'am…here…please give us a brief about you and your family. How have you met Mr. Varma…how you discussed business…and all that. We'll ensure to print it in the main page", came voices behind Sharada to which the entire villagers, her daughters and to her satisfaction, even her husband Gopala Swamy were pushed aside by the raging media.

"What are you going to do Gopalam?" Subbu asked his friend as they started towards their jeep.

"Firstly, I am going to dye my hair", said Gopal Swamy.

Chapter - 33

WAVES AND TIDES

"Did you give that village woman the share to negate the negative publicity we faced sir?" Surya (RV India's CMO) asked. "Do you think it will help us?"

"I hope it negates the negativity. As to whether it helps us, I am sure it will help people invest in others' dreams too" Raj spoke unconcerned. He was just looking out from his car. He was in the front seat as his CMO drove. Varma senior and Manoj were in the back seat. Varma kept asking every 5 minutes if they left the village, and the villager inside kept asking if they had left the kallu compound yet. He was not particularly happy with his son's decision to 'uplift' the kallu compound. But Varma was now ok with the voices as they no longer concerned him, but were just like consoling him.

"No issues Surya. If in any case you require help, just call me. I'm ready to dance with the Indian actresses at your restaurant. And what's more, we'll stick that Rajagopal's clown face on the buffalo's back and me and the actress will be throwing cow dung on the photo and enjoying it. It will create the correct persona of him, and will also bring back the positivity", said Manoj all the while checking back how far they have come from the village, and if any car of Gopala Swamy is following them.

"Let's pray that our car doesn't get punctured now mama, like it happened when we were entering. And these guys are thinking you did the negotiation to neutralize the negativity? Such fools you got in your office" whispered Manoj into Raj's ears.

"Did you recognize these folks and places, Varma?" Surya asked Varma.

"Yeah, sort of. Nothing has changed since. Except of course that kallu compound grew much bigger", he said as they saw the compound towards their left as they approached the seashore. The villager inside kept nagging for a vat, while Varma just smiled to himself.

He patted Raj's shoulder, "I have no idea how you did what you did, or how you convinced that devil of a woman, or how you guys got to all those godforsaken deeds and still made it out alive. But please do not let me face any such ordeal ever again, where I would have to deal with this village or its occupants. And I assure you we will have that huge party I owe you once we reach New York"

"That's great Varma. Raj, why so silent? Are you tense about your results?" Surya winked.

"What results uncle?" Manoj asked.

"Vogue always announces the list of winners in the 'Most Eligible Bachelor' thing a fortnight before the edition prints come in. Going by this, his results are due today or tomorrow", Surya answered.

"Oh yes, Maggie did seem to tell me she would call me once they are out", Varma now started to remember all that seemed too trivial to pay attention to.

"Anyway I think Raj needs some diversion. So tell me man, did you recognize any places from this village of yours?" Surya asked.

"Stop!!!" Raj shouted as they just turned a corner along the shore.

Surya stopped the car suddenly and the car received a bump from the convoy behind.

"Mama, not now please. We have not yet crossed the village. Don't tell me we forgot something. Please let us just get out of here", Manoj became a child again.

"No, I didn't forget anything, I just remembered something", Raj said.

"What Raj? What now? Can we just talk after we leave this village?" Varma trembled.

Raj replied, "Nothing Pops. Let me face the breeze. Not able to get the feel of the air from the glass. Already faced a lot of heat."

"NO! NO! NO! Stop", cried Varma and Manoj while Raj got out signaling his bouncers not to come out.

That place was like a photocopy in his mind where he could see a younger Varma without anything, not even money to buy food, looking worried. Alongside him was a toddler, who was gazing at Varma to say something and with no response, kept toddling along the sea. The place he visited with Sharada Devi was not it. She never saw Varma at the sea, she saw him at the field. So he guessed she just showed him some place near so that he would get her back home soon.

When his father narrated the deal that day, the village was just a distant vision to him, he couldn't remember it's name. But the shore and the sea were a distinct vision to him. He could remember feeling hungry, angry and painful that day. All emotions which he no longer felt once he migrated away. He had to come back to his village to get angry again, had to get arrested to wait to be fed, and had to fight to feel pain. It was like the waves of the sea. Once they retreat, one might think they would never come back (just like his father and Sharada), but they always do. They come back to feel the shore again. Once they take enough sand with them they go back, only to come for the sand again. Also, alternately, however close and deep they might come onto the shore, they can't remain there, and should return to their depths.

It was that basic lesson of nature which many miss or forget or choose to forget. Raj thought to himself.

Think of his father. He was a wealthy, luxurious businessman from the outside. But was a basic cook born in a village, who likes to cook, drink and use native swear words to express any of his emotions, on the inside. But, he never accepted it or respected it and always thought of running away from the truth. In the end, he was forced to return to the shores of his village, face the truth and it saved him from his worst fears.

Then comes another villager Sharada Devi, the woman with such an intelligent mind. Well educated and courageous, she could have taken her village and her family to great heights had she wished to. But she was surrounded by the village folk whom she considered ignorant and careless, without a goal (including her husband). She couldn't take it and considered it as a punishment to get married and remain in the village rather than accepting and embracing it. She too was forced now to accept her upbringing, to announce her roots before the entire village and media, and this won her a share in the billion dollar MNC.

Manoj was pushed out by Varma to get his cousin's ass back on to the car. As Manoj cautiously put one step ahead of the other, looking all ways a million times, Varma lit a cigar.

Ring…. Ring…. Ring….

"It's Maggie", Varma announced to Surya. Surya honked the car in excitement to alert Manoj and Raj to get back. But Manoj was halfway towards Raj who was looking at the horizon as though enjoying the view, or a wilder romantic would say contemplating suicide.

"Chief, guess what. He didn't make it to the top 100", Maggie started.

"What!!! Not even to the top 100?" Varma blinked as Surya's face fell.

"No, not even the top 10", Maggie held her breath.

"I don't get it. What parameters have they based their rankings on? Those crazy elite bureaucrats, just decide on the few posh jargon used during the interview. I should lend them some of my swear words", Varma barked.

"Chief, he made it to the very top!!! He is the most..." Maggie shouted.

"Don't you say, he is the most eligible bachelor now?" Varma dropped his cigar as Surya let out a whoop in surprise.

"YEEESSS Chief", Maggie shouted back. "Get yourselves back soon, we should have a blast."

"Hey you idiots!!!" shouted Varma as Surya again honked.

"Mama!!! Let's get back now. Stay here for a few more minutes and we won't be leaving. Come on mama, let's leave. I never want to come back here for the rest of my life. Don't tell me you want to" Manoj kept tugging Raj back. "Even though I haven't got any time with those Indian chicks, I know they are not worth all the trouble. Say something bro, don't scare me. Don't you want to go back?"

"I do", said Raj, still watching the kid take his 12th, 13th, 14th and God knows how many rounds.

"And you want to come back?" Manoj asked as Raj faced him at last. The setting sun lit one side of Raj's face, and the other side was darker.

"Maybe I want to", said the villager inside the most eligible bachelor's head.

THE END

www.ingramcontent.com/pod-product-compliance
Lightning Source LLC
LaVergne TN
LVHW061538070526
838199LV00077B/6833